THE GHOST OF GRACIE FLYNN

First published 2022 by
FREMANTLE PRESS

Reprinted 2022.

Fremantle Press Inc. trading as Fremantle Press
PO Box 158, North Fremantle, Western Australia, 6159
fremantlepress.com.au

Cover image by Agata Sztarbala / Trevillion Images
Designed by Nada Backovic, nadabackovic.com

 A catalogue record for this
book is available from the
NATIONAL LIBRARY OF AUSTRALIA
National Library of Australia

ISBN 9781760991258 (paperback)
ISBN 9781760991265 (ebook)

GOVERNMENT OF WESTERN AUSTRALIA

Fremantle Press is supported by the Western Australian State
Government through the Department of Cultural Industries,
Tourism and Sport.

Fremantle Press respectfully acknowledges the Whadjuk people of
the Noongar nation as the Traditional Owners and Custodians of
the land where we work in Walyalup.

THE GHOST OF GRACIE FLYNN

JOANNA MORRISON

 FREMANTLE PRESS

For my family

1

The first person to know your father was dead was a woman. A young woman. Early twenties. Emerald eyes and a dark mass of hair.

Imagine her eyes now closed—eyelashes dark against her pale skin. She's lying on her back, her hair spread out around her head.

When she wakes, there's a gurgling sound and a briny smell coming in on the breeze. She opens her eyes and a throb of pain spreads from the back of her head to the front.

Slowly, a shape comes into focus, white in a sea of darkness.

The moon.

A mast reaches into the night sky, sails furled up tight.

The woman sits up and the throbbing intensifies—a blinding flare behind her eyes. Through the ache, she sees lights over on the shore, rising and falling with the rocking of the boat. Their reflections slip in and out of the water's skin.

Not that far away.

She pulls herself onto her knees, and that's when she sees it: a shoe. A black shoe, on someone's foot, pointing up at the sky. Fear moves through her like a slow, augmented arpeggio. Barely breathing, she studies the shape of him. He's long. His clothes are dark. On his left hand, which is pale and still, a wedding band catches the light from the shore intermittently. Like a lighthouse. A warning pulse.

She recognises him then. It's Sam. Sam Favier.

Yes, your father.

He's taken her out on *Stargazing* before, with the water stretching out dark around them, like this, restless in the moonlight.

Tentatively, she touches the cool skin of his face. His dark hair merges with the shadows. Holding her hand over his slightly open mouth, she feels for warmth but there's nothing. No sound either—just the gentle slap and surge of water against the sides of the boat.

'Wake up,' the woman says, her voice thin and fearful. She feels for a pulse. Her own is tearing along, but not Sam's. At his wrist, up under his jaw—nothing.

The lights are still there on the shore, but they have no answers. The moon is silent too. There's only panic for guidance, and the panic says *swim*. She steps up to the top of the ladder and looks down at the water—so dark and unsteady—then she jumps before she can think too hard about it: about how far she has to go and exactly how deep the water might be; about leaving Sam alone. Worse than alone. Gone.

2

It's a glorious Saturday morning: a bright sky brushed with clouds, a fresh westerly. You and your parents are at this great little café around the corner from home. A funky spot, with exposed brick walls, and devil's ivy in pots suspended from a high ceiling. Sunlight filters in through large windows, casting everything in a dreamy glow—all the diners with their sourdough toast and poached eggs; smashed avocado and bacon; muesli with yoghurt and raspberries.

Sam sits back in his chair, so full he can hardly move. He watches your mum feeding you buttered toast, and feels contentment tugging at him. Inviting him to drift into a doze, right there at the table. It's surreal. As if he's been dropped into a parallel version of his life: one moment a bachelor touring Europe to flog a new bestseller; the next, a husband and father, trying to get out of his seat so he can pay for breakfast.

'You okay there, Sam?' Tori says, wiping crumbs off her fingers. It still takes him by surprise sometimes, her accent—steep and swooping. Regal. 'You look like a man brought to his knees last night.'

'She's two-thirds owl, this kid,' Sam says, yawning and stretching his arms over his head. 'Aren't you, Isla?' He smiles at you, then stands up and heads for the till, stooping to kiss Tori as he goes. They linger over the kiss and you grab his hair, and for a moment he's stuck, laughing while Tori disentangles him from your sticky paw.

When he reaches the queue, he recognises the guy in front of him. His sandy hair is shorter now, and he's lost weight since Sam saw him last, but the turtle tattoo on his neck is a dead giveaway.

'Cohen,' Sam says.

Cohen turns. The woman beside him does too, pulling her hair behind her ear and smiling. Expressions flit across Cohen's face, settling into an uneasy smile.

'Sam,' he says. 'Wow, long time no see.'

'Too long, mate,' Sam says, holding out his hand. 'I hardly recognised you.'

'The ravages of time,' Cohen says, shaking it.

'Not at all; you're looking well.'

'This is my wife, Jewel.'

'Pleased to meet you, Sam,' Jewel says, extending her hand.

Jewel is a local celebrity. A social media consultant and influencer who's managed to build an empire out of the brand she's turned herself into. With an army of followers, she's attracted swarms of sponsors, meaning she probably won't have to spend another cent on swimwear, clothes or shoes for the rest of her life. But she's taken it further than that, using her brand to create, curate and sell a dizzying array of desirables, to the point where now she's raking it in, hand over delicate fist. Can you tell I'm not too fond of the woman? It's nothing personal really; it's just that, in my head, Cohen is still mine.

What do you care about these things, Isla? The light and the shadows of the human heart? Nothing yet, I know. But you will, one day. And that's what this story is about—the light and the shadows. I'm hoping that if I whisper it to you while you sleep, you'll absorb it somehow, even though you've no vocabulary of your own yet. Call it esoteric osmosis, if you like. If you need a name.

'We're about to order breakfast,' Cohen says, nodding an apology to the waiting cashier.

'Of course,' Sam says. 'Sorry, yes. Do what you have to do.'

'But you two should catch up some time,' Jewel says. 'Why don't you swap numbers while I order?'

'Yeah, okay,' Cohen says, perhaps reluctantly, though Sam can't be sure. He finds him difficult to read. Not like the old Cohen, who shared everything with him—all his fears and hopes. All his self-doubt, of which there was plenty.

They exchange numbers and find things to say to each other, avoiding a few possible topics along the way. They don't mention me, for example. Also, Sam avoids asking after Cohen's mum, Libby. In case the news is bad.

Jewel finishes ordering and rests her hand briefly on Cohen's forearm.

'Good to go,' she says, smiling goodbye to Sam and heading towards a table at the far end of the café.

It's agony for me to watch Cohen go after her. It should be me with him, choosing a table, scanning the menu. It should be *us*, sharing observations about life, the universe and buddha bowls. Instead, he's spending his life with this polished little woman with her glowing tan and carefully chosen accessories. And when I say carefully chosen, I'm being diplomatic. The woman will spend hours picking out what to adorn herself with. Hours.

Sam, too, watches them go. It's amazing, he thinks, how Cohen's managed to master such a casual air over the years. No one would guess now how hard it was for him, once, to be in the world. To move through life.

◆◆◆

Sam and Tori walk home alongside the wide band of river. Tori's hair smells sweet: floral with a hint of breastmilk. She's beside Sam, under his arm, while you sleep against his chest, snug in your carrier. This is happiness, Sam thinks. If he could, he'd bottle it. Store it at the back of the cupboard. For leaner times.

'I'm still bummed you didn't introduce me to your friend,' Tori says. 'It's been what, eight months since we got here? And the only people I've met are your mum and your grandparents.'

'You were the one who insisted on a registry wedding in London, remember? I wanted to show you off here, properly.'

'Yeah right, in all my pregnant glory.'

'Absolutely. See, Isla's nodding; she agrees with me.'

'No, she isn't. She's looking for boob.'

'Fair enough, too.'

'You know these are only temporary right? Soon as she's weaned I'll be right back down to zilch again.'

This is probably true, but what Tori usually lacks in the breast department she easily makes up for everywhere else, thanks to a combination of genetics and eight years' dancing on a West End stage.

'Fine by me,' Sam says.

'I think what you meant to say was: *not zilch, babe.*'

'Exactly what I meant to say.'

You're growing agitated, realising you've been attached to the wrong chest for the walk home.

'Nearly there,' Sam murmurs, giving you his little finger to tide you over. Fortunately, the three of you have reached the street that runs along below the front of your house, between Charles Court Reserve and a cluster of hillside mansions overlooking the Swan River. Nearly home.

'So, was it nice to see him again?' Tori asks.

Sam opens the gate at the bottom of the path up to the house; it's single-file only up the sleepers embedded in the hillside, cutting through the dense bush.

'Cohen?' he says. 'For sure. He's changed quite a lot. Physically, I mean. Used to be quite overweight.'

Sam's idea of overweight is a little misguided, if you ask me. His benchmark is every muscle clearly delineated, enough to cast a shadow. Cohen's leaner now, yes, but his body was just fine back in the day. Perfect, even.

The overgrown path from the river to your house opens out onto your backyard—a gleaming pool embedded in a long stretch of turf, dwarfed by the glass-walled house beyond.

'How long since you saw him last?' Tori asks, unlocking the sliding door and going in, dumping her bag on the kitchen benchtop. She plumps up the cushions on the sofa to support her back while she feeds you.

'About eighteen years.'

'Wow. What happened?'

'Why should something have happened? People lose touch.'

'True, but … it's a long time. Anyway,' she laughs, 'you'd better pass me that baby before she puts her neck out. Look at her.'

Sam unclips the carrier and pulls you out, warm and wriggling. He holds your soft cheek against his own for a moment then hands you to Tori, who nods towards her bag on the benchtop.

'Forgot to grab my water,' she says. 'Can you pass it to me? It's in the bag. My phone too … side pocket.'

'Too easy,' Sam says, fishing them out.

A message pings through on the phone as he carries it over, lighting up the screen. He glances at it—a reflex, but long enough to read what's there and who it's from.

When can I see you again?

Sam hands your mother the phone and watches her read until she makes reluctant eye contact.

'Who's Pete?' he asks.

'It's nothing,' Tori says, putting the phone face down on the sofa beside her.

'Who is he?'

'Sam …' Tori says wearily, leaning back into the cushions, closing her eyes.

Sam sits on the armchair facing her. He repeats the question calmly though his heart feels quick and heavy.

'He's my ex,' Tori says at last. 'He's having a hard time letting go.'

'Letting go? Why have I never heard of him?'

'Have I heard of all of your exes?'

'No.'

'Well then …?'

'*When can I see you again?* I mean …'

Tori sighs, adjusts her position.

'Why *again*?' Sam says. 'Have you seen him recently?'

'When, Sam? How? He's in London.'

'What else has he been saying? Can I see?'

'Why? What difference does it make?'

'I want to know how far back it goes. Why he thinks he still stands a chance.'

'He doesn't stand a chance.'

'Clearly he thinks he does.'

'Well, he doesn't.'

Sam heads towards the window. Down below, the wide band of river glistens in the sunlight, skin-like and smooth though puckered in seemingly random places, like snail trails on glass. Small boats are dotted here and there, rocking gently, drifting around their anchors. Others cut through the water, white froth streaming out behind them.

'Sam,' Tori says, pulling you up off her breast and rubbing circles on your back. 'Honestly, there's nothing going on between us.'

'I'd let you read my messages, Tori.'

'I'd never ask to, Sam. Seriously, you have to be able to trust me or this whole marriage thing is never going to work.'

Sam watches her speak. Massages his forehead with his fingertips.

'How long were you two together?'

'Nine years.'

'Nine years? That's ... Makes us seem like an after-thought.'

'We're not an afterthought; we're a balmy island after a long and harrowing journey. Pete and I were awful together, Sam. Intensely wonderful sometimes, but not enough to make up for the mostly awful.'

'Are *we* intensely wonderful?'

'Of course,' Tori says, but there's a pause first, a beat just long enough for Sam to know she's layering something over the truth.

'We're not, are we? I'm just a safe harbour. Somewhere to catch your breath.'

'What's wrong with being safe? That's exactly what I want.'

'Right now it is, but what happens when the novelty wears off? Are you going to head back out there? Crank up the adrenaline?'

Tori lays you back down on the feeding pillow.

'I'm married to you, Sam. We have Isla ...'

'Did Pete ever ask you to marry him?'

'Sam, I'm tired ...'

'Did he?'

'No, he didn't.'

'Would you have said yes if he had?'

'God, Sam, I don't know.'

'Would you?'

'Probably, yes. But he didn't, okay? Thank God.'

Sam looks at the two of you on the couch, his belly churning. He shakes his head.

'It was an awful, unstable relationship that I should never have allowed to go on as long as it did,' Tori says. 'But I was young, and there was this charge between us. He made me laugh. But he could be cruel … the things he'd say sometimes. I should have stayed away, but I kept going back. I was young and stupid.'

'When did you break up?'

'Around September, I think. A year and a half ago, nearly.'

'That's like … a month before we met.'

'Please don't let this become a thing, Sam. He's my past, okay?'

'Not according to him, if that message is any indication.'

'But he is. According to me, he is.'

Sam scratches the stubble on his jaw. 'I'm just the rebound guy.'

'The rebound guy is the best guy,' Tori says quietly. 'Come on, Sam. What's the difference? Really?'

'The difference is everything,' Sam says, standing up and heading for the door.

3

Sam steps outside and even the sky has changed, as if a filter has fallen away. He's not used to being second best. To feeling vulnerable like this. It's deeply unsettling for him. I'm not saying he's been walking around in his marriage going, *Yes, this is good, I am at the helm*. But, consciously or otherwise, that's where he likes to be. Steering the ship. Not flung about like a deckhand in a storm.

He heads down the driveway and exits via the pedestrian gate beside the electric one. A little way down the road, there's a path to the river between two neighbouring properties, overgrown with Geraldton wax and melaleuca scrub. He strides down to the foreshore, for want of a better plan, and then he walks, thinking about Tori and their first date at The French House in Soho.

He got there early, to settle in with a drink and steady his nerves. When he saw Tori come into that dim, old pub to meet him—her cheeks flushed, her thick auburn hair in a low ponytail—he felt something stir inside him: excitement, desire, and an optimism he hadn't felt in ages. It wasn't that he'd been suffering a dry spell; women were always eager to hear what he had to say, to lap up what he was willing to give. But few of them, if any, made him feel the way Tori did.

Their eyes met and she waved at him before buying a glass of wine at the bar. She was so elegant, so charming to the barman.

When she reached the table, Sam stood and kissed her on the cheek. She smelled like roses. Her eyes looked a little red-rimmed, but Sam put it down to the crisp autumn air. Now though, it seems more likely she'd been crying. Almost certainly over Pete.

Clenching his fists in his pockets, Sam curses under his breath. This memory, and all the others, will have to be recalibrated. Where to even start?

Meanwhile, Cohen and Jewel are back home after their breakfast. Cohen's sitting on a pool lounger, watching Jewel swim laps in their infinity pool. He likes watching her swim. In most other activities, she's poised and restrained, but in the pool she's fierce and strong. Cohen has her phone beside him, ready to take pictures when she gets out. She's promoting her new line of bathers and her usual photographer is territorial about weekends, so it's up to Cohen to capture her today, toned and invigorated, for her multitude of followers.

Jewel pauses at the far end before launching into backstroke. Cohen takes a few snaps, checks them, then picks up his own phone. He resisted all through breakfast, but now he surrenders and types Sam Favier into his search engine. Sam has a website promoting his books and events, and he has several professional social media accounts, full of book-related stuff. His personal social media is roped off to the plebs, but his profile picture shows him with his arm around the woman who was at the café with him today, and their baby between them.

Sam Favier, family man.

Guess people change, Cohen thinks, looking across the pool at the palatial house he calls home, and the woman who married him, now pulling herself out of the water. Circumstances mutate. Sometimes beyond recognition.

1998 Friday, 17th April

Brown leaves accumulate in gutters and gardens. Woodsmoke drifts across the still-blue sky. In their two-bedroom cottage, Cohen's mum, Libby, is gearing up for her fortieth. She's having it at home, in the backyard. Her friends who play in a folk group will perform their mix of covers and originals long into the night while a pig turns on a spit, and nearly everyone in town will be there. Her friends complain of being skint all the time, but somehow tonight—guaranteed—there'll be an endless supply of beer and whisky and bourbon and weed, and whatever else they can get their hands on.

Sam's been around to help. He and Cohen have been hanging lights, fetching ice, squashing redbacks with sticks and sweeping their webs off the outdoor chairs. They've set up the spit on one of the old tables out the back and made sure the sound system is working.

'Cheers for helping out,' Cohen says, brushing his hands on his jeans. 'What do you want to do now?'

'We could bike out to the forest?'

'Or we could play Monopoly?'

'Nah, Monopoly is for losers. I might go home for a bit; I have to chop some wood for my mum. I'll see you later.'

Libby's finished cleaning the kitchen and is stirring a giant pot of vegetable curry, humming away, drinking an icy Jack-and-coke.

'Hey, Coh,' she says when he leans in to smell the curry. 'All them jobs done already?'

'Yep. Sam's gone home for a bit.'

'He'll come back with his mum later?'

'Yeah.'

'I'd better get ready. Can you stir this for me? Just for five minutes, then turn it right down.'

Cohen takes the wooden spoon and watches the curry work its way to boiling point while Libby tops up her drink.

'Dad coming?'

'Bloody hope not. I haven't told him about it; fingers crossed no one else has.'

Cohen stirs, thinking about his father, Danny: funny and chiselled and loved by everyone, except the people who actually know him. He left Libby and Cohen two years ago, having found a new woman to pin to the wall with his forearm, should the spirit move. There's been no official divorce, but Cohen's stopped grinding his teeth at night and gnawing on his fingernails. Now that he's not bracing for unchecked violence all the time, he's noticed a kind of happiness moving in. A lightness to things. It feels delicate, as if it could break at any time, but it's there.

After five minutes, he turns the gas down low, puts the lid on the pot and the spoon on a plate next to the stove, and heads out for a walk. He likes being in town in the evening, especially when the summer heat is backing off for real. People are milling around, kicking the footy on the oval, watching their kids muck around on the swings.

When he gets back home, Libby's back in the kitchen, putting the rice on. She's wearing her best dress—a blue floral one with a long, swoopy skirt—and her blonde hair is draped over her shoulder in a loose braid. She smells of her sunflower perfume and the cigarette burning in an ashtray by the window.

'Party time, Coh,' she says. 'Time to get the tunes cranking.'

People start arriving with their eskies and glad-wrapped bowls of potato salad and coleslaw. They tell him how big he's getting then they move on out to the back, where Libby's new boyfriend, Gary, is building up the bonfire ready to be lit. Sam and his mum arrive too. Cohen likes Sam's mum. She always seems happy to see him.

As daylight fades into night, the banter gets louder and the band kicks off.

Sam and Cohen eat roast pork and potato salad, and Sam nicks a beer for them to share. They're playing ping-pong on the weathered table when suddenly all the chatter and guffawing around them falls away. The music cranks on, but everyone is staring at the man walking through the screen doors.

Danny doesn't mind the attention; you can see he's calculating how to make the most of it while he scans the group for his wife.

'Thanks for the invite, Lib,' he calls out, when he spots her near the fire. She's paralysed where she stands, torn between cowering behind Gary and getting between him and her husband. In the end, it doesn't matter. Danny's heard about Gary on the grapevine, and he's been seething ever since.

He walks across to an esky and selects a cold beer, which he opens and raises in a toast. 'To the birthday girl,' he says, taking a swig. Then he leans over the trestle table and picks up a slice of pork. He eats it slowly, acknowledging people's stares until they look away and tentatively resume their own conversations.

Cohen watches, dread throbbing in his gut, as Danny makes his way over to Libby and Gary and the others gathered around the fire. Standing there, shifting his weight from one foot to the other, Danny makes a big show of listening to whatever's being said for a while, then he says something to Libby that Cohen can't hear. It must've been designed to provoke a response from Gary though, because Gary frowns and steps in. Says something back.

Danny takes another long drink of his beer. Then he smashes the bottle against the fire pit and holds the jagged rim up to Gary's jugular. Libby screams at him to stop, but he presses his new weapon against Gary's skin until blood begins running down the glass onto his hand.

Suddenly, he drops the bottle in the fire and lunges for Libby, grabbing her by her hair and forcing her across the patio, into the house. It's all so fast, so shocking, nobody does anything to stop him. Gary's on his knees, holding his bleeding neck, and everyone's just standing there.

Cohen's the first to snap out of it, but he's not quick enough to stop Danny dragging Libby into the bedroom and locking the door. He can hear her through the wood, placating and pleading.

Cohen drives his shoulder uselessly against the door. Some of the blokes run over. One of them body-slams the door. Another tries a standing kick to the side of the knob, but the lock holds.

There's a scream and a thud from the inside.

A woman is on the phone in the kitchen, calling the cops. She's shouting the address. Cohen feels hopelessness wash through him, ice-cold. Then he hears Sam's voice, telling everyone to move over.

He has something in his hands. The crowbar from the garage.

Sam uses his foot to flex the door open at the base, then he wedges the tool into the gap between door and frame. He drops his weight below the crowbar and pushes upward until, thank Christ, the lock gives.

Cohen runs to where Danny is standing over Libby in the corner. She's crumpled against the wall. Not moving. Blood all over her mouth and down the front of her dress.

Danny seems dazed as the men grab hold of him and pin his arms behind his back. Cohen drops to the floor, touches Libby's face, takes her hand.

'Mum, I'm here. We're here.'

She murmurs something, opens her eyes a little and squeezes his hand feebly. 'Cohen,' she whispers. 'I'm okay, mate. It's okay.'

It feels like forever, but at last, the police and an ambulance arrive. The paramedics assess Libby and take her away on a stretcher, telling Cohen he should stay at home, get some sleep. The cops lock Danny in their van and take statements from Cohen, Sam and the guests, then they leave, saying they'll send one of their liaison people around soon.

Slowly, the guests leave too. Sam's mum is the last one there. She cleans up the blood in the bedroom, then she wraps up the leftover food and puts it in the fridge.

'How about we stay over tonight?' she asks. 'Would that be good?'

Cohen nods and offers her Libby's bedroom, trying to hide his relief.

'Don't you worry,' she says. 'They'll put him away for real this time.'

Outside, the party lights are still on and the fire's not quite dead. The boys stand staring down at the embers.

'How'd you know how to do that?' Cohen asks. 'With the crowbar?'

'Someone did it in a book I read.'

Cohen sits on a bench, his legs suddenly shaky.

'You okay, mate?' Sam says, sitting down next to him. 'That was pretty intense.'

'I'm okay, I think.'

'Maybe you should lie down?'

Cohen shakes his head.

They sit for a while, staring at the chairs, arranged all nicely by Libby, and the empties on the table. Used napkins on the ground. Then Sam stands up and heads inside. Cohen gets up too and digs a couple of soft drinks out of the ice bucket before going in.

Sam's standing over the dining table, doing something. He turns when he hears Cohen come in, and Cohen sees he's set out a game of Monopoly—board, money, cards.

'You wanna be the dog or the boot?' Sam says. 'Looks like they're all that's left.'

4

Jewel walks up out of the pool at the steps. She squeezes water from her hair then loosens it up with her fingers.

'You ready, Cohen?'

'Two seconds.'

She backtracks into the water to recreate her emergence. Cohen, up off his seat, catches her from several angles as she walks to her towel—a slow, feline walk.

'Here you go,' he says, handing her the phone and leaning in for a kiss.

'Thanks, babe,' she says, offering him her cheek before scrolling through the shots and heading into the shade for a better look. Cohen watches her go then turns away. He's looking at the water, considering a swim, when his phone lights up on the lounger.

It's Sam.

Heading to Leighton for a swim and a coffee. Thought maybe we could catch up?

◆◆◆

Sam's already there when Cohen pulls into the car park that afternoon. He's leaning on the wooden fence, near the picnic gazebo and the steep steps that lead down to the beach. There's a fair queue at the coffee wagon—a timber-clad caravan with a sea-facing servery—and the footpath is busy with dog-walkers and cyclists.

'You made it,' Sam says, holding out his hand. Seagulls perch on the shade umbrellas or squall overhead. 'Coffee?'

If you were to ask Sam why he's called Cohen up now, I think he'd struggle to explain it. He could've tracked him down easily enough over the years, after all. But the urge hasn't been there. Or at least, it's never been loud. If you ask me, it's because he's had the marital rug pulled out from under his feet. He's been set adrift, and he's looking to Cohen for anchorage.

They order two flat whites and step aside to wait.

'So,' Sam says. 'How've you been?'

'Good, yeah. Can't complain. You?'

'Not bad,' Sam says, glancing over at a young family at a table nearby—three kids squabbling over a packet of chips, their parents escaping into their phones.

'Something to look forward to,' Cohen says, following his gaze.

'Don't know about that.'

'You think you'll stop at one?'

'I think so, yeah. Might not have a choice in the matter, actually.

Tori and I … something weird happened this morning.'

'Sounds ominous.'

'Yeah, a little bit.'

'Want to talk about it?'

'Two flat whites for Sam,' the barista calls.

'Maybe later,' Sam says. 'Let's take these down and hit the water.'

2000 Wednesday, 23rd February

It's strange to think there was a time before I knew Sam or Cohen. A time before their lives intersected with mine. But there was, and it was fine. You know, ordinary—parents, a brother; highs and lows. After high school, I found an ushering job at the Windsor and an apartment to share with some friends—a little place not far from campus, on the top floor of a whitewashed three-storey building. I liked it a lot: the light and the art deco curves.

It's orientation week and I'm lying on my bed, officially reading, but actually watching a fly buzz at the window, over and over again, like a tiny blind drunkard. It's distracted me from my book because now I'm wondering which marine life form might be considered its counterpart. Some kind of micromollusc, I'm guessing. Or a copepod. This line of thought is not unusual. Since childhood, I've been drawn to the sea, watching life unfold in rock pools: miniature crabs frozen in my shadow; slow-creeping anemones and crevice-wedged urchins; fish darting over craggy submarine cliffs. I've devoured books about seamounts and underwater landslides; about phonic lips and subaquatic echolocation; about the swift and intricate brutality of the marine food chain. I just love the ocean—that wild, hidden place, far richer and more fascinating than anything you'll find on land. Which means I've surprised exactly no one by enrolling in Marine Science at UWA.

The fly has taken a brief hiatus and is wringing its wiry legs when I hear the other girls come home, laughing and talking loudly.

'Hey,' Marla says, standing in my doorframe. 'You ready to get ready?'

'I was born ready to get ready.'

'Well, we have one hour to figure out how to get these sheets wrapped in a way that says *toga* but also *hot*.'

Julia mixes some punch and we're half tanked by the time we leave. It's a short walk to campus, but long enough to finish off the punch on the way. We're laughing and Julia is singing Ani DiFranco loudly, and I feel like I may never have to push through loneliness or insecurity ever again.

Lit by stadium lights, the oval is full of sheet-draped students, shouting and dancing and lurching about. Loud music blares from four or five speakers on stands next to the trestle tables, which are stacked with plastic cups and kegs. We three girls queue up for wristbands and beer, and before long we're out there with the others, dancing and sloshing our drinks around. I'm lining up for more beer when a guy comes up to me in the queue. Leans close to speak into my ear.

'Pretend I'm with you,' he says, smiling at me. He's tall and smells of aftershave. His skin is tanned and smooth. My attempt at a cool response—'Why would I do that?'—is, if anything, flirtatious. It's all in the tone, isn't it? The tilt of the head.

'Because you're kind and good,' he says, putting his arm around me, 'and I need a beer *immediately*.'

The heat of him pulses through me like new blood.

'Fair enough,' I say, 'old friend.'

He laughs and pulls me closer, and it should be unwelcome—too familiar—but I'm pissed and open to all things bold and spontaneous. That's what O-week is all about, after all: radical ice-breaking. Sanctioned transgressions.

We buy more beer than we need, to avoid having to queue up too soon, and take it back out to the party. Jostled about by revellers and soaked in spilled beer and sweat, we dance closer and closer to each other, and I think we're going to kiss, when suddenly Marla is there, pulling me away.

'Thank God I found you,' she says, dragging me towards the darkness of trees. 'Julia's hurling her guts up. We have to get her home.'

'What? No,' I say. 'I met someone.' But Marla's grip is firm and, away from the mass of people, I suddenly realise how drunk I am. The stars are spinning.

'Sorry, babe,' Marla says. 'He was hot, but hoes before bros, yeah?'

We stagger home with Julia propped between us, stopping twice to let her heave in the bushes.

The semester begins for real the following week. Days pass in a jumble of course outlines and expectations and social events. Weeks go by in a cycle of labs, tutorials and assessment crunch-times. Now and again, I think I catch sight of the guy from the toga party, but he's always disappearing into the Arts building and our paths never cross directly.

Sometime in May, Julia starts talking about a girl she's met in her Maths lab, Erica. Erica is smart and sassy and interesting. They spend a lot of time together, and when Erica's cousin has a house party, Julia drags me along. It's in a sagging share house in Nedlands—lots of little rooms off a small entry hall. Strangely dim lights. Lurid carpets.

Pearl Jam is blaring from somewhere. We work our way through the people and the smoke towards the kitchen at the back, where Julia makes sure I have a beer before Erica whisks her off to meet some other people. I'm standing in the kitchen, watching three drunk people make a concoction of some kind in a blender, when a guy comes over and offers me some chips. He's half a foot taller than me with broad shoulders and sandy hair.

'Hungry?'

He's solemn about it, as if my discomfort is no laughing matter.

'Starving,' I say, taking a handful.

'There's heaps of food outside,' he says, and I follow him out to where a table is loaded up with buns and more chips and sausages and sliced watermelon.

'Here,' he says, handing me a paper plate before filling up his own.

'Thanks,' I say, grabbing some of everything and following him to some plastic chairs.

'What's your name?'

'Gracie.'

'I'm Cohen.'

He smiles then. His eyes are grey-blue.

'This your place?'

'Yeah. Me and some mates.'

Cohen is studying History and Philosophy, but he loves the idea of Marine Science. Says he almost went that way himself, owing to his love of fishing and stingrays, but in the end, he followed his fascination with humanity.

'No other species swings from idiocy to genius like we do,' he says. 'We're uniquely mental.'

A bloke comes up to us carrying a box of wine and a large plastic cup. He has long black hair and is wearing a patchwork waistcoat over his bare torso.

'Cohen,' he says. 'Who's your friend?'

'This is Gracie. Gracie, meet Matty.'

'I've got some wicked shrooms,' Matty says, lowering his voice and leaning in close. 'If you're keen?'

Cohen glances at me. 'Not for me, thanks,' he says. 'Cheers.'

'I've also got some trips, and some new designer shit if you're into that?'

'I'll pass,' I say. 'Thanks.'

'No worries. Let me know if you change your mind.'

Matty turns and moves on to a group sitting a little way off. There's a notebook wedged into his back pocket, quite a big one.

'He came with the house,' Cohen says, watching him go. 'No idea how long he's been living here. Studying Geology, allegedly.'

'What's with the notebook?'

'He calls that his logbook—records every drug he takes and reflects on the experience ... Perth's answer to Hunter S. Thompson. Can I get you another beer?'

'I'll come with you.'

As we're approaching the food table with its understorey of eskies, I recognise someone coming down the stairs. It's the guy from the toga party, with his arm around a girl who looks as if she can't believe her luck. She says something in his ear and goes off to talk to some people sitting on a blanket.

I look away before he notices me staring, and take the beer Cohen's holding out to me.

'Cohen, mate,' the guy says, punching him on the upper arm. 'How's things?'

'Can't complain,' Cohen says, punching him back. 'D'you get more ice?'

'Sure did. And who's this?''

'This is Gracie. Gracie, this is another of my housemates, Sam. He didn't come with the place, but he may as well have.'

'Gracie,' Sam says, 'come find me when you're bored, okay? We can reminisce about Ancient Greece.'

He winks at me, and for a moment, I'm back in that drunken throng on the oval, smelling freshly cut grass and beer and wondering if he's going to kiss me … but then I'm back at this party, next to Cohen.

I glance from one to the other, then slip my arm through Cohen's.

'I think I'll be okay, Sam, thanks anyway.'

'Time will tell,' Sam says, ruffling Cohen's hair, then he saunters off to find the girl he came with. Though any girl will do, I imagine.

◆◆◆

The next time I see Cohen is a week or so later. It's half-price Wednesday and I'm serving popcorn and snacks at the Windsor.

He's there to see *Mission: Impossible II*.

'You often come to movies on your own?' I ask, handing him his choc-top.

'Sam was meant to be here,' Cohen says, 'but he piked. Not that I mind too much.'

'I like watching movies on my own too,' I say.

'Maybe we should catch one alone together sometime.'

I laugh, but the idea is not ludicrous; he's got this spaciousness about him.

I'm still working when his film is over, but he says he'll hang around and walk me home. Just after ten, I step outside and there he is, leaning against the wall, reading a battered copy of *The Outsider*.

'How was the movie?' I ask as he slips the book into his backpack.

'Entertaining,' he says. 'Not amazing.'

We walk along the highway, past the pub and down the hill, stopping in at the service station to buy water. I remember we need milk at home, so I grab some of that too. When we reach my apartment block, I stop at the stairs and face him. My intention is to say thanks and goodnight, but instead I find myself asking him up.

Upstairs, the girls are watching a movie. I make coffee and we take it out onto the balcony. There's a small table with chairs out there, but there's also a low couch with a coffee table, and that's where we go, sinking back into the cushions.

We drink our coffee and talk. There's a frisson between us as we sit out there in the dark with the light of the film flickering inside. Cohen takes my hand. We sit for a moment, then he looks at me, that TV glow catching his eyes and the side of his face.

I feel exhilarated, but also safe—as if we're suspended together in a low-pressure stillness; cocooned in the eye of a storm. I guess he sees enough to know I won't mind if he leans in and kisses me, because that's what he does, and I'm rapt. Spellbound. I hope he never stops.

5

I need to introduce you to someone else: Robyn. Robyn Tinsley. She's an old friend of mine. Cohen's too. And Sam's. Number four in our tight little group.

She lives in London now. A foreign correspondent for the ABC. Before London, she was based in South Africa, and before that, Istanbul. Six years all up since leaving Perth. She's found it hard. Really difficult work. But she's stuck with it, feeling like she owes it to all those people whose traumas she's reported on over the years.

And to her father, back home. She thinks of him now as she watches the dark innards of the city flash past the windows. Pictures his head bent over his old laptop. Wonders how he's holding up today.

A hot tunnel wind snakes through the train from end to end; there's a distant howling sound, an eerie drag of steel on steel.

Robyn closes her eyes to imagine sunlight on her face. The quiet rhythm of the ocean. Salt in the air.

Stepping off at Camden, she's drawn into the surge of people heading through the white-tiled labyrinth of tunnels and stairs, making for the relief of open sky. Though it's not that open. More a smothering greyness accompanied by a fine drizzle and a bracing wind off the Channel.

◆◆◆

Her phone rings as she climbs the steps to the front door of her flat— a small, borrowed sliver of the city with a damp winter smell that will hang around all through spring. If spring ever comes.

'Dad, hi,' she says, rummaging in her bag for her keys.

'Robyn. How are you?'

It's good to hear his voice, the flat Aussie emphasis he gives the *are*.

'I'm okay. You?'

'Not bad, not bad. Heard you on the news this morning, your terrorism story.'

'Yeah, I made a meal of it.'

'Sounded fine to me.'

Frank isn't one to sugar-coat things. If he says it was fine, it was fine. But Robyn's in a bleak place, emotionally, and not in the habit of being kind to herself.

'Not my best work,' she says.

'Don't be too hard on yourself, love. This is always a rough day.'

He's not wrong: she wades through the fourteenth of January each year like someone lost in a mire. Every step is arduous; every encounter frightening. Time dissolves and she's eleven again, watching her mum leaving the world. Taking everything good about it with her. Leaving nothing but desolation behind.

Desolation and Frank.

He was a beacon. A place of safety. Robyn's grief was the darkest, coldest desert—oppressive sky; obliterating winds—but then Frank would give her a hug or make her a cheese toastie, and she'd glimpse a future in which she'd feel okay again. He was everything. He was also a brilliant journalist. Formidable. Far better than Robyn could ever hope to be. If she could've made one complaint, it would've been that he was too good. Too committed. Either shut in his study or running out the door with a folder under his arm, grabbing his keys from the hallstand.

When he was there with her—properly there—it was like bathing in a warm rock pool with the sun on her skin. He taught her how to thread a worm on a hook, murmuring, *Sorry little guy*; how to build drip-castles on the beach; how to touch-type. He was so steady. So patient. Only, so easily stolen away. If something happened in Nepal or down the street, he'd be off finding a new angle on it, some way to shape it before filing it with the mothership.

'Sorry, mate,' he'd say, tousling Robyn's hair while her shoulders drooped. 'You'll have to take it from here.' So she would. And she'd make sure that when he came back, she could show him how she'd nailed it.

Just as she's doing right now, in London. Nailing it.

It's all she's ever wanted to do: travel the world as a foreign correspondent, meeting people and telling their stories. But she never anticipated the way your ears ring after a bomb's gone off around the corner; the way bodies look when they're strewn across the street; what it's like to walk over the rubble of people's homes while the stones are still warm. It's gutting, and it burns, in an existential, cosmic way. She's beginning to suspect she's missing that thing some journos have, whatever it is that stops the images from haunting you. For instance, the little boy she saw sleeping in an inner-city doorway, his tiny foot hanging out from beneath a collapsed cardboard box. He was so small, so alone in all the world, his dirty toes in danger of being kicked or trodden on, and that was the least of the dangers he surely faced. Buying him a pie from a nearby fast-food place full of middle-class kids on the piss—not their fault either, all the shit they'd inherited—broke her heart because a pie might fill his tummy tonight, but what about tomorrow? And the day after that?

'Did you visit Mum today?' Robyn asks, locking the door behind her and heading through to the kitchen with its lime-green tiles. She pictures Heather's plaque, set into a free-standing memorial stone under a tree in Karrakatta cemetery.

'Yes,' Frank says. 'I took her some roses. We had our usual chat while I did some weeding.'

'I still miss her.'

'Me too, love. Every day.'

Robyn stares up at the water stains on the ceiling, their soft edges creeping ever outward.

'I'm coming home,' she says, surprising herself with the words.

'Oh?' Frank says. 'New assignment?'

'No. No new assignment. I've lost my balance, Dad. I'm falling.'

And so she is. Palpitations, panic attacks, the works. It's time to go home, to turn her back on all the wounds of the world and nurse her own for a while.

2001 Saturday, 3rd March

It's a stifling morning in Perth. Must be forty degrees out there, and not much cooler in the apartment, aside from in the lounge room, where our reverse cycle aircon unit is working overtime. We're trying to make the most of the weekend, given that the semester starts on Monday, so we've been to the beach already— hot white sand; gleaming cold swell—but the air feels too hot to breathe, much less move around in. So we've admitted defeat, which amounts to lazing about on the sofas drinking cold water and lemonade. Robyn's suggested putting on a movie, but so far, it's in the too-hard basket.

She's a first-year to our second, and she's been living with us for about a week. Julia scooted off for a gap-year in Melbourne, so we needed someone to take her room. We put a poster up on campus and had heaps of interest, but there was something about Robyn. She arrived for the interview—slight, with a blonde ponytail and glasses—in black dungarees over a teal T-shirt.

'Why do you want to move in here?' Marla asked her across the dining table.

Robyn looked around at the white walls and Marla's indoor plants. My posters of sea turtles and whales on the walls.

'It's clean and close to campus,' she said, 'and you both seem nice.'

'We do,' Marla said. 'But are we?' Wriggling her eyebrows.

Robyn smiled, looked past her out the window.

'Course you are,' she said. 'Plus, my dad wants me to make friends and let loose.' *Let loose,* pronounced as if in inverted commas. 'It's been just me and him for a long time.'

'No mum?' I asked.

Marla looked at me as if I'd crossed a line, got too personal too soon, but Robyn met my gaze and shook her head.

'Cancer,' she said. 'Six years ago last month.'

I look at her now, over the rim of my lemonade glass. She's leaning back on the sofa cushions, feet up on the coffee table, flicking through one of Marla's celebrity-gossip magazines. Every so often, she makes a scornful comment—*Why do we care? Who writes this stuff?*—and I just can't imagine losing my mum. Or anyone I love.

The phone rings. It's Cohen, suggesting a board game. He and Sam can be here in half an hour, armed with beers and wine and Carcassonne.

Marla rolls her eyes and heads out to meet her boyfriend at the movies, so it'll just be the four of us, expanding our influence via tiles and meeples on the table.

Robyn and I give the flat a bit of a tidy up, listening to Blondie, then we give ourselves the same treatment—showers, makeup, something cute to wear: in Robyn's case, a long, black dress; in mine, white shorts and a butter-yellow singlet.

'Hey,' Cohen says when I open the door. He kisses me and goes to put the game and wine on the table. Sam has two sixpacks under his arms. His hair is damp and he smells of sandalwood.

'Space in the fridge?' he asks me.

'Should be.'

He has to move a few things around, but he gets there, and when he comes back to the living space, Robyn is standing next to Cohen, listening while he gives a brief summary of Carcassonne.

'Robyn,' I say. 'This is Sam. Sam, Robyn.'

'Hello,' Robyn says.

'Hi,' Sam says. 'Cohen making sense?'

'Sense enough. I need to actually play the game for it all to sink in, but I get the gist.'

I can see she's impressed by Sam. She hides it quite well—a steady gaze, a nonchalant posture—but I know a faint blush when I see one.

6

Let's leave Robyn to her packing in London and dip back in on Sam. See how he's holding up. In a nutshell, not very well. It's nearly a week since he discovered your mum's secret tether to her past, and he's still smarting.

This Friday night, we find him at Mojos Bar in North Fremantle, with Cohen. After their coffee and swim on the weekend, he's called Cohen up twice. He suggested a movie for their next catch-up, or a game of squash, but Cohen proposed beer and live music instead. Less intimate, somehow.

Mojos is dark. Welcoming in a way that only a low-ceilinged pub with a red velvet stage can be. Sam still feels a little awkward, sitting beside Cohen, but after several beers, despite the weight of years and bravado, he tells him everything he couldn't bring himself to say the other day at the beach—a slow, cathartic pour.

'Tori still wants to be with you though?' Cohen asks when he's finished.

Sam shrugs, fidgets with the label on his beer. 'She says so.'

'And you want to stay married to her?'

'Of course. I mean, there's Isla to think about.'

'Then I reckon you'll get over it.'

'That's your prognosis?'

Cohen shrugs. 'All that's happened is that the reality doesn't match the idea and you're having a hard time adjusting. Happens all the time. But you will.'

Sam would never admit it, but Cohen's always been good at advice. He has a knack of summing up a tricky situation in a new way, one that makes more sense.

'You have a wife who loves you, and a child,' Cohen says. 'Don't take that for granted.'

Sam nods slowly, mulling it over. 'When did you get so wise?'

'Day I was born, mate.'

Sam laughs. It feels good, this. Been too long.

'Jewel appreciate your wisdom?'

It's a meaningless comment, straight out of nowhere, but Cohen looks sprung.

'Yeah, I guess,' he says, looking away, back at his drink.

'Hey, sorry, I didn't mean to hit a nerve.'

'No, you didn't hit a nerve. It's all good. Things are a little strained I guess, but it's mostly work stuff. You know what they say about working with your wife.'

Sam studies Cohen for a moment, trying to figure out where his friend might fit within Jewel's empire. He doesn't need to vocalise his confusion; the loose fit is not lost on Cohen.

'I'm basically her finance guy.'

'Didn't you major in Philosophy?'

'And History.'

'Well qualified then.'

'Good evening,' someone says from the stage. A woman, her voice soft but sure. Cohen turns to see what the stamping and whistling is all about. Sam does too and that's when he first sees Skye Culhane, on stage.

It's only fair, I think, to issue a small warning here: about the unexpected ways a person's life can veer off course; about the ravines a man can encounter, and the ways he might try to cross them. Such ways are not always honourable. And you're not always going to like them. In fact, some of them will cut so deep you'll spend the rest of your days running your fingers over the scar. But they're there, Isla; they happen; and you've got Buckley's or none of avoiding them.

The music starts and Skye begins to sing, murmuring a melody in a low register while the bass guitar climbs and falls and climbs again over the steady, slow beat of the drums. Long, dark hair, eyes closed, she could almost be asleep she's so still. But her voice is doing wondrous, intergalactic things. Skye herself seems transformed by it, as though she's channelling it from some other realm. Sam *feels* it, like something soft brushing against him. It makes him want to close his eyes and drift on it, like a cloud over a dark, blue world. Goosebumps ghost across his skin. Across hers as well—he sees them, the hairs on her arms backlit by the stage lights. And that's when he knows he's in trouble.

✦✦✦

Skye curls her fingers around the microphone as the drummer thuds a slow pulse on the kick drum. Jim's lead guitar melody slips over Kiyo's bassline like silk, both of them riding on the rhythmic whisper of Jethro's brush on the snare.

She looks out over all those faces lifted towards the caress of her voice. She's used to it. Likes it. She's under no illusion anymore that it's *her* they love so much as the *idea* of her, and knowing this has taken all the pressure away. She knows what they're all here for now: only a little magic, a little transportation away from ordinary life. They don't need her soul.

Having said that, most of the men in the audience wear a calculating look, as if they're trying to work out how well her stage presence will translate in the bedroom. Because that's what a lot of them think. They think she's up there offering herself to them—a prize for whoever buys her the most drinks after the show or comes up with the most ardent expression of admiration for her performance. It escapes them that she might be up there for some other reason. Like maybe it's a calling. A vocation. Maybe it feeds something inside her that nothing else can reach.

When she first notices Sam watching her, Skye can tell that he gets it. He understands the drive to make something beautiful and send it out into the world. He's not merely watching her. He *sees* her. Such is the power of this realisation that she almost stops singing. She has to close her eyes to find her way back to the song.

She manages to sustain her focus, more or less, for the rest of the gig only by keeping her gaze clear of him. Though he remains a vague shape in her peripheral vision, his presence a thread that tugs at her from the inside.

Later, while the others are packing up their gear, she makes her way to the bar and collects the round of beers that's part of their payment. Wrapping her fingers around the four cold bottlenecks, she turns back, glancing at Sam though she's been determined not to. He's tall, dressed in black jeans and a navy jumper, his hair a dark mass of curls and shadows.

She pulls her eyes away and takes the beers to the waiting band.

'Thanks,' Jim says, flicking down the latch on his guitar case. 'Good gig.'

'Yeah, went well I think.'

Jethro takes his beer and taps it wordlessly against the base of Skye's then turns away to continue packing up his drum kit. He hasn't managed to say much to her recently, not since she had to explain that their brief relationship was over. Already. She'd hoped it might be more; that his quietude might belie fascinating depths; that being with him would feel like submerging herself in crystalline waters after a long hike. She'd had enough of tears and slammed doors and squealing tyres. Of endless discussions about love and never really knowing other people. She'd thought a relationship with Jethro might be different. Better. Calm and cruisy. And it was, but too calm, too cruisy. So here they are, in this awkward lagoon.

Kiyo's bass is already packed away. She's winding a cord back and forth from thumb to elbow, and she looks at Skye, smiling, one eyebrow raised.

'Who's the guy?' she says.

'Which guy?'

'Oh, you think you're subtle, do you? So who is he? Is he here?'

'Godsakes, woman,' Skye laughs. 'It's like living with ASIO.'

'Too right, and your attempt at diversion is not going to fly. So, spill.'

'Over by the door. In a blue jumper. Talking to his friend about something heavy, by the looks of things.'

'Just leaving?'

Skye turns to see Sam following Cohen out the door. He glances back in her direction as he goes. Their eyes catch and it's there again, that thread. That pull.

Kiyo smiles, loading cables into her nylon bag. They don't mention Sam again, but his face inhabits Skye's mind for the rest of that night—the look in his eyes when she caught it.

◆◆◆

Later, Skye locks her guitar in Kiyo's boot and heads back toward the pub. The street is quiet, but for the odd car gliding past.

Jethro steps outside, carrying his pedals and snare to his ute.

'Skye,' he says as he goes. Could be he's trying to sound upbeat, but it comes out officious. Skye wishes she could reclaim the former easiness between them. The way it was before—the gentle banter, the quiet flirtation. Now there's this awful, brittle coldness between them. Wildly, she contemplates pressing him against the shop window and kissing him, just to see his face lift for a moment.

'Jethro,' she says.

The hope in his eyes when he turns back is brutal. 'Yeah?'

'I'm so sorry about everything, you know?'

He looks away again, slides his gear along the metal trailer base.

'Jethro, I hate this too. What can I do to make things better?'

'Nothing,' he says, turning to face her, brushing his hands down his denim thighs. He hasn't met her eyes properly for weeks, and now that he does, the anger that's been brewing back there is like a slap. 'I'm sorry you hate this,' he says, almost whispering, 'but if you're reaching out to *me* for absolution, you're even more arrogant than I thought.' He pulls a trembling hand through his hair then returns it, clenched, to his side. 'I had all my cards on the table, Skye. And you were just trying me on so you could peel me off again, like something in a dressing room you didn't like.'

'Jethro,' Skye says. 'I'm sorry. I didn't mean to mess you around.'

'Well, I'm sorry too, Skye. Sorry I wasn't good enough for you.'

'It's not like that, Jethro.'

'What's it like then, Skye? Tell me.'

'You don't know what it's going to be like with someone, you know? Even if you know them; even if you think there's enough chemistry … Sometimes there just isn't.'

Jethro shakes his head. 'If there was nothing there, Skye, why did you keep coming back?'

'I was being optimistic.'

'Optimistic? Fucking hell … you're nasty, d'you know that?' He shakes his head again, muttering as he climbs into his ute and slams the door.

He tears off down the road, but he's failed to latch his ute canopy down properly; the back falls open and his kick drum falls out with a metallic thwack on the bitumen. Skye watches as he picks up the damaged piece, puts it back in and locks the trailer gate. He looks back at her, then he climbs in and roars away.

7

You're very sweet when you're asleep, Isla. Your eyelids flicker, and your breathing is the loveliest rhythm that ever existed. I'm working hard not to let it make me sad; I always thought I'd have a little person like you in my life. One of my own. Maybe two.

Cohen and Sam are in Sam's car, heading home from Mojos. Cohen is a little worse for wear, head flopped back against the headrest and mumbling about things being blurry. Six beers and two double bourbons will do that to you. Sam glances at him as they cruise along the dark streets of Peppermint Grove towards the river, hoping he won't be sick in the car.

Before long, they pull up outside an eight-foot wall. Beyond the gate is the place Cohen calls home, but really, it's Jewel's domain, artfully curated and scrupulously maintained. A breathtaking lair.

After a prolonged search for his keys, Cohen aims the remote at the gate and thumbs the magic button. The gate glides open and Sam drives in, pausing at a fork in the driveway.

'Which way?'

'Left to visitor parking, right to the underground garage ... the lift and whatnot.'

Sam steers them left through a dense avenue of glossy greenery until they emerge at the foot of an architectural ode to symmetry and scale. He leans forward over his steering wheel, trying to see where the house ends and the sky begins.

'Coming in?' Cohen says.

'It's late ...'

Cohen squints at his watch, blinking slowly.

Sam looks at him, laughs. 'Okay,' he says. 'I'll come in, but only for a minute.'

They cross the driveway towards the portico with its Grecian columns and carved oak door. Sam tries not to be too obvious about it, but he's gawking as they head through the vast entrance hall and past the formal lounge en route to the kitchen. Cohen doesn't see it anymore, this lavish display of wealth and style. Which is a blessing really, because when he takes it all in, he feels ashamed of it. Buried deep within him is a resistance to opulence he can't shake, no matter how hard he tries. And he does try, because God knows he'd rather live like this than return to his childhood spent in that place that smelled of mould and weed and beer-soaked carpets. Jewel doesn't understand the struggle. She grew up in this part of town. For her, this is the natural way of things. No less than she deserves.

'So, what's your poison?' Cohen says, opening the fridge. 'We have beer, wine, gin ... a rainbow of gins ...'

'Coffee thanks.'

'Good call,' Cohen says, fumbling over the coffee machine

before heading to the fridge where he grabs the milk and a can of soft drink.

They take their drinks outside. Eucalypts tower over them as they lean back into their seats, surveying the manicured lawn that stretches out into the darkness.

'It's all Jewel, this place,' Cohen says, resting his can on his thigh and closing his eyes. 'She's worked so hard; she's amazing.'

As you can imagine, Isla, I hate it when he sings her praises. Makes my stomach turn. But I put up with it. Not only because I have no choice, but because I know that while he cares about Jewel—while he admires and desires and respects her—he'll always have that turtle tattoo on his neck. He got it with me, *for* me, when we'd been together six months. To match the one I had on my shoulderblade. And now, all these years later, every day, he reaches back and touches it, whispering, *Hey Gracie*. Whatever Jewel means to him, there's a place in his heart she will never reach. A sanctuary, locked away, with my name carved into the key.

Sometime later, Cohen wakes up alone. The house is silent, hard surfaces gleaming in the moonlight. Sam's gone, but he must've helped Cohen to the couch and covered him with one of Jewel's soft throw rugs, because that's where Cohen is now, and he didn't get there by himself.

He contemplates sitting up, but contemplation is as far as it goes.

Jewel's car growls up the driveway. A minute or two later, he hears her coming upstairs, that ping as the elevator reaches the ground floor.

Lying there, head throbbing, he watches her slip her shoes off and tiptoe to the kitchen for a long drink of water. She's undeniably beautiful—even I'm mesmerised by her sometimes, the way she moves. Light-footed, smooth.

Cohen closes his eyes again, marvelling at the inadequacy of alcohol to fix things, and his apparent inability to accept this basic fact. Instead, he returns again and again to the altar of booze, attempting to drown his fears. Of which there are many, because it's all teetering: the house, the business, the marriage ... all of it ... about to plummet away beneath his feet, leaving nothing but a cloud of smoke and a feast for the gleeful tabloids. He can imagine the headlines now. Has been imagining them for weeks.

Jewel puts her glass quietly beside the sink then pads past Cohen, making for the stairs. She doesn't spot him there. He wonders if he should alert her to his presence but decides against it—he almost certainly reeks. Also she'll probably laugh at him. One of those laughs that may or may not be contemptuous; it's hard to tell these days.

Watching her disappear into the dawn-lit stairwell, he remembers like a flare in the dark his conversation with Sam, outside, under the trees. Must've been hours ago now.

Cohen had just finished singing Jewel's praises.

'It's impressive, for sure,' Sam said, admiring the festoon-lit patio, the trees, the fountain.

'It is, and she's going to kill me,' Cohen said, making a sweeping, sideways gesture with his free hand. 'When she finds out it's all fucked. Everything she's built ... the foundations ... all fucked.'

Glancing at the house, Sam frowned. 'What, like … termites?'

'No mate, like fraud.'

'Fraud?' Sam asked, smiling until he realised Cohen wasn't joking. 'As in …?'

Cohen looked at Sam, thinking maybe it would be a relief to tell someone. And as he began to offload, I could almost see him regressing in front of me, back to a time when Sam would find him throwing stones at trees or piling rocks up in the river, and he'd join in. Without asking questions. Sam could be callous sometimes, but in those moments, he was a lifeline.

'As you know,' Cohen said, slurring a little, 'I'm new to the world of finance … something I probably should've told Jewel, right? I let her think I was all about the money …' He scoffed. 'Didn't take long for me to get us into a bit of a hole. I was trying to win money to make up for shortfalls … horses, dogs, cards … Total shitshow. I remortgaged the house to settle the debts, but then I needed to do something about the mortgage before Jewel cottoned on.' He took a long sip of soft drink. Blinked slowly. 'I created this investment scheme around bitcoin. It was on the rise and people were mad for it, but they didn't know how to get their hands on it. So I offered to invest in it for them. The more people I got on board, the more money I had to work with. They'd get some returns but mostly all I did was send them graphs and things, suggesting their stocks were on the rise. It was too easy, Sam. Seriously.'

Sam was watching Cohen with eyebrows raised.

Cohen's initial relief began to dissipate. 'I paid off the mortgage again and put some money away, so the business and everything is back to rights … but then the investors started to hassle me about getting their money out. I don't know, something spooked them.

I made excuses, but they started to get suspicious and whatever, and so now I've had to …'

'You set up a Ponzi scheme?'

'Well, I guess you could call it that.'

'Jesus Christ, that's some serious shit, mate.'

'I know.'

Cohen felt unwell. He'd said too much, and he had no idea what Sam was thinking.

'Who are your investors?'

'People I hooked up with on forums, mostly. Your average type, looking to get a leg-up. And they would send friends and family my way.'

'Jesus.'

'Yeah, look, I'm not proud … But I'm going to fix things.'

'Have they figured out it wasn't legit yet?'

'Judging by some of the emails, yes.'

Sam shook his head.

Cohen's face felt hot. His heart thudded in his throat. Saying it all out loud for the first time had gone from cathartic to nauseating.

'It's not as if I killed someone though, is it?'

'Not unless one of your investors tops themselves,' Sam said, 'when they discover they've lost everything to a shitty scam.'

Cohen closed his eyes. 'As I said, I'm working on paying them back.'

'What if they've gone to the cops already?'

'I've covered my tracks pretty well.'

'They can trace anything, mate. You should turn yourself in. For real.'

Cohen shook his head. 'Jewel would lose her shit.'

'She'll lose it more if she finds out from someone else, don't you reckon?'

Sweat was beading on Cohen's upper lip. And his forehead.

'I realise I've been an unprincipled bastard,' he said, 'and I'm probably on the verge of a long prison sentence. I get it. Can we move on?'

Sam looked at him, eyebrows up. 'Of course,' he said. 'But Christ Almighty … make sure you think through your next move very carefully.'

Shit, Cohen thinks now, sitting up on the couch. Shit, shit, shit. What's he done, telling Sam about all that? He was planning on taking it to the grave, not offloading it at the first sniff of an old friend and a big night. Seems he forgot how it is; how he can't keep his bloody mouth shut when Sam's actually listening to him.

'Idiot,' he mutters, forcing himself to stand up. He fills Jewel's glass with water, drinks it down then heads upstairs. He needs to fess up. Tell Jewel everything. Give her a fighting chance to fix things before the ship goes down, so to speak. But not now. Not yet. First he needs to lie beside her. Absorb her warmth and soak up what's left of her love for him. He'll tell her soon. Once he's ready for the end.

Tattoo or no, it takes it out of me, watching the man I love climbing into bed with someone else every night. Someone who feels only a fraction of what I feel for him myself. I hope you never have to know what that's like.

8

Emerging from the airport's air-conditioned limbo, Robyn finds herself under a sky so bright it hurts. It's been six years, and the heat is suffocating, like a blanket over her face, but she's home.

Her taxi cruises towards the tunnel, meandering west until at last they reach Cottesloe and the rise of Grant Street. From the highest point, you can see the ocean—that vast expanse of glittering blue. She'd forgotten how magnificent it is.

Flanked by mansions, they approach the coast and turn south onto the promenade. They crawl along Marine Parade, past the hotels and restaurants and ice-cream shops, past the pine trees and the golf course, until they reach the southern end. The houses are less ostentatious here, the coastline a little wilder. They pull up outside a narrow double-storey house—white paint grubby, front yard unkempt. Robyn's childhood home.

She rings the doorbell then realises she has a key, tucked away in her wallet somewhere. Frank opens the door before she can start hunting for it.

'Robyn,' he says, his smile creasing his deeply tanned skin. He's still tall and broad, if a little more stooped than he was last time she saw him. His hair is no less unruly, the grey winning now over the blond. 'Home at last.'

He takes her in for a hug. It's a moment before she works out what's missing: instead of his usual dense smell of tobacco and cologne, he smells only mildly of the sea.

'You ditched the smokes?'

'I did,' he says, picking up her suitcase and leading the way down the passage towards the stairwell at the centre of the house. 'Eight months and counting.'

'Impressive,' Robyn says, following him in. She stops halfway down the passage, snagged by the photographs on the wall. First there's her nan and pop posing stiffly, side by side in black and white. Then there's Robyn herself, progressing from infanthood through her sullen teenage years to the first day of her cadetship at the local daily. Seeing her life mapped out on the wall like this reminds her of how she once longed for a sibling, someone to share the maternal spotlight with. With Frank so immersed in his work, Heather's love for her was intense. And then it was gone.

She moves on to the portrait of Frank and Heather on their wedding day. She's always loved her mum in this picture—there's such lightness in her eyes and in the carefree tilt of her head. Robyn remembers the fading of that light. The cold softness of Heather's hand in the moments before she died.

'Good flight?' Frank calls down from upstairs.

'Fine,' Robyn says, blinking back tears.

Frank is up in her old bedroom. It's the same except there's a row of boxes labelled *Robyn* against one wall and a double bed now instead of her old single one. There's no sign of the quilt she grew up with either, the one Heather made for her.

'It's in the cupboard,' Frank says, seeing the look on her face. 'I kept the bed too—it's in my study. I probably spend more time on it than I do at the desk, if I'm honest.'

'That's good, isn't it? A restful retirement and all.'

'You're my daughter,' Frank says, heading for the door, 'so I'll forgive you this time, but if you say the R-word again in my presence, I can't guarantee your safety.'

He winks and leaves the room, calling out that he's made dinner but she doesn't have to eat it if she'd prefer to sleep.

She wanders around the room, touching familiar things—the mahogany desk, her books on the pine bookshelf, the hedgehog Heather knitted for her when she was five. A framed photograph catches her eye, on the wall beside the Escher print Frank gave her on her fourteenth birthday. It's a picture of her and Sam. She takes it off the wall and studies the two of them in that moment, caught forever by the light, and by Cohen with his Canon, most probably. For some long-forgotten reason, she's holding a copy of *Bleak House*, examining it with a comedic look on her face. Sam's laughing. His hair is longer than she remembers it.

I would've been there too, just out of shot. After that first boardgame in our apartment, the four of us spent a lot of time together. We drank beer and played cards, talking politics and future plans late into the night. Cohen and I were saving up for a ticket to London right after graduation. The plan was to earn some pounds there before heading over to Europe. We'd see as much as possible before the money ran out—Paris, Barcelona, Rome—then we'd stop and work again until we had enough for the next leg: South America, USA, Canada.

Robyn and Sam would listen to our plans with enthusiasm—travel was top of the list for all of us—but whenever possible, they'd steer the conversation back to films. All films were worthy of their analysis, but mostly they liked the art-house ones. They connected over literature too, always swapping books and talking about dialogue and narrative arcs. I'd watch them sometimes, if Cohen was off buying drinks or using the bathroom. They'd be engrossed in whatever it was they were discussing, but then Sam would catch my eye. He'd hold me there for a moment, suspended, then he'd look away and I'd hate myself. For having enjoyed it. For looking forward to the next time.

Robyn frowns at the picture and considers not hanging it back up again. She could put it in a drawer instead, spare herself the cocktail of nostalgia and regret. But she decides against it; an empty picture hook is just as likely as the picture itself to remind her of what was there.

2001 Saturday, 14th April

Two days into the Easter study break, Cohen and I head down to his mum's place in the forest for a week. Woodfires, red wine, long walks along winding tracks; I love it down there. The cool freshness of it. All the birds.

Back in the city, it's Saturday afternoon and Robyn is working on an article for the student newspaper: a piece about the student union needing more funding and less interference from the chancellor. She's going through her interview notes, kicking herself for not double-checking some of the surname spellings on the spot—a schoolgirl error—when someone knocks on the door.

Marla is out on a pub crawl so Robyn drags herself away from her desk and opens up. Sam is standing there in a blue hoody, looking handsome, if slightly worse for wear.

'Robyn,' he says. 'How's it going?'

'Good thanks,' Robyn says, wishing she'd had a shower that morning instead of pulling on last night's jeans and getting straight to work. 'You?'

'Went out with Matty last night, which is never good for my health.'

'Up and functioning by three pm, though—not bad.'

'You got anything to drink?'

'I think we have juice in the fridge.'

'Thanks,' he says, opting for a soft drink he finds at the back. 'There's a fundraiser screening of *Lost Highway* on at Luna tonight,' he says, cracking it open. 'In Leederville. I was thinking of heading over there in a bit. Thought you might like to come?'

'Definitely,' Robyn says. 'Do I have time for a shower?'

'Yes,' Sam says, checking his watch. 'We have an hour.'

He stretches out on the sofa, and that's where Robyn finds him twenty minutes later, snoring gently. She kneels down beside him and studies his sleeping face—the cleft between his nose and his mouth; the soft twitch of his eyelids. He smells of body wash and cologne. She hasn't been this close to him before. Has to resist an urge to lean in and kiss him.

'Sam?' she says, shaking him gently. 'We still going to the movie?'

He stirs and rolls onto his side, struggling to open his eyes.

'We don't have to go,' Robyn says. 'If you need to sleep it off?'

'Hmm?'

'*Lost Highway*?'

'Yeah.'

Robyn leaves and returns with a warm washer. Drapes it gently over his face.

'Hmmm, magic,' he says after a minute, his voice muffled through the cloth.

In the cinema, they share a box of popcorn, and Robyn feels Sam looking at her. She turns to look at him too and he leans in to whisper in her ear.

'You have the sweetest profile.'

Robyn frowns. Whispers back, 'Really?'

'Really.'

A few minutes later, he reaches across for her hand. For the rest of the film, that's all there is—her hand, resting in his, trying to embody a nonchalance she doesn't feel.

After the film, they find a table in a restaurant down the road.

'Don't you love the way Lynch messes with time and logic?' Sam asks, once they've ordered a pad thai and a green chicken curry. 'It's like a window into someone else's subconscious.'

'I don't know,' Robyn says. 'I mean, if that's what you want from a film, fair enough, but … I feel like anyone can conjure up weird nightmare vibes and be all symbolic and mysterious, but what's the point if it doesn't mean anything? His films are trippy and atmospheric and everything, but in the end I'm always dissatisfied. Like, I have nightmares too—big deal. You know? Where's the story?'

Sam leans across the table and says, 'You dare to question the grand master Lynch? In some circles, that'd get you killed.'

'What can I say?'

'I like that about you, Robyn. You're subversive, but no one would ever guess it to look at you.'

After dinner, they stop in at the bookshop across the road. Robyn's scanning the blurb of *The Remains of the Day* when Sam wanders over.

'Robyn,' he says, watching her read. 'You do realise I'm going to have to kiss you, don't you?'

She turns, momentarily bewildered. 'Are you?'

'That okay with you?'

'I'll have to think it over,' she says, smiling up at him, returning the book to its place on the shelf.

2019 Tuesday, 22ⁿᵈ January

Robyn struggles to keep her eyes open over dinner with Frank. She brushes her teeth in the shower. The exhaustion is like a cave, dark and beckoning.

In the strange embrace of her new bed, she glances at the photograph on the wall again, its shape emerging once her eyes have adjusted to the darkness. She tries to remember the moment around the image, to resurrect it. In particular, she wants to recall what I was doing at the time. I'd have been there for sure. Goofing around, laughing with her at everything and nothing. That's the way she prefers to remember me—the way I was before, when the future sprawled before us, as endless as one of those afternoons we spent down by the river.

She hasn't done this for a while—thought about me on purpose. It's nice; I've missed it. At first, she thought she owed it to me to mull things over a lot. To imagine my final hours forensically: a kind of penance. But she doesn't do it much anymore. Self-preservation kicked in somewhere along the line. Still, there are times when memories sneak up on her, usually when songs we loved are playing, or in this liminal time between sleep and waking.

After my funeral, the three of them did their best to salvage things. They went to a couple of films together and played Scrabble, drinking cask wine and discussing current affairs. But they knew it was futile. Cohen seemed hell-bent on self-destruction; Sam wanted to pretend nothing had happened; and Robyn couldn't stop pointing out what I would've said or done if I'd been there, which made everything worse. In the end, it became easier for them to stop trying. To pick their way through the remaining semesters of university, and try to move on.

9

Robyn wakes late in the morning. The heat of the day has invaded her bedroom already, pushing past the glass and the heavy blinds and curtains. Gradually, objects in the room become familiar—the pictures and posters on the wall, the row of boxes, the books on the shelf. She listens for Frank moving around downstairs but everything seems quiet.

Her body feels like a sack full of sand, but it's nothing a little coffee can't fix. She pulls back the covers, drags herself up and heads downstairs, pausing to take in the familiar band of ocean from the arched window on the landing.

Frank is seated in an armchair in the living room, gazing out the back window into the grey-stone courtyard, newspaper on his lap.

'There's a better view from upstairs,' Robyn says, heading into the kitchen. 'Endless sea and sky instead of King Arthur's tiny courtyard.'

'Morning, merry sunshine,' Frank says, glancing at the clock. 'Only just, though. Sleep okay?'

'Very well,' Robyn says, yawning and flicking the kettle on. 'Coffee?'

'No, thanks. I'm thinking about lunch right now. Coffee bags are next to the kettle, with the teabags.'

'What happened to the moka pot?'

'The what?'

'Mum's stovetop brewing thing. Or the plunger? I can only handle one coffee a day; I like to make it count.'

'Might have chucked them out ... or they might be at the back of the pantry somewhere.'

Robyn opens the stacked pantry with its layers of cans, sachets, sauces and dry goods, and closes it again. Settles on a coffee bag after all.

'Why only one coffee a day?' Frank asks when she sits at the table with her steaming mug.

'My heart starts racing if I go too hard on it. Or too hard in general. Doctor says I'm burnt out. Probably from the job.'

Frank studies her for a moment, frowning. 'Did the doctor say anything else?'

'Not really. Only that I should probably take more time off. Do some meditation. Find a better balance.'

The coffee is weak, as expected, and less than satisfying.

'Well then, I'm doubly glad you're home for a while,' Frank says, shuffling his paper into shape before folding it double. 'Got any plans for today?'

'I've teed up a meeting with Adira, my old news editor,' Robyn says, glancing at her watch then up at the sky through the kitchen window. A breeze has blown a thin strip of cloud across the blue.

'You don't mess around, do you?' Frank says, eyebrows up. 'What about a break, like the doctor said? Doing things for yourself for a while?'

'I'd go nuts without work.'

'Work ethic on steroids.'

'Must be hereditary.'

◆◆◆

Adira greets Robyn in the reception area. She has more grey hairs than before, but her gaze is no less penetrating.

'Welcome back, Robyn,' she says, holding out a new access card on a lanyard. 'Here you go. I used your old photo; hope you don't mind. We can update it whenever you like.'

'Thanks, Adira, fine by me.'

'Test it out,' Adira says when they reach the elevator.

Robyn presses her card against the scanner; the door slides open.

'Now,' Adira says as they arrive upstairs, 'do you remember your way around?'

'More or less,' Robyn says, taking in the enormous open-plan space with its rows of cubicles, most of them occupied by reporters tapping on keyboards or hustling over the phone.

Light floods in from the wall of windows on the south side.

They head towards a glass-walled office at the centre of the open space.

'Come in,' Adira says. 'Take a seat.'

Robyn lowers herself into a leather chair while Adira settles behind her desk, a stretch of oak stacked as always with the nation's dailies.

'Good to be home?' That searching gaze.

'Yes, thanks.'

'We're so excited to have you back, Robyn. Pinching ourselves. You did good work out there; we kept an eye on you.'

'Thank you.'

'I won't ask you to go into it, but I imagine it must have been tough.'

'It was rewarding in lots of ways, but I'm ready to slow down for a while.'

'Well, their loss is our gain. You sure you want to start next week? You can wait a couple of weeks if you like? Settle in a bit?'

'No, Monday's good.'

'Monday's a public holiday.'

'Tuesday then. I'm ready.'

10

Late in the afternoon, having spent the morning on the beach, Robyn borrows Frank's car again and winds her way down to the Nedlands foreshore. She parks in the shade near the riverside restaurant, and cuts across the oval, between rugby posts and soccer goals, towards the water. The lawn is full of tiny divots. Machine-dug.

Reaching the footpath, she takes in the great sweep of river. It's calming, the way it looks so still even as it stirs and drifts towards the sea. The air is fresh, though scented with brine and traces of oil. With one hand shielding her eyes, she looks ahead along the footpath, towards the yacht club: the route she and I used to run, back when we were at uni. She'll have to walk it for now, but maybe after a few months, once she's established a routine of some kind, she can work her way back to her former fitness.

Some way along, she walks beneath the low-hanging

peppermint branches and into the dense shade of the enormous ficus trees. It's always a few degrees cooler here. She runs her hand along the trunks, feeling their scars: layers of names and initials carved into the wood. She's always loved these trees, these quiet and patient survivors, with their dense canopies and low, sturdy branches. Out on the water, the huddle of sailboats emanates a constant clinking sound. It's like a windchime. Floating and incidental, weirdly hypnotic.

She should have known it would happen, given that this was one of our favourite picnic spots, but even so the nostalgia catches her off guard. She remembers lying right there on a blanket, listening to the three of us talk while she drifted, close to sleep on one of those long afternoons. Over there, on the grass, is where she proved to us that she could walk on her hands, which earned her loud applause from me, though she was so light and nimble it wasn't much of a surprise. And there, right under the trees, is the bench she sat on with Sam, the day she first suspected he wasn't hers to keep.

2001 Friday, 12th October

Robyn knocks on the share house door in Nedlands. There's movement beyond the leadlight window, then Matty opens up, eating a bowl of cereal.

'Sam here?'

Matty chews and gestures with his head towards Sam's door, then he turns and goes back to the kitchen. Robyn can see his notebook open on the table, next to the milk.

She knocks lightly, then lets herself into Sam's dim, airless room. He's asleep so she closes the door, slips off her shoes and climbs into his bed, tucking her hands inside her jumper sleeves so they won't startle him. Putting one arm around him, she pulls herself in close and lies there for a while, waiting for him to wake up. Wondering how to say what she has to say. Whether she should.

At last, he stirs. Minutes pass, and then he reaches back to touch her head. He turns to face her.

'Morning,' he says, struggling to open his eyes. 'How long have you been here?'

'I'm not sure. A little while.'

'Don't suppose you brought coffee and some of those pastry things?'

'No, Mr Breakfast,' she says, nudging his chin with her jumper-wrapped fist. 'I did not.'

'Shall we go get some?'

+++

They take their takeaway cups and paper bags down to the bench by the river, beneath the peppermint trees. Black swans glide around and between the moored boats on the water.

'I had to see you today, Sam,' Robyn says, fidgeting with the lid of her cup.

'That's okay,' he says, nudging her with his elbow. 'You're only human.'

'My period is late.'

Sam places his coffee cup carefully between them on the bench. Clears his throat.

'How late?'

'Two weeks.'

'That's bad?'

'Possibly quite bad.'

Sam rubs a hand across the back of his neck. A man jogs past in bright blue nylon shorts.

'Have you done a test?'

'Not yet. I thought maybe we could go to the chemist today and get one.'

'Isn't that something you'd do with a girlfriend?'

'I thought you'd want to be the first to know.'

Sam shrugs. 'Okay,' he says, standing up. 'Shall we go now, then?'

'Wait,' Robyn says, taking hold of his arm. 'I want to know what we'll do if it's positive. What would you want us to do?'

He scratches his skin behind his ear. Watches clouds move slowly across the sky.

'I don't want kids, Robyn,' he says. 'I don't like kids.'

'What, as in, all kids?'

'All kids. They're noisy, and sticky ... and nappies? No thank you.'

'Do you like *me*, Sam?'

'Of course I like you, Robyn. But I'm not settling down and raising a family right now, if that's what you're thinking.'

'Do you think that's what I want? Some kind of suburban nightmare with a guy who doesn't want to be there? But if there's a baby already ... I mean, maybe we have to adjust our plans.'

'I'm not adjusting anything, Robyn. I'm only just getting started.'

◆◆◆

They stop in at the chemist on the way back to Sam's place. He waits outside and Robyn goes in, trying not to look terrified.

She takes the test in Sam's share house bathroom—a room with tiny tiles and grimy towels and a sliver of soap on the edge of the basin. When it's done, she carries it through to his bedroom on a wad of toilet paper.

They wait, sitting side by side on his bed. Not talking.

When the time is up, Robyn checks.

There's only one line.

'Thank Christ,' Sam says, hugging her tightly.

'Yeah. Phew!' Robyn says into his shoulder. She's relieved too. Deeply relieved. She doesn't need the complications of parenthood right now, obviously. And yet, she feels weirdly disappointed. Until recently, babies have been little more than a perambulated blur out on the periphery, but these past two weeks, she's been looking at them more closely. Noticing things about them. They have nuanced facial expressions, for one thing. And they're not above sucking on their own hands if it makes them feel better. In this way, carefully, she's been teasing out the idea of a tiny Sam. Imagining what he might look like, or how he might feel in her arms. As prospects go, she's found it not too terrifying. Almost lovely.

But she knows she'll get over it—now is not the time for motherhood, let's be real.

What's harder to move past is her new awareness that things are not as she thought in her relationship with Sam. When she met him, her ache for him was almost immediate. The glow of his attention, once she had it, was so luminous, she never stopped to question its sincerity. Now, though, how can she not?

The sand beneath the swings is strewn with curling leaves dropped by the trees above. Maggies chortle and croon in the branches while cockies fly in and away then back again, scrapping over territory. Kids trundle their skateboards around on the ramps, jumping and slapping their wheels on the concrete.

Robyn walks on. That's when she spots Sam, as if she's conjured him out of memory. Just there, beyond the small jetty, where the sand meets the water this side of the yacht club. The afternoon light is blinding behind him. Seems to splinter through and across him. Almost as if he isn't there at all.

But he is there, and he's holding a baby—you, Isla.

Unable to work out which impulse is stronger—the one to get closer or the one to flee—Robyn does neither. Instead, she watches as Sam sits down in the sand at the water's edge. He holds you out in front of him, feet in the water, as if you're standing on your own, though you can't yet. You dip and lift your feet, in and out, one at a time, as if you're dancing. It's almost unbearable— your quiet way of savouring the experience. So much newness, discovering things about the world the rest of us have long since taken for granted. The properties of water, for example. The way it glistens.

Sam's quiet too. Letting you get on with your sensory brain-wash. Letting your mind grow on the inside, taking in all that sky.

Robyn's just chosen *flee* when Sam turns towards her. He hesitates, surprised, then lifts a hand in greeting.

'Robyn,' he says, standing up as she approaches. 'Holy moly. Long time no see.'

'I know. Not since graduation.'

Looking at him—the line that creases his cheek, the light in his eyes—Robyn remembers why she had to remove herself from his life. And from Cohen's. It was too hard to be near them without me.

'This your daughter?'

'Yes, this is Isla.'

'Cute.'

'Thanks.'

'What happened to Sam the rolling stone?' She keeps her tone light, squint-smiling into the sun. 'No moss, no mortgage, no nappies?'

'Things change, I guess.'

White cockies screech in the trees overhead.

'So what brings you home?' Sam asks. 'Didn't I see you on telly the other day, in Istanbul or Johannesburg or somewhere?'

'London. I've packed it in for a while.'

'Oh,' he says, looking at her for a moment in case she wants to say more. 'Well, welcome home.'

'Thanks. And you? You've been doing all right for yourself.'

'Yes, it's been a dream run. Professionally anyway.'

'Not personally?' Robyn says, glancing down at you on the sand.

'Well, we're very blessed with Isla, but … yeah. Things are a bit complicated at the moment. How long are you in town?'

'Not sure. I've got my old job back, which is good, but … I'm not very good at staying put.'

Sam studies her, an inscrutable look on his face.

'What?' Robyn says.

'Nothing. It's just … it's weird running into you like this. I bumped into Cohen the other day too. At a café, having breakfast.'

'You two don't hang out anymore?'

'Not for years. Although I've seen him a few times since the other day.'

'How is he?'

'He's fine. Different.'

'Maybe we should all get a coffee sometime.'

'Yeah,' Sam says after a moment. 'Okay. Here, give me your phone, I'll add my number.'

You begin to make cranky noises, jerking your arms around furiously and grinding your legs into the sand.

'We'd best head back,' Sam says, handing back Robyn's phone and stooping to gather you up and brush sand off your feet. 'Come on, Strawb. Let's go see your mum. Good to see you, Robyn.'

He heads off in the direction of home, a tall sprawl of glass and concrete, high on the embankment, surrounded by bush. Robyn watches him go, remembering the torment of loving him. She shakes her head, finds herself smiling. Despite the uneasy, discarded feeling it's given her to see him with a baby after all these years, there's something enchanting about the sight of him with you. Something uplifting. She wonders when he lost his determination to stay free, though. And what the woman who tamed him is like.

11

It's early evening, and Cohen is in his upstairs living room, fretting. He was always a good fretter. Not something you want to be when you grow up, Isla; a waste of time and energy. But try telling him that.

The curtains are drawn. Jewel is in the shower. Cohen sits forward, perched on the edge of a green velvet armchair, his knees unsteady beneath his elbows. He turns his phone over and over in his hands, waiting for it to ring or chime or do something. It's been fifteen minutes since he left Sam a message inviting him to the pub again tonight. Fifteen minutes is a long time to wait when you're in the kind of headspace Cohen's in. For nearly a week it's plagued him: the question of how much Sam drank last Friday night; how much of their late-night conversation he's likely to recall.

Cohen has no idea whether what he's done can be traced to him. He's been careful, but really, how hard can it be to trace someone nowadays? Particularly if Sam decides it's his duty to look into things and turn him in. Currently Sam seems preoccupied with his own domestic shit, but that could resolve itself at any moment, and then what?

All week, Cohen's kept his cool, waiting for Sam to make contact again, but today he's snapped. Reached out first. And now, he waits.

He needs a plan, in case Sam brings it up. Should he pretend he knows nothing about it? Imply that Sam imagined the whole conversation? What if Sam insists on going to the authorities, or making Cohen do it himself? That's the most likely scenario—he'll push Cohen to come clean, first to Jewel, then to the police. And maybe that's the way forward: Jewel can help navigate through the public-relations nightmare, and perhaps if Cohen acknowledges full responsibility and commits to a repayment plan, the courts will be lenient. He can play the inexperience card, plead panic and temporary insanity or something. Because that's what it was, really. How else can you explain it?

But Jewel might just as easily wash her hands of him. She's been so cool towards him lately, who knows how she'd react if she found out how spectacularly he's ballsed things up? And if his own wife turns her back on him publicly—which, as we know, is how she does things—he could end up in jail. After which, he'd emerge with nothing. With no one. Exactly where he started.

'You all right, Cohen?' Jewel says, tying her robe and lowering herself onto the chair opposite him. She pulls her legs up, slow and sleek.

'Never better.'

'You look jumpy.'

'I'm waiting to hear back from a broker.' The lie slips out so easily he almost admires himself for it; maybe he's found his true calling at last. He stands up to give his legs a chance to go still. 'It's a new investment; there's a bit of competition so I'm keen to jump on it, but I need the go-ahead from James.'

He goes to the window and pulls the curtains open, stirring up dust and letting the light cut in.

Jewel stands, lifting a hand to block the evening glare. 'Let me know how it goes,' she says, heading back to the bedroom.

'Will do,' Cohen says, momentarily struck by the shape of her body in her silk robe.

Downstairs, the intercom buzzes.

Cohen checks his watch and heads down.

It's a man from Australia Post outside the gate, with a package to sign for. Cohen assumes it's for Jewel—these things usually are—but then he remembers, this one's for him. He signs the little grey screen and says, 'Cheers, mate,' while the delivery guy climbs back in the van, then he shuts the front door and studies the package in his hand. It's slightly battered and kind of small, considering how big it is, figuratively speaking. He should open it, check it's what he ordered. He's about to, but his phone vibrates in his pocket.

It's a text from Sam.

Sure mate, see you there.

Cohen hides the package behind his toolbox in the storage room under the stairs and grabs his jacket.

'See you later, Jewel,' he calls up. 'Heading out for a bit.'

He waits for a moment in case she replies, but there's nothing, just a distant electrical hum and the kitchen clock ticking through the quiet.

Cohen gets to the pub first. It's a long, narrow space, nearly at capacity already, with a bluegrass band setting up on a small stage in the corner.

Sam arrives a few minutes later. Thumps Cohen on the shoulder and claims the next barstool along. 'How's it going?'

'Good,' Cohen says. 'You?'

'Yeah, all good. You pull up okay on the weekend?'

'Eventually. Thanks for getting me home.'

'Any time.'

Not sure how best to proceed, Cohen orders a couple of beers.

'Hey, listen,' he says while they're waiting. 'The stuff I said on Friday night ...' He leaves it there, open-ended, until Sam nods. 'Do me a favour,' Cohen continues. 'Try to forget it, okay? I'm a little out of my depth, but it's nothing I can't fix.'

'Are you sure? You seemed more than a little anxious.'

'Par for the course in this job, believe me. I'm learning the hard way.'

They get their drinks and the band kicks off with a frantic number that gets a handful of women up off their stools. The already close space draws in more tightly around Cohen.

'Game of pool?' he says.

They head for the table at the back, where at least there's a window.

'Did I tell you I ran into Robyn?' Sam says. 'This afternoon, on the foreshore.'

'Isn't she overseas? I've seen her on the news.'

'She's home now. Seemed a bit over it.'

Cohen remembers Robyn. Small and serious. Fine features—the kind you had to keep looking at to be sure you weren't imagining them. Too good for Sam, really. Considering his reluctance at the time to pick a lane, so to speak.

'She said we should all get together,' Sam says. 'The three of us.'

Cohen lines up the break. 'Not sure I'm up to it, mate,' he says. 'Bad enough having *you* back in my life.'

Only half joking.

'Yeah, you're right,' Sam says, bending low to take aim then sinking solid purple in a corner pocket. 'Been awful seeing you again.'

His easy sarcasm, the casual way he lines up his next shot—they turn something in Cohen's gut. An old resentment he thought was well-buried.

'Do you ever think about her?' Cohen says, dropping a ball of his own: yellow, side pocket.

Sam, obtuse when it suits him, deflects. 'Now and then … but we weren't that good together.'

'I'm not talking about Robyn.'

Sam swivels his cue on its base. 'You mean Gracie?'

Cohen closes his eyes; he hasn't heard my name said aloud for nearly eighteen years.

'I wish I hadn't gone down south that weekend,' he says. 'If I'd been here, she wouldn't have gone out alone.'

'Your uncle died, Cohen; course you had to go home. Anyway, she went out with her housemate.'

'If I'd stayed, she might still be here.'

'Not necessarily,' Sam says, dropping green in the far-left pocket as the band picks up the tempo again. 'Have you ever thought of seeing someone, Cohen? It was a terrible thing, losing Gracie, but I hate to think you're still in that place.'

'Gracie loved me,' Cohen says. 'In a way no one else has before or since. And I loved her.'

'I know you did, mate. She was a great girl.'

'I still have dreams about her. Sometimes, when I wake up, I wish I'd died instead of her.'

Sam moves around the table, considers his next shot. 'Seriously, mate, a grief counsellor might help.'

Cohen necks his drink and lowers the glass to the table edge, his hand trembling. This was a bad idea.

'Think I'll go home,' he says.

'Can I give you a lift?'

'No. I'm good.'

Cohen walks through the pack of people dancing and jostling for service at the bar, then out into the night air. He pulls out his phone and orders a ride.

Leaning up against the wall, waiting for the car, he thinks about how cruel life is. For letting him love me so hard, then taking me away. For allowing him to suffer all the old feelings so acutely while stripping out most of the details. So much of me has faded for him now. He still has fragments of course. Tiny, torn-out pieces—my laugh; my Dove-soap scent; my weird addiction to wasabi peas. He remembers a certain look in my eyes, any time I was thinking about the ocean. And the way I could always make people laugh. Even Robyn at her most serious. Seemingly over nothing.

Interesting that Robyn's come home, he thinks. Now, just as

Sam's also re-entered his life. One of life's weird coincidences. He wonders if she's home for a break or taking off her correspondent hat for good. Surely the former; she was always so focused on that career, it's difficult to imagine her packing it in.

In the car, he taps into social media. There are multiple Robyn Tinsleys on Facebook, but none he recognises. He searches more broadly and finds her profile on Twitter. There she is, same old Robyn, only now with that flinty look in her eyes. Most of her tweets link back to her stories on the news website. He scrolls through them idly then taps on the feather icon to send her a message. Nothing more than a few words and his number.

She replies almost immediately.

Good to hear from you, Cohen. How've you been? Love to catch up.

For sure, Cohen types. *We'll grab a drink some time. I'll be in touch.*

And he will; it'll be good to see her. Find out what's what. He hopes she's not putting down the mic forever. He's enjoyed watching her over the years, articulating one faraway crisis after another. It's sometimes made him anxious to see her out there, so alone, but he's always come away with a sense of triumph. Because as careless as Sam was with her already wounded heart, and as shattered as she was by my death, there she's stood, out in the world, strong and direct. Unflinching. It's been a comfort to Cohen, knowing that his instinct to protect her is unwarranted.

We're approaching the week-long study break in the lead-up to exams, and there's plenty of work we should be doing, but the weather is too perfect, so we head down to the foreshore for a picnic instead. Sam and Cohen stop at the servo for chips and chocolate. Robyn's made chicken drumsticks and a pasta salad. I'd have made peanut butter sandwiches and called it a day, but Robyn's right at home in the kitchen. Has been since she was a kid.

Once we've all sat down, Robyn sets the food and paper plates out on the rug and Cohen pulls a large plastic bottle and four paper cups out of a cooler bag.

'Your favourite, madame,' he says, filling my cup with premixed bourbon and cola.

'Merci, monsieur,' I say. Walking here was thirsty work, and by rights we should be back at home, bent over our books, which means the booze goes down extra well. Before long, it's time for refills.

'So,' Robyn says, leaning back against Sam. 'Are we all looking forward to next year?'

'Let's get through the exams first,' Sam mutters.

'Not to mention the summer holidays,' I say. I'm lying with my head in Cohen's lap, looking up into a peppermint tree: long, narrow leaves and tight clusters of fine, pale flowers.

'I can't wait for next year,' Robyn says. 'Some cool units coming up.'

'Such as?' I ask, blissing out as Cohen massages my scalp. Sam watches us for a moment then sits up, forcing Robyn to adjust her position.

'Literary Journalism,' Robyn says, pulling herself upright

and crossing her legs. 'Media Law and Ethics; Feature Writing. Though I might do a broadcasting unit instead of that last one. Not sure yet.'

'I'm thinking of deferring,' Sam says, squinting towards the river.

Robyn gives him a long, quiet look. 'And doing what?'

'Not sure. Might head over east for a while. My cousin's in Byron Bay, so I could stay with her. Matty reckons you can get some amazing stuff over there.'

We all know what he means by *stuff*. He's become fixated, recently, on the idea of altered states of consciousness. On transcending his so-called perceptual limitations.

'Matty's full of shit,' Cohen says.

Some people, Isla, are born knowing their path. They know it, they trust it and they follow it. For others, like your father, predictability is an almost existential threat. Sam wants mystery and magic and all of life's colours; to go everywhere, read everything, know everyone. And as infuriating and entitled as it is, there's a beguiling innocence at its heart. An energy—a kind of glow—that's sometimes hard to resist.

'What we see now?' he says. 'It's only the surface of things. We're just knocking on the door.'

'Right on,' I say in my most exaggerated American accent.

Cohen laughs.

'We've only dipped our toes into what the human mind is capable of,' Sam says. 'Don't you want to see what else there is?'

'I'm good, thanks,' Cohen says.

Robyn's staring at the rug, no doubt wondering what she'll say if Sam invites her along. What she'll do if he doesn't.

'You'll come back with dreadlocks,' I say. 'So baked we'll have to soak you in milk.'

Sam smiles at me. 'Maybe I won't come home at all, Gracie,' he says. 'Maybe you'll have to come find me.'

12

It's a scorcher, the mercury topping out at thirty-nine degrees Celsius. Late in the day, Tori feeds you outside on the deck, catching the evening breeze off the river.

Sam watches you both while the kettle boils for tea; you've started waving your hand around while you feed, grabbing at things. Frustrating for Tori, but kind of adorable. Like a tiny monkey.

He looks away, bleakness sweeping across his heart like a lighthouse beam, only dark. He fights the urge to turn and leave the house without another word. It's been nearly two weeks and he still can't look at your mum without thinking about that message from Pete. And not just that one, but all the other ones, the ones she won't show him. Does she smile, he wonders, when she gets them? Those backlit words of devotion?

He knows he needs to get over it. To stand taller if he's to survive being diminished like this, by a man he's never met and who Tori swears is no longer important to her. But how can he? He feels dwarfed. Outdone. In all the important categories—passion, duration, potency. Pete wins them all, and Sam can't smile and say it doesn't matter, because it does. It matters so much that he would've walked out by now if it wasn't for you. Because of you, he has stayed, and he will stay, though the marriage feels ready to implode.

He's found that it helps him to picture Skye, though he doesn't know her name yet. Ever since he saw her, he's been returning to the memory, to the caress of her voice. It's been soothing. Helps stave off the panic.

He takes the tea outside.

Tori holds you up across her shoulder, patting you gently on the back. Watching you bliss out in the evening sunshine, Sam marvels at the way such loveliness can bring on this searing, aching sense of loss. He lowers the cups to the table next to Tori and offers to take you. You bleat at being handed over—reach back for your mum—but there's comfort in movement and soon you're cooing at the sound of his voice as he sings you a fragment of something.

Tori rolls her shoulder and rubs at a knot there.

'Mind the gap,' she says, adopting the disembodied tone of the London Underground. She's referring to the gap between the deck and the concrete that runs the ring of the pool. It's been there since they bought the place, and they're still trying to work out how to fix it: a second pour of concrete, or another row of timber to create a border, make a feature of it. Something needs to be done. Sam says nothing, though once he might have hammed it up, stepping over the gap theatrically, hoping to make Tori laugh.

He glances over at her, leaning back against the chair with her eyes closed; she's accepted his silence. She's resigned, though it's her duty to fight. With Sam, *for* Sam—either one would be good.

He can't bear it, this cruel interplay of love and sorrow.

You cling to his shirt with one fist as he hands you back.

'Come here, little sausage,' Tori says, using her thumb to release your grip on your daddy.

'I'll see you later,' Sam says.

'You heading out?'

'Yes.'

'But you just made tea.'

'I don't want it,' Sam says, heading for the sliding door back into the house.

'When will you be home?'

'Not sure.'

'Where are you going?'

'Not sure yet.'

'Will you call me? Let me know?'

He looks back at her on the sun lounger, holding you on her belly with her knees up. Maybe this is her way of fighting for their marriage: this half-hearted interrogation. If so, it's not enough, because that string of messages remains. Why won't she show him, if there's nothing to hide? Can't she see that by refusing, she's choosing Pete over him?

He holds on to his anger as he walks down by the river, as the sun goes down and the mosquitos start whining out of the gloom.

He books a ride and nurses his ire all the way down Stirling Highway. It's uncomfortable—a heavy pressure in his chest—but he can't seem to throw it off, until they pull up outside Mojos and adrenaline floods in to dilute it.

Stepping out of the car, he looks up at the sky: thin grey clouds against the darkness, the odd star blinking through.

Skye's band isn't there yet; he's early. But that's okay. Gives him time to sink some Dutch courage. Seems he needs courage to achieve the simplest things these days. Including this: sitting at a bar on his own. It's not something he's done in a while; he feels exposed. Fleetingly, he considers calling Cohen, but he decides against it—too needy. So he sits there, feeling watched by the sound guy, and the barman, and the small clusters of other patrons, all of them some years younger than he is. Jesus, he berates himself. Shake it off. Chill out. Have a drink.

Two beers in, the band arrives. The drummer comes in first, taking several trips to bring in his kit with the help of one of the guitarists—a dark-haired guy in torn jeans. Some minutes later, the bassist walks in, slight in her skinny jeans and off-the-shoulder top. She's done something different with her hair tonight: looped it up into nodules, nineties-style. Finally, Skye arrives, guitar strapped to her back. She's dressed in black jeans, leather boots and a shredded, rose-coloured shirt. Sam can't quite tell what gives her hair the shape it has. It's long and thick but somehow weightless.

She clocks him at the bar as soon as she walks in. Doesn't stop walking, but keeps her eyes on him long enough to suggest recognition. He's not sure, but he thinks she smiles. A small one. It's mostly in the tilt of her head and her eyes—green and thickly lined. Then she looks away and joins the others setting up on stage.

Sam fights an urge to leave. Like a diver at the bottom of the sea. But he tells himself to stay: he's here now anyway, and there's no crime in visiting a bar on your own to watch a band you like.

He turns back towards the bar and contemplates its offerings. Not because he wants anything—his beer is still full, still cold—but because he can't very well sit there watching her set up. For one thing, it might freak her out. And for another, there's still time to prove to himself that she's not the whole reason he came here tonight.

He looks over his shoulder at the door out to the courtyard. Wonders if there might be someone up for a game of pool with him out there. He stands and takes his beer outside, and it takes every ounce of willpower he possesses not to glance back at the stage as he goes.

There are a few people out the back, and a game of pool already underway; he might have to think of something else. Dinner next door maybe, at the burger joint. He should eat something.

For want of a better plan, he fishes out a two-dollar coin and places it on the table. He nods at the guys wielding the pool cues and steps out of their way. Then he finds a place to sit, though it's only marginally less awkward than standing.

He sinks what's left of his beer fast, assesses how much time he has before he's up for a game—plenty—and heads back inside to grab another one.

There she is at the bar. Sam has to remind himself to keep walking, not to stand there in the doorway staring at her like a man on day-release. The door swings shut behind him and he takes a spot beside her, though not too close. It's not like they're acquainted yet, though the way she looks at him, it's as if they know all they need to know already.

'You're back,' she says. Her voice is low and sure, same as when she sings.

Sam nods, not sure if she's referring to his presence at the previous gig or just then, before he went out to the courtyard.

'I am,' he says. 'And so are you.'

'We're here every Friday for the next couple of months. Doesn't pay too many bills, but it makes us feel less deluded about our chosen career path. Which is something.'

'You guys are good though. I've paid to see you again and this will be my third beer, so that's around thirty bucks you've earned this place already.'

She nods. 'We're doing them a favour, aren't we, just turning up?'

'You are,' Sam says, also nodding. She smiles then, and this time it does reach her mouth.

The barman brings the band's rider—four beers—and she curls her fingers around them as if that's what fingers are for.

'Well,' she says. 'Best get these across. I'm Skye by the way.'

'Sam.'

'Pleased to meet you, Sam.'

◆◆◆

Watching Skye on stage, Sam feels that internal pressure lift. He forgets himself and finds himself, both at once, and it's clear to him why he came back: he wants to be disarmed. Like this. By her.

Afterwards, she finds him at the bar. Stands beside him as if it's a given that she should. He points at his near-empty beer, she nods, and he waves the barman over. Orders two more.

'So?' she says. 'How did we do?'

'Loved it. You're really good.'

'We dropped the ball once or twice, but …'

'I didn't notice.'

'Well, that's good.'

'Have you recorded anything?'

'We have some stuff online—I can send you a link.'

Sam notices the drummer watching them. He's standing with the others beside the stage, but while the others are packing up their gear, he's staring at Skye, his snare drum in one hand, sticks in the other. Seeing that Sam's noticed, he looks away and looks around before bending to put his sticks in his bag. After that, he does his best impression of a man interested in what the small gathering of friends and fans has to say.

'Do you play pool?' Sam says, remembering his coin on the table, though it's sure to have been used by someone else by now.

'Do I ever,' Skye replies. She lets Sam pay for the drinks then takes him by the hand and leads him out to the courtyard. It feels wrong, her hand in his. Wrong but good. It's a strong hand. A guitarist's hand. And though his first impulse is to pull away, he resists. What's the harm, after all? It's not like he's being unfaithful. Not really. There's still time and space for this to be nothing more than an innocent interlude. Easily explained away.

It's not long, though, before that space falls in on itself. Collapses, like a sinkhole. Fresh coin on the table, they're waiting for their turn, Sam leaning against the wall and Skye there beside him, her thigh resting against his. He's mulling over the relativity of things—the way the lightness of her touch is anything but light—when she turns to face him, so close he can smell the perfumed oil in her hair.

'We *could* play pool,' she whispers. 'Or you could come home with me instead?'

And there it is. He must make his choice. What will it be: harmless flirtation or all-out adultery? He looks at her face. The certainty in her eyes. How can he let her leave without him? How can he say no to this? He knows what will happen if he tries: he'll stay awake all night, outside, watching the water, wishing he'd done otherwise.

But then he pictures you—asleep in your bassinet, unconsciously working your arms free of your swaddle. He imagines Tori switching off the TV, her lit-up face going dark. She'll be lowering her plate into the sink, filling a glass with water and tiptoeing upstairs in preparation for the dream-feed.

'I can't, Skye,' he says. 'I really can't.'

She glances at his left hand, not for the first time, and nods.

'Fair enough,' she says, pulling a pen from her bag and printing a number onto her beer label. 'If you change your mind …' She leaves the bottle on the windowsill and doesn't look back, not even to check if he's plugging her number into his phone. He hopes this is a reflection of her willpower rather than a sign of indifference.

Either way though, he doesn't care, right? He's a husband, and a father. And though he peels the number off the bottle, he tells himself it's to protect Skye from some other creep getting hold of it. He has more integrity than to be chasing after some singer in a band.

13

Robyn and Frank head into Subiaco to the growers market, stocking up on spices and fresh coriander. They'll be making chicken tikka masala tonight, Heather's favourite recipe. It's a ritual they both hang on to. For the flavours, and the memories.

It's Australia Day, so everywhere you look there are Aussie flags fluttering from car windows, wrapped around shoulders or worn as dresses, belted at the waist. Many of the market stalls have added patriotic stubby holders and novelty hats to their offerings, and tonight, there'll be fireworks over the river.

Frank is eager to get home. This day has never sat right with him. He loves this land as much as the next person, but in his view, as histories go, there's not much to crow about.

They're back home playing checkers when a message from Cohen comes through on Robyn's phone.

Hey, Robyn. Let me know if you're free for that drink tonight. Good view of the fireworks at my place.

'You should go,' Frank says. 'I always had a lot of time for that Cohen. Good kid.'

'But we're cooking Mum's curry.'

'We can do it another night. Easy. Go on, have some fun.'

◆◆◆

Dusk is closing in when Robyn rolls up on Cohen's driveway and leans out to press the intercom buzzer. The gate looms over her, almost medieval with its curved spikes against the darkening sky. I can't tell you how I envy her, about to drive up and see Cohen. Be *seen* by him. She imagines him hesitating, finger over the button, leaning against the wall. It's the old Cohen she sees there, up inside the house beyond the gate: slightly stooped, dark blond hair all messy. Sam may have been mystified by my interest in Cohen back in the day, but Robyn knew exactly what I liked about him: his dark sense of humour; his solid calmness; his secret love of classical music. He was like an opal fossicked from the dirt: a rough grey stone shot through with glimpses of glorious colour.

At last, the gate begins to grind open. Winding her way up the driveway, Robyn marvels at how lush it is. Large ferns lean in over the car. Eucalypts tower behind them. The house, too, is enormous, a study in curves and angles and planes of white, all lit up by carefully placed spotlights.

Robyn scarcely recognises Cohen when he opens the door. He's more carefully put together than he used to be.

'Robyn,' he says, his smile a shadow of his old impish one.

'Cohen, it's good to see you. It's been a long time.'

'It has,' he says. 'Come in.'

He doesn't offer himself for a hug, but Robyn gives him one anyway, surprised by the surge of affection she feels for her old friend. As if he embodies all the good times we shared, back when things were simpler. When the shadow over her life was concise and singular. All those rambling conversations, the sense of belonging ... he's been keeping them all here, safe, to dose her up on them when she got home. Like an infusion.

He smells of beer and the new-denim scent of his dark jacket.

'Got started early?' Robyn says.

Cohen smiles ruefully. 'You're a little late.'

Robyn follows him down the hall then up a flight of stairs into an enormous living area. On one end, an austere kitchen asserts itself on the rest of the space, all smooth surfaces and integrated appliances. The living room is carefully stylish, with pale grey sofas arranged around a gas fire and flanked by elegant lamps. Blooms of subtle colour fill enormous canvases on the walls, complementing the view of the city beyond the floor-to-ceiling windows.

'Drink?'

'Red wine, if you have it.'

They take their glasses out to a large concrete table on the sprawling balcony, where they sit side by side in comfortable chairs, facing the view. Trees are silhouetted against the sky beyond a glass balustrade that emphasises the property's height above the river and the pool below. Cohen drinks his beer fast while Robyn relishes the rich flare of wine on her tastebuds.

'Prime spot for the fireworks,' she says, looking at the lights on the water—a school of boats, whose owners have motored them out and dropped anchor.

'My wife and I sometimes have people over for the show,' Cohen says. 'But she's gone out tonight. Watching with some friends.'

'You weren't invited?'

'I was, but I hate all that national-pride shit.' He looks down at his drink. 'Jewel was unimpressed, of course. My mother would've been too. She loved a good party.'

The first firework sings up into the sky and explodes in a shower of fine green fronds.

'So, your wife's name is Jewel, then?' Robyn says.

'Don't laugh,' Cohen says, but he's smiling too. 'You seeing anyone then? Someone with a good, proper name?'

'Nope. Work's been pretty intense.'

'Married to the job?'

'I guess you could say that.'

'You here for a while?'

'I think so.'

'Taking a breather?'

'For now, yeah.'

There's a series of smaller explosions, purple and red, followed by a glittering shower of blue. Cohen glances over at Robyn. She looks tired. Deeply so.

'You were too good for Sam,' he says. 'You know that, don't you?'

'He wasn't so bad.'

Together they watch a row of synchronised flares streak across the sky.

'Maybe not,' Cohen says. 'But he wasn't that good either, was he?'

2001 Saturday, 3rd November

It's swot vac, and Sam's driving us down to stay in Yallingup for a week, in his grandmother's holiday house. Yallingup is three hours south of Perth, down where the south-west coast kicks up into the Indian Ocean—a kind of westward pout—before edging into that long, east-bound stretch. We have exams to study for and essays to work on, which means lugging books and notepads and pens along with us. Other than that, we don't need much: bathers, towels, sunscreen. Cardies to throw on when the wind picks up.

Once we've loaded everything into the car, Sam straps his surfboard to the roof. Pulls the ropes tight.

'What about you, Cohen?' Robyn asks, once we're cruising along the open road, listening to Radiohead and the flap-flapping of ropes against the roof. 'You surf too?'

Cohen, up front in the passenger seat, says, 'Not anymore.'

'Lost his nerve,' Sam says.

'Guess you could say that.'

'He got a concussion a few years ago,' I tell Robyn. 'Came off his board and lost it in the surf, only to have *it* find *him*. Right in the temple.'

'Ouch.'

Cohen nods. 'In a nutshell.'

'I used to surf too,' I say.

'I didn't know that,' Cohen says.

'My dad used to take me. I was pretty good, actually.'

'So what happened?' Robyn asks. 'Why'd you stop?'

'I sold my board when I was saving for a car.'

'And you still haven't got a car,' Robyn laughs.

'I've got a couple of spares down there,' Sam says. 'If you're keen.'

He catches my eye in the rear-view mirror. Just a glance, but it stirs something in me that it shouldn't. I lean forward against the seat in front of me, reaching around to rest my hand on Cohen's chest. I feel his heart beating in there, and the warmth of his hand as he places it over mine.

✦✦✦

Sam's grandmother's place is perched high among the windswept melaleucas and the dense coastal scrub overlooking the wide bay of Yallingup Beach.

Sam pulls up at the back of the house. We bring the bags in from the car and dump them on the dining table before opening all the windows to let the breeze clear out the musty smell. Unlike some of its more expansive neighbours, the house is just a wide, worn deck with some bedrooms and a kitchen tacked on behind it. But it's more than luxurious to us: we're staying rent-free and have bedrooms to share, like fully fledged couples; we certainly aren't complaining.

Out on the deck, we stand for a moment, marvelling at the endless stretch of water beneath a vast sky. Dazzling beaches aren't new to any of us of course, but a view like this never gets old.

'Let's go get some supplies,' Cohen says, putting his arms around my waist and burying his face between my shoulderblades.

While we're at the general store, and once we're back at the house, I notice Sam's gaze lingering on me a bit longer than it needs to. And though part of me is wary of him, another part of me … I like it. I like his brooding gaze. I know it's loaded, and he's not what I want for myself, but it's still difficult to resist. Whatever negativity you harbour towards him evaporates when he smiles at you or stands a little closer than he should. Which is to say, I don't discourage his attention. Maybe I even encourage it. By not looking away.

Each night, we have a barbecue out on the deck. The sky dips from evening blue into indigo, then deeper still as the stars begin to appear. I can still see Cohen now, standing at the barbecue, turning the sausages, hair curled against his skin all smooth and sunburnt in the flickering light of citronella candles.

In the mornings, we swim and have a fry-up, then we sigh and stretch and find places to do our work.

One morning, after an evening spent drinking and talking late into the night, Sam and Robyn are sleeping in. I think I heard them arguing after we went to bed, though I couldn't make out the words. Cohen and I swim and eat, then Cohen sits at the worn pine table in the corner of our room with his History notes while I gather up my readings and essay notes and head to the dining table. I have the space all to myself for a while—just me, the humming fridge, and that view, framed by the flaky old window frames— but before long, as I'm working away on a tricky conclusion to a beast of an essay, Sam emerges from his bedroom, closing the door quietly behind him.

'Robyn still asleep?' I ask, glancing up from the page.

Heading towards the kettle, he nods. 'We were up late, talking.'

He makes a pot of coffee, fills two mugs and places one in front of me.

'What are you working on?' he asks.

'Oceanography essay.'

'Going well?'

'Yeah, you know. It's one of three I need to write this week, so it's not going to be brilliant.'

Sam yawns over his mug. 'I'm sure they'll all be brilliant.'

'What did you bring down?'

'English Lit, Theatre Studies, Media Studies … But it's enough to just bring it down, right? Or do I actually have to do it?'

'I'm sure bringing it down is mostly what they'll be looking for.'

There's nothing disloyal or suggestive in any of those words, but you can learn everything you need to know from a glance— the way it trails its warmth along the inside of your skin.

I look back at my work and force myself not to watch him—his sleep-mussed hair, the muscles in his back—as he stands up, makes two more coffees and heads back to where Robyn is sleeping.

It's nothing, really. But I feel bad about it when Cohen comes out for a break and rests his head momentarily on mine, massaging my shoulders. And again, later, when I'm alone with Robyn, talking as we walk along the beach towards the northern lip of the bay, gathering shells and dried seaweed trees as we go.

◆◆◆

The next morning, before the sun's properly up, there's a tap on our door. So gentle, I wonder if I dreamed it. I look at Cohen, but he's asleep, one arm across his eyes.

'Gracie?'

It's Sam in a loud whisper.

I carefully pull back the covers and head to the door. Then I open it and slip through the gap.

'Hey,' I whisper. 'What's up?'

'I'm going for a surf. Thought you might like to join me. I already chose you a board.'

Beyond the windows, the sky is growing lighter. You can hear waves pounding on the shore, and birds beginning to warble.

'Sounds big,' I say.

'Sounds perfect,' he says. 'But we'll go somewhere smaller if you prefer.'

It's been too long since I paddled out in the early morning. Felt the push of water beneath my feet through a board. So I nod through a yawn and grab my bikini and towel off the line while Sam finds me a wetsuit.

'Shall we leave a note?'

'Why?' Sam says. 'I don't need permission. Do you?'

Smiths Beach is one bay to the south—a short drive through the national park then west again at the Canal Rocks turn-off. We don't speak in the car, allowing space for the sacred hush of early morning.

The view of Smiths from the rise is spectacular—a wide blue bay with shadowy reefs beneath the surface. We pull off into the car park at the bottom of the hill then take the stairs, carrying our boards up over the dune and down to the water's edge. Six or seven surfers are out there already, black wetsuits rising and falling with the waves, waiting for a good set.

'Let's go,' Sam says, then he gives a whoop and runs out, diving onto his board and paddling fast. I do the same, though my whoop is more of a gasp in the bracing chill of the water. Paddling hard, duck-diving as needed, I finally reach him out back.

I'm unsure on the board. Last time I tried this, I was small and light. A whole lot nimbler. I wait out the whole of the next set, watching the others. He's good, Sam: strong and confident. Rides those waves as far as they'll take him. They're not big, only a couple of feet, and I'm feeling guilty that he's missing out on something bigger around the reach of rocks to the north, but he makes them count anyway.

After a good wave, he gets back out to where I'm waiting—not for him but for my courage to kick in—and pushes his hair back off his face. 'Sensational,' he says, then he glances at the swell behind me. 'This one has your name on it,' he says. 'Come on, Gracie, gun it.'

So I do, and he's right—I'm in the sweet spot. I paddle hard. Muscle memory kicks in and somehow, I'm on my feet, knees bent, gliding along in the pocket while the water churns behind me. My rusty technique is still sharp enough that I can stay ahead of the lip, even pull a cutback before I lose momentum and drop back into the water.

My heart's pounding when I come up for air, sending that same elation I saw on Sam's face pulsing through my veins, out to every cell in my zinging body. He gives me a thumbs-up from the back.

After an hour or so of being tumbled by the waves, with the occasional good ride thrown in, plus a nasty reef-scrape to the shin and a gallon of salt water up my nose, I find I'm spent, and hungry.

'Must be time to head back,' I say, picturing Robyn and Cohen back at the house, wondering where we've got to.

'For sure,' Sam says. 'One more set and we'll head in.'

Back on the sand, shot through with adrenaline, we peel off our wetsuits to the waist. The breeze is a caress. Water glistens on Sam's skin, runs off the curves and dips of his shoulders as he bends for his board.

I look away, head back first up the stairs.

Back at the car, Sam chucks our dripping wetties in a bucket and straps the boards to the roof. I'm wrapped in my towel, leaning back against the window, still riding the inner rush.

'Glad you came?' Sam asks, wiping his sandy hands on his boardies.

'Very.'

Sam reaches past me for the key, which he left on the wheel. I can smell sunscreen and the sea on him. I should move away, at least avert my eyes. But I don't, and when he stands back up, he reaches out with his free hand to push a strand of salty hair over my ear.

'Sam,' I say.

'Gracie.'

'We should go back.'

But I don't move. And he doesn't either, except to lean closer. Grit between my toes, dopamine still surging, I know he's going to kiss me. I can already imagine confessing to Cohen, seeing the dismay in his eyes, but it's as if some kind of spell has been cast— by the sea; by my surrender to it—and I want Sam anyway. Dark-haired, easygoing, inscrutable Sam. I want to know how it feels to kiss him. To feel his skin against mine. Sink my hands into his hair.

We kiss against the car, long and slow and salt-drenched. It's lush and electrifying, and while it's happening, there's no room for regret.

✦✦✦

When we get back to the house, Robyn's in the kitchen, beating eggs. There's oil heating on the stovetop, and trays of bacon and sliced tomatoes in the oven.

'Good surf?' she asks, pouring the eggs sizzling into the pan.

'Amazing,' Sam says, stepping behind her and kissing the top of her head. She looks surprised, but she reaches back for him. Turns to kiss him. I grab a loaf of bread from the pantry. Make some toast. Act like nothing happened. What else do you do with a memory that pulses like that, swollen with pleasure and guilt?

✦✦✦

That afternoon, as I sit bent over my work at the table in our room, Cohen comes in and lies on our bed, arms behind his head. He wants to talk to me, but he can see I'm concentrating, so he waits till I'm ready. When I'm satisfied with my work, or satisfied enough, I lie down beside him. He strokes my upper arm with his fingers and kisses me on the forehead.

'Fancy a walk?' he says. 'Maybe a drink up at Caves House?'

It's a stately old gem, the Caves House Hotel, not far from Ngilgi Cave. Steeped in colonial history, for better or worse, it overlooks a vast, manicured backyard: a dreamscape of undulating lawns and wedding gazebos sheltering beneath a towering benevolence of trees.

'Sounds good,' I say, turning my face towards him. 'What about the others?'

'Don't know what they're up to, but I'm happy to sneak off and leave them to it, whatever it is.'

The quickest approach to the hotel is to head south along Valley Road, turning left near the small cluster of shops and the café and making for the southern scoop of the small seaside town. Here, the road delivers us to a path that dips into the wonderland of the state forest, just for a short while—a dense limbo glade between the town and its historic hotel. It feels magical in there, beneath that lush canopy of twisting branches and paperbark trees, the groundcover glowing green in the dappled light.

As we descend into that cooler, darker place, Cohen takes my hand.

'Is there anything you need to tell me?' he asks.

He knows something happened down at Smiths, but he doesn't want to breathe life into it by giving it a name unless he has to. As for me, I know a lie is more corrosive than any truth, but how do I tell him *this* truth? It was only a kiss. It has no bearing on my feelings for him; if anything, I love him more than before. And if I were to tell him, I'd have to trade one lie for another to make it bearable—I'd have to say it wasn't great and I regret it, when the truth is, it was, and I don't. It was a one-off delicious enchantment, and I don't want it to mean anything. I want to keep it in its own little pocket somewhere, a silken pouch, undisturbed and inconsequential. Confessing will make it ugly. It'll break Cohen's heart. And for what?

There's no anger in Cohen's eyes. No jealousy. Instead, there's fear. Sadness. I put my hand to his face.

'I love you, Cohen. You know I love you?'

I've never said it before.

He smiles, rests his forehead against mine and closes his eyes. 'I love you too, Gracie. More than life.'

2019 Saturday, 26th January

Cohen refills Robyn's glass and his own as fireworks whistle into the sky and burst open, lilac sea urchins hanging in the air before ghosting away. Robyn's never seen them from a height like this before, reflected loosely like that on the water.

'I thought Sam was your friend anyway, Cohen,' Robyn says, taking the glass he's holding out to her. 'Why the slagging off?'

'He was there for me as a kid,' Cohen says. 'Most of the time. But later on, I don't know. Sometimes I wondered if he even liked me.'

'I know what you mean,' Robyn says, watching the display escalate towards a frenetic finale. 'But I think that's his way. He seems laid-back, but he keeps his cards close, you know?'

'That's true.'

'Plus, Cohen … I hope you don't mind me saying this … but it can be really triggering to see someone who reminds you of a shitty time. Maybe that's what's going on.'

Cohen looks away then shuts his eyes. Robyn wonders if she's overstepped the mark.

'I know how much you loved Gracie,' she says. 'I loved her

too. I hate that someone did what they did and got away with it.'

Cohen is silent for a long time, then he clears his throat. 'Me too.'

'Did you ever get grief counselling? Someone to help you through it?'

Cohen shakes his head. 'Mum tried to convince me, but unless it could bring Gracie back or take me away, I wasn't interested.'

'And now?'

'Nothing's changed. I mean, a lot has changed, but also nothing.' He downs the rest of his drink.

'Maybe we could do something together,' Robyn says.

'I've never seen a therapist, Robyn, and I'm not about to start.'

'Actually, I was thinking about a memorial gesture of some kind. Just, casual. We never gave her a send-off, you know? And now we're all here ...'

'A send-off? As in, bon voyage, have a great trip?'

'As in, closure.'

'Closure means letting her go.'

'Yes, in a way.'

'What if I'd rather not?'

'It's been nearly twenty years, Cohen; is that what she'd want for you?'

'I don't know what she'd want. I'd give anything to ask her.'

Robyn looks at him. He's staring at the sky, now dark and quiet, as if he's forgotten she's there. She looks away. Decides not to push it. Listens instead to the distant buzz of boats being steered back to their moorings, happy voices drifting through the air.

14

Robyn is in her cubicle at work: four grey planes of laminate to call her own. She sits there, typing and squinting at the scrawled notes and quotes in her notebook. The story is taking shape. She's accounted for the fundamentals, checked the flow, checked her spelling and added a little pizazz in the form of a punchy opening line. Pulling together a story like this one—about the shift in inner-city demographics, complete with a human-interest angle featuring a divorcee and her one-bedroom apartment on Murray Street—is a walk in the park. Exactly the kind of change she came home for.

Nearly time to file it for the subs to butcher.

She's thinking about Cohen, wondering if he's considered her memorial idea, when someone clears his throat beside her.

It's Jon. Jon Ellis.

He hasn't changed. Still has that dark flame of hair, perpetually standing up owing to his habit of resting his forehead in the palm of his hand. And those grey-green eyes. No doubt he still has the same way of talking, his words having to hustle to keep up with his ideas.

'Jon,' Robyn smiles. 'Hi.'

'Robyn,' he says, leaning on his elbow over the side of her cubicle. 'Never thought I'd see the day.'

'But then the sun came up and there it was: the day.'

He laughs, that quiet laugh Robyn hasn't heard for six years, though she's thought about it. Missed it, even.

'I heard you were back,' he says.

'Good news travels fast.'

'Liam saw you in the canteen this morning.'

'Scuttled over to warn you, did he?'

'He did. Made me run through a few drills ... revise the brace position. You're a scary lady, Robyn Tinsley.'

'Thanks,' Robyn says, standing up.

'How goes the newshounding today?'

'At a feverish pace. How about you?'

'Actually, I'm doing a lot less hounding these days. Deputy Editor Jon Ellis at your service.'

'Well, brilliant. Congratulations.'

'Thank you. A nice change. Actually, I'm needing an election piece on the young guns who've toppled the old guard, if you've missed the warm glow of local politics ...?'

'Sounds great, Jon, but I'm too busy squeezing human interest stories out of an endless pile of press releases.'

Jon looks surprised. 'I'm sure Adira's just getting you warmed up,' he says. 'She'll be happy to shift those on to an intern if you wanted to pick this one up for me?'

'I asked her for them. I wanted to ease my way back in.'

'Fair enough. I'll find someone else.'

Which should bring a natural end to the chat—an ideal time for Jon to say, 'See you later.' But that's not what he says. Instead, he says, 'Do you have any plans for Friday night?'

Robyn considers her Friday-night options: a chance to cook with Frank, or, if he's out, a packet-laksa for one and something on TV. Or she could touch base with her old housemate Marla, catch up over a bottle of wine. But she dismisses that idea. Just thinking about trying to be her old self makes her bones ache.

'I do have plans, as it happens,' she says, standing up to take her empty mug to the kitchenette. 'What about you?'

'Well, I did, but they kind of relied on your not having any.'

Robyn looks down at the mug in her hands.

'I know what you're going to say,' Jon says. 'Lots of water under the bridge and all that, but I'd love to talk about it.'

Robyn turns from him and heads for the kitchen, past cubicles so suffocating in their uniformity it's enough to make her want to run far, far away. But she tried that already; look where it got her. Instead, she looks beyond the desks, through the floor-to-ceiling window at the lake across the road. Maybe a good, long walk is what she needs.

'We talked things through a lot, Jon,' she says over her shoulder. 'Inside, outside, from all angles. It always came back to the same thing.'

'We argued too much, I know,' he says. 'But that was a long time ago. We talked it over from where we were standing *then*. I think we need to talk it through from where we're standing *now*. I mean, I've had a lot of time to think, and I've had a few insights while you've been gone.'

Robyn stops and turns to face him but he keeps going, nodding in the direction of their hawk-eyed editor's office. Within the soundproof glass walls, Adira sits behind her heavy desk, flicking at pace through her stack of dailies.

'Insights?' Robyn says, following him. 'Such as?'

'You want an example now?'

'Yes please, if it's not too much trouble.'

'Okay, let me think,' Jon says, stepping into the galley kitchen and making room for Robyn to access the sink.

'Right, okay,' he says, glancing at the desks closest to them; no one appears to be paying attention but he lowers his voice anyway. He's a journalist—he knows their best listening is often done whilst they're supposedly engrossed in some other task. 'You used to say I never showed you any affection in public, right? Like, I wouldn't even hold your hand outside the house.'

'Yes, I remember,' Robyn says, rinsing her cup and filling up the kettle. 'You weren't going to be some kind of parent surrogate.'

'Well, I figured out that it came from having extremely controlling parents. They used to grab my hand the minute we left the house.' He holds up both hands to demonstrate, one hand squeezing the other. 'My dad's grip was like some kind of stony torture device crushing my fingers. I think I came to associate hand-holding with suffocation.'

Robyn flicks the kettle on.

'It wasn't about other people's perceptions,' Jon says quietly. 'I was always proud to be seen with you.'

'Oh, well, thank you kindly. Shall we bow toward each other now or something?'

'See now, you're being sarcastic. Which means somewhere in there you do still care.'

Robyn opens an upper cabinet, hoping to find a stash of herbal tea.

'Of course I still care, Jon,' she says, locating a fruit blend and dropping the pyramid sachet into her cup. 'But I don't have the energy for all this again.'

The kettle boils and Jon lifts it off its cradle, pouring steaming water over the teabag. Robyn gazes at the cup, watching the pink pomegranate essence swirl slowly out into the water. Jon reaches across and gently smooths the frown from her forehead.

'I'm sorry,' he says, pulling his hand back. 'I'm coming on a bit strong here. I'm just … you've been away so long.'

Robyn smiles and raises her eyebrows in resignation. 'So what's happening on Friday night then?'

Jon gives a small fist-pump, the kind of understated slapstick that always made Robyn laugh.

'Well,' he says. 'I have a media pass for two to a show at Fringe. We can eat dinner from cardboard plates and drink beer under the stars.'

'Sounds okay.'

'So will you be my plus one?'

'All right, I'll come with you. But it's not a date, okay? It's a debriefing, looking back on our tangled-up business from a more mature standpoint, et cetera. With a show thrown in.'

'Right. Exactly. Excellent. You won't regret it.'

'I hope not,' Robyn says, lifting the mug and blowing steam off the tea as she heads back to her desk.

Jon gives her a nod and walks on, making for his office. Hands in his pockets, shoulders slightly stooped, he smiles as he goes, giving one colleague a wave and stopping to talk to another.

'Mr Popularity now, are we?' Robyn mutters, lowering her cup to the desk and sinking into her seat.

It's difficult to choose which release to work off next—most of them have a tenuous relationship to what Robyn would consider to be actual news. Plus the competition for most-tedious-item-requiring-highest-number-of-dull-telephone-interviews is stiff.

'Lord save us,' she murmurs, leafing through the pages. She needs to get back to real stories again instead of these endless mind-numbing pieces that pad out the paper. She should've taken Jon up on his election story. But that would've meant talking to people, face to face, asking difficult questions. Hearing difficult answers. She's had enough of that, at least for now.

15

We need to drop back in on Skye now. I imagine she's not your favourite person in the world, but, actually, I quite like her. I mean, she's not done much to endear herself to you, of course. But she has an energy I like. It's calming. And she's self-sufficient. Had to learn to be, being the unplanned daughter of a woman who was rather too fond of oblivion in all its many guises. Meaning everything Skye is, or has, is down to her own hard work. Which has to count for something, don't you think?

We find her alone in her single-bedroom unit this Thursday night, not far from the university campus where she's studying music. Skye's no stranger to melancholy, but when she picks up her guitar, all the shadows and bleakness fall away. It helps if there's a drumbeat to carry her, a little blues harp on the side. Throw in a thumping bassline and she can do better than find her way back to herself; she can find her way into someone else. If that's not freedom, what is?

Sitting on her couch, she's picking out a new melody on her steel-string, thinking about Sam. It's nearly a week since she gave him her number, but it's only a matter of time before he calls; she can feel it.

There's a knock on the door.

'Hello?' she calls, standing up and placing the guitar carefully on the couch.

'Skye?'

'Jethro?'

'Skye, I'm sorry,' he slurs mournfully beyond the door. 'I was such a dick the other night. Can I come in? Please? I want to talk to you. I just ... I need to apologise.'

Skye looks at him through the peephole. He's had plenty of opportunities to apologise before now, but she's been called worse things than *nasty*, and he's not the first person to ever swear at her. He looks so forlorn out there, with the night sky behind him and that unfamiliar stoop to his frame, she can't help feeling sorry for him.

'Skye,' he says when she opens the door. 'Can I come in?'

'Of course you can.'

He steps forward and takes her in for a hug. He smells of whisky and cigarettes. Skye pulls away and gestures towards the sitting area.

'Smoking again?' she says, filling up a glass of water for him.

'Nobody likes a quitter.' He holds a hand across his eyes at the brightness of her lights.

'So where've you been tonight?' she asks, handing him the water. He looks at it as if he's never seen the stuff before, then, seeing her watching, takes a gulp before placing it on the coffee table.

'Where haven't I been?' he says, wiping his shirtsleeve across his mouth.

'Got your kick drum back yet?'

'Still waiting on a quote,' he says, gazing at Skye with a look that has little to do with the words that come out of his mouth. 'The rental's okay, but yeah … not as good …'

'It fell pretty hard.'

'Gave me a fucking heart attack.' He nods towards her guitar on the sofa. 'You been writing something new?'

'I have.'

'Want some feedback?'

Skye looks at him, studies the expression on his face. It's hard to tell what he's thinking, given the slow-blinking, booze-soaked state he's in. She wants the old easiness between them, but she doesn't want him getting his hopes up again.

'It's probably too early for that,' she says. 'It's just a little lick …'

'Go on, it's never too early,' he says. He reaches out for the guitar but misjudges the position of the coffee table and loses his balance. He hits the ground hard, banging his forehead against the foot of Skye's desk.

'Jesus, Jethro.'

He sits up, holding his head.

'Are you okay?' Skye asks, squatting down beside him.

'Fuck, that hurts.'

'Come on,' Skye says, taking him by the shoulders and urging him up off the floor. 'Lie down, will you? Before you really hurt yourself.'

'First off,' he says, pulling himself up, 'I'm not an idiot.' He squeezes his eyes shut and presses his hand to his head. 'But also, that's a bloody good idea.'

'Drink more water first, yeah?'

'Yeah, okay.' He gets most of it down then lowers himself onto the couch, frowning at the pain in his head. Skye pulls her woollen throw over him and moves toward the freezer to grab some ice.

'I'm sorry I told you to fuck off at rehearsal the other night, Skye,' Jethro says, keeping his forearm over his eyes. 'You were right; I was playing too loose. Too many beers. I hope you know I never want you to actually do that.'

'I know, Jethro …'

'I love you, Skye. You know?'

'I never want you to fuck off either.'

'But you don't love me.'

Skye wraps the ice in a towel and places it on Jethro's swelling forehead. He flinches.

'I care about you, Jethro,' Skye says.

He takes hold of the ice pack and turns away from her.

'You're an amazing guy.'

'Yeah, I know,' Jethro mutters into the couch. 'So you keep saying. If you keep saying it, maybe one of us will believe it.'

✦✦✦

In the morning, Jethro's gone. There's no sign he was ever there, aside from the blanket left on the end of the sofa. That, and Skye's phone lying on the coffee table instead of on her desk where she left it charging overnight. She picks it up and her heart lifts at the sight of a waiting text from Sam. Sent through in the early hours of the morning.

Film at Paradiso tonight? Sam.

The brevity would usually be enough to put her off. If a man can't be bothered being at least conversational in a text—especially his first—what does that say about his willingness to put energy into other aspects of the relationship? But it's different with Sam. Everything's different.

16

The heat of the day has persisted into the evening; Robyn feels a bead of sweat trickle down her back as she approaches Jon. He's waiting for her near the Pleasure Garden's temporary box office, set up on the southern end of Russell Square, beneath one of the park's giant Moreton Bay fig trees. There's perfume in the air, mingling with the fragrance of woodchips and stage makeup. A man on stilts goes by, followed by a small group of women dressed in leather corsets and fishnet tights.

Jon is wearing a collared shirt with a small pencil and a notebook tucked into the pocket. He kisses Robyn on the cheek, enveloping her in the familiar scent of his cologne.

'So what are we seeing?' Robyn asks.

'It's a circus act. Something-something *Cirque Noir*. It's had great reviews.'

They buy drinks—mercifully cold—before joining the queue

outside the De Parel Spiegeltent. A man in a tutu and leather knee-high boots is handing out small paper fans; a lovely gesture, but the trapped heat inside is stifling and the smell of sweat is strong. Robyn would once have been right at home, but it seems her singed nerves don't respond well to noisy confinement. She downs half her beer in a few long gulps, eager to take the edge off. Then she takes a slow, deep breath and exhales as discreetly as she can, not wanting to alarm anyone—they're all crammed in so tightly, who knows what could happen if someone got spooked?

She distracts herself by glancing across at Jon. It's strange—kind of nice—being pressed up so close to him. It's been a long time. And yet it feels like just the other day that they were laughing together, picking ideas apart, arguing; that she was kissing the place where his jaw meets his neck while his fingers trailed slowly down her spine.

The show is a detective-themed romp, with aerial displays and burlesque flair. It's entertaining and masterfully executed, but Robyn is glad to escape the sweltering closeness of the tent once it's over.

'What did you think?' she asks Jon, once they're out and making their way to the food corner.

'Pretty good.'

'That's a lukewarm review if ever I heard one. I thought you said you were easy to please.'

'When did I say that?'

'Maybe never.'

'Definitely never.'

The next twenty minutes are best described as fraught. Robyn tries to enjoy the festive vibe of the place—it must be named the Pleasure Garden for a reason—but the need to make food-related decisions while standing in queues that literally cross over other queues at right-angles generates an unsettling static in her brain.

'Jesus, make up your mind,' she mutters as a woman ahead dithers over her choice of sauces.

Jon looks at her. Raises an eyebrow.

'What?' she snaps.

'Nothing,' he says, hands raised in surrender.

'Go on, Shakespeare, spit it out.'

Her use of the old nickname takes them both off guard.

'I'm not used to seeing you so agitated, that's all,' Jon says. 'On a balmy night out at the Fringe. Used to be your bag, this kind of thing.'

'I know. It's … I'm not great company at the moment, Jon. Maybe we should call it a night.'

'No way,' he says quietly. 'I'm ordering my pulled pork and coleslaw if it's the last thing I ever do.' Robyn looks at her feet. Has to laugh. 'And I think you should too. Come on; you'll feel better for it.'

Finally, food in hand, they find a couple of seats at the edge of a long wooden table and sit facing each other over the food. Which is not bad. Tasty and tender. And now that the jostling and wrangling is over and they're sitting under the night sky, Robyn feels the tension lift a little.

'So, Shakespeare, hey?' Jon says, jabbing at his food with his flimsy fork. 'I'd forgotten you called me that.'

'I'm glad—so cheesy.'

'And miles off the mark, all things considered.'

'Did you not finish that collection? Flash fiction or prose poems or whatever it was?'

'Bit of both, but no. They're still stacked up in my virtual basement ... like the BFG's gallery of dreams.'

'You should submit them somewhere.'

'What, and let someone else read them?'

Robyn laughs. 'You're insane, Jon. You know that, don't you?'

'Yes. And so are you, which is why we're such a good fit.'

Robyn contemplates him for a moment, remembering the look on his face when she told him she was leaving Australia six years ago. Leaving him.

'Are we?'

He nods, holds her gaze. 'I think we are, Robyn. I do. I mean, I know things went to shit and everything, but that was then. We've got six years on our former selves. We'd handle things better now.'

'Would we?'

Jon hold his hand out across the table.

'Only one way to find out,' he says.

'You know I didn't come back here for you, right?' Robyn says. 'I didn't get a job at the paper because I knew you still worked there. In fact, if I'd known, I'd probably not have applied.'

Jon curls his fingers back up. Pulls his hand into his lap. Resumes eating.

'Not that I'm not glad to see you,' Robyn adds, lowering her face to catch his gaze. 'But I would hate you to think I was chasing you down.'

'Heaven forbid.'

'Exactly.'

'So why did you come back?'

Robyn looks at her food in its cardboard vessel. The light wooden fork in her hand.

'I couldn't hack it anymore,' she says. 'I was filing stories that made my stomach turn, every day, delivering them with poise and brevity, all the while thinking, Jesus, what am I doing? How can I be refining my syntax over here while over there, a mum is weeping over the bodies of her children? While a grandma is shooing a fly off the face of her orphaned grandchild because he's too weak from malnutrition to swat it away himself? And tonight, three hundred factory workers won't be going home to their kids because the boss was too stingy to build the place properly?'

Some people only half-listen when you talk, leaving themselves open to distraction, waiting for a good moment to interrupt. Not Jon. He leans into Robyn's words, watching her in that earnest way of his.

'I told myself it was important work and it needed to be done properly, if change was ever to happen. But change doesn't come, Jon. It never comes. I kept seeing myself as all those people must've seen me, in my buttoned shirts and neat hair, working with our high-tech equipment—the market value of which would probably feed them for months or help them afford life-saving medicine—and I kept imagining them thinking: *Go home, lady. What do you know?* I got sad. And scared. I was becoming a liability to the crew. They'd have to stay longer than was safe because I kept stuffing up my pieces to camera.'

'You did great work,' Jon says. 'Your stories were always dead-on—balanced, challenging, accurate.' He puts his hand on the table again, and this time, Robyn takes it.

17

Robyn and Jon are not the only ones in Northbridge. Jethro's there too, having spent the day stewing in a feeble state of hungover dejection before finally showering and making his way into the city. His plan? Rather formless. All he knows is that he has to see for himself the man behind that text message—the one he saw through a pounding headache early this morning at Skye's place. More importantly, he wants to see if Skye shows up.

Seated in an Italian restaurant, around the corner from the Pleasure Garden and opposite the Paradiso, he rests his elbows on the table and his chin in his hands, unmoved by the scent of parmesan cheese riding on the thick aroma of tomato and basil sauce. He hasn't ordered anything yet; no appetite. He's only there for the view.

If all goes well, Sam will be some guy pacing along the street outside the cinema's double glass doors, checking his watch and sweating over the rejection and humiliation Jethro has come to know so well. This possibility releases the vice grip around Jethro's chest and jaw, enough that he can take a breath, a deep one, drawing in the smell of pasta sauce just delivered to a couple two tables down.

The place is heaving; the whole of Northbridge is heaving. Jethro had forgotten about Fringe. Not really on his radar. Skye's well into it though; he remembers her discussing it with Kiyo, planning which shows to catch … God, how can he love her so much when she feels so little for him? And how can she play so callously with someone she supposedly cares about then drop him so easily? He's tried everything, hasn't he? He's tried venting his anger, thinking maybe that will bring in a little respect. No result. He's tried remorse; he's tried showing her where it hurts. Nothing. Only that concerned expression on her face, which doesn't even come close to what he wants from her.

It's not as if he hasn't done that kind of thing himself. He's disappointed plenty of women who thought they were onto something with him. It's shithouse. It feels bad. But what feels worse is knowing that Skye might look at him the same way he looked at those women, when he was the one doing the dropping: with pity and distaste. There's nothing less enticing, is there, than neediness.

It makes him thump the table, sending salt and pepper cellars juddering along its surface. Good. He'd like to see them fall off the edge and hit the tiles, breaking into ugly shards. All the better to reflect the state of his heart. Then again, if they were to break he might be asked to leave—the manager is already eyeing him from behind the till—and then he'd lose his vantage point. Time to chill out a bit.

Jethro picks up the menu and scans it. Chooses some kind of penne dish, and a beer. He looks over his shoulder and catches the eye of a waitress.

She arrives and he mutters his choice, using the nail-bitten tip of his finger on the menu to point it out.

He waits. Pours more water. Fiddles with the salt and pepper cellars, tilting them to create a pivot point and twirling them slowly on the table.

At last, a possible Sam arrives across the road. He looks older than Jethro and more refined—hair casually groomed, a smart shirt. In fact, he looks familiar: the man Skye was talking to at Mojos the other night.

Outside the cinema doors, Sam checks his watch and begins to pace, just as Jethro imagined he would. Hope leaps in Jethro's throat as the minutes pass, to think that Skye might stand him up.

Sam checks his watch again, peers up and down the street and pulls out his phone. Jethro smirks.

But then Sam stops pacing.

Jethro, his heart thumping darkly, catches hold of the spinning salt cellar. Sam gives a little wave before looking up and down the street again and ducking inside.

So much for refinement, Jethro thinks; even *he* would have waited for Skye and held the door open for her. Then again, maybe Sam's ducked in to buy tickets because Skye's late and they'll otherwise miss the start of the movie. Or—and this seems more likely somehow—maybe he wants to minimise the chances of being seen with her. Which means he shouldn't be with her at all. Jethro has no way of being sure, of course, but the idea falls into place like a tongue in a groove: Skye is his bit on the side.

And there she is. Emerging from the crowd of mugs and freaks as if parting the waters. If this were a slapstick comedy, her hair would be billowing out behind her and the plebs would be falling over sideways in her wake.

Of course she's here, Jethro thinks. Sam is the walking antithesis of Jethro—how could she possibly resist?

Skye disappears through the doors just as Jethro's beer and pasta arrive.

He drinks, trying to douse the resentment burning in his gut. He'd like to get up and leave, but with the food already on the table … it's not like he can afford to pay for something and not eat it.

The chewing and swallowing seem to go on forever, but in the end he gets it all down. Afterwards, he settles his bill, thanks the watchful manager and heads to the pub next door.

In there, he buys a drink and finds a spot at the stand-up bar overlooking the street. He stands there, stewing. Trying to remember his life before he met Skye. It was good; he was happy, jamming with friends, hanging out, smoking weed and talking crap. He hasn't seen that crew for a while actually. Should touch base. Life was easier then. For one thing, he was capable of thinking about something other than Skye. His happiness was not contingent on her laughing at his jokes or holding his gaze; hope wasn't invariably followed by disappointment, with a nice little dose of self-loathing stirred in.

A woman arrives to stand beside him at the bar. Blonde hair to the shoulders. She places her glass of wine on the bar and smiles up at him before looking away to dig in her bag. Pulling out her phone, she checks it before placing it carefully beside her drink.

There's an air of expectation around them now. She's chosen her spot carefully, singling him out for this strange pantomime.

It's sweet. Maybe. She looks sweet.

But she's not Skye. And if she's interested in Jethro, that says something about her judgement, doesn't it? Namely that it's a little off. Because if he's not good enough for Skye, he's not good enough full stop. And how messed up is that anyway? That he should have aligned his opinion on all things—including himself—so closely with Skye's that now he has no perspective of his own. And no matter how much he critiques all this, he can't seem to bloody change it.

Eventually, getting a better reading on Jethro's solitude, the woman retreats. Finds a table on her own, where she sits, trying not to look as if she minds.

Three, maybe four beers later, Sam and Skye emerge through the cinema's glass doors. They seem to have forgotten their initial cunning strategy of not being seen together. Skye is looking at Sam in a way Jethro's only ever imagined for himself. They're not touching in a bodily sense, but in every other way—whatever such ways may be—they're all over each other.

'Getting your chemistry now, are you?' Jethro says, draining his glass and making his way to the exit.

◆◆◆

Meanwhile, Robyn marvels at how uptight she was at the start of the evening. Already, it seems long ago and far away. Nothing like a little alcohol to loosen her up. That, and a warm hand across a table.

She still has the warmth, except now it's Jon's arm around her shoulder. They've left the Pleasure Garden and are walking in the direction of the train station, approaching the Paradiso, one of Perth's smaller cinemas. It's dated but kind of classy, making it a little out of place in Northbridge. Sure, Northbridge is a buzzing place, a vibrant hub, but nothing good ever happens there after ten or eleven at night. The bad fairy godmother waves her wand and clouds move in across the moon. Mascara runs down cheeks; lipstick gets smudged; high heels break and violence spills out of venues like blood from a wound.

Right now though, it's Sam, spilling out of the cinema with a woman beside him. Robyn's first impulse is to shout hello but she holds back, thinking maybe he and his wife are enjoying a rare evening out together, trying to make the most of the time alone. He might not appreciate worlds colliding. But something's not right. The woman he's with seems too young. And there's something between them, a tension that doesn't gel with the idea that they're a married couple with a baby.

Robyn watches them. Sam is smiling. The woman is slender. Quite tall. Her hair is thick and dark, the kind of hair you can twist up in a coil and it'll stay that way for a while before gradually returning to its ordinary shape. Robyn makes a mental note to get online and search for pictures on social media of Sam with his wife. The chances are slim that they will exonerate him, but it's worth a try.

'You okay?' Jon says.

'Yeah, all good.'

She tries to ignore what she's seen. Tells herself not to jump to any conclusions. The woman could easily be Sam's wife. Not all new mums have full breasts and soft bodies. Some are back in shape within weeks of the birth. And some don't breastfeed. So what's to say this is not his wife?

Nothing. Nothing more than instinct. The way they're looking at each other seems illicit. They share some kind of secret. And as they walk, Sam extends his left hand ever so slightly towards the woman's right and brushes his finger against hers. Just that. Nothing more, but Robyn can feel the electricity from here. She knows the nature of that secret as plainly as if they were having it off right there in the street.

She's not sure what she feels, but it's akin to loss. Something inside her retracts, the same thing that just moments ago was unfurling ever so slowly, like a cat in the sun: a sense of wellbeing. Trust. A feeling that everything actually might be okay.

Jethro keeps to his own side for a while then crosses over as Skye and Sam approach the Brass Monkey on the corner of James and William. They stop on the corner and stand there, being careful, very careful, not to be in any way demonstrative. It's pointless though, considering how obvious it is that all they want to do is get each other alone. Jealousy courses through Jethro at the thought of it. Hot and dense, and there's nowhere to put it, because no amount of fury is going to bring Skye back onside. If she wants this guy, with his expensive shoes and carefully dishevelled hair, she's not going to be thinking even for a second about having another go at things with her good friend Jethro. Good old drummer Jethro: always there, ready to catch the crumbs before they hit the ground.

People are giving him looks now, the way he's standing there in the middle of the pavement. That's not how it works; you don't just stop. Some of them brush past him, but most keep their distance, as if he's one of those types you don't want to mess with. He edges sideways to lean up against the wall, out of the way.

'There you go,' he murmurs to no one in particular. 'Happy flowing.'

Sam waves down a taxi and he and Skye get in. Jethro moves fast and flags one down for himself. It's an indulgence, but this is important. He has to know where they're going.

His taxi is some way behind theirs for a while, but as they approach a red light, it pulls up right behind them.

'Follow them, okay?' he says to the driver.

'Okay. Friends of yours?'

'Yes.'

In the backseat up ahead, Sam and Skye are making no effort now to keep their hands to themselves. Jethro watches, wondering what she smells like tonight—that Moroccan shampoo she uses, or the perfume oil? Sam's hand is buried in her hair, holding her head while he kisses her. God knows where his other hand is.

Jethro's jaw begins to hurt, he's grinding his teeth so hard. Seething is what he is. Enraged. And Christ, it hurts to watch them at it. He pulls his eyes away and looks out his window sideways until at last the light changes and the cab in front pulls away.

Anger feels better than dejection. So much better. Stronger. So he feeds it, listing words he'd like to paint up on Sam's wall, if he knew where the prick lived. Where are those kids spraying giant dicks on people's cars? He'd like to commission one of them now, just for the satisfaction of knowing Sam will have a hard time scrubbing some mindless shit off his paintwork.

The taxis in convoy wind their way past Kings Park, in the direction of UWA, until at last, still about a hundred metres ahead, Skye's cab pulls up in the car park below her place. It idles out front, at the foot of the stairs.

'Stop here,' Jethro says.

The driver pulls up alongside the nearest verge.

'Turn off the lights please, mate.'

'Everything okay here?'

'Yes, all good.'

'You seem not good.'

'I'm fine.'

The taxi in front is still idling. This is good. This is great.

Skye climbs out, leans in for a moment then pulls away, shutting the door and giving a little wave. She blows a kiss that turns something sharp in Jethro's gut, then she heads up the stairs.

'Thanks mate,' Jethro says to his driver. 'I'll get out here.'

'You sure?'

Jethro hands over his bank card.

'Of course.'

'She a friend of yours?'

'Yes, she is.'

'She with someone else tonight?'

Jethro scratches the side of his nose. 'Maybe.'

'She meant to be yours though?' the driver asks, running the card through his machine. He talks on into Jethro's silence. 'Happened to me once. Best thing to do is to go home, sleep it off, feel better in the morning. Serious. You're dodging a bullet, mate.

Keep on rolling on, you know? Don't let it ruin your life. And definitely don't try to talk to her tonight, yeah?'

'Why not?'

'Mate, look at yourself.' He's studying Jethro in the rear-view mirror. 'What's she going to prefer—someone calm and collected playing his cards smooth, or someone in a state like you? Seriously. I know women, mate. Four sisters. Stay away. I'll take you home if you like. No charge.'

He turns to face Jethro then and hands back his card.

Jethro thinks it through. Imagines opening his front door and going into that shithole share house. Trying not to touch anything in the feral kitchen that is apparently not the responsibility of anyone living there. Having to talk to his housemates about some inane shit or other, all the time wanting to see Skye. Ask her about Sam. Make her promises, whatever it takes to make her see that he is the better option. For so many reasons. Surely she doesn't want to be some douche's second woman? Surely she must be reconsidering now, having been unceremoniously turned out of the taxi before it whisked prince turd-boy away to his better life, wherever it is. Jethro would never do that to her. Not ever.

'It's not like that,' he says to the driver. 'I'm good here. Seriously.'

'Okay, mate. Be calm, okay? Don't hurt the lady.'

'What? Why would I do that?'

'Anything happens to her, I will tell the cops I left you here in this state, okay? Take care now.'

'Jesus, nothing's going to happen to her, all right?'

Jethro slams the door too hard, gestures an apology for it, then heads towards Skye's place.

The driver watches him go for a while, until Jethro looks back and waves him off. Then he shrugs, turns on his lights and pulls off into the night.

18

Standing on a dark street two blocks away from the Fringe revelry, Jon and Robyn are waiting for her Uber.

'Would it kill you to show me your cards?' Jon says. 'Or just one of them? Any one. Even your worst one.'

'You always do that, Jon.'

'What?'

'Take a sweet old metaphor and run it into the ground.'

'Does that mean my days of being likened to Shakespeare are numbered?'

'Afraid so.'

Robyn peers down the street, checking for her ride.

'Is there any way I can persuade you not to go home yet?'

'I'm super tired, Jon.'

'Let me drive you. I could make sure you get home all right.'

'I'll bet you could,' Robyn says, eyeing him in mock suspicion.

'An outrageous slur.'

'I'm sorry, you're right. I'm sure you have nothing but the purest of intentions.'

'Well, I wouldn't go that far,' Jon says. 'No man worth his hetero salt could say his intentions towards you were one hundred per cent impurity-free.'

'Well, thank you,' Robyn says. 'I think.'

'Any time.'

'Where can I get some of that hetero salt?'

'You trying to tell me something? Something change while you were away?'

'No. I just think hetero salt sounds a little tasty.'

'Guess it does.'

A blue sedan pulls around a corner and slows to a stop in front of them.

'Tonight's been fun, Jon. Thanks for putting up with my … disposition.'

'I've never had to put up with you, Robyn. That's not how I roll anyway.'

'Well, thanks, and I'm sorry if I've ruined your evening.'

'Not at all. There's a stand-up session I might stick my head in on. Down at the Brass.'

'Okay, well, better you than me, I reckon.'

'Yes, I am better than you. Except at most things. And even then …'

'If I don't get into this car now, we'll keep talking shit all night. So I'm going to get in now and go, okay?'

'If you insist.'

'I insist. Thanks for tonight.'

'Any time Adira gives me free tickets, you'll be the first person I'll call.'

'Well … I might say no next time. Take me swimming instead.'

'Thanks for the hot tip.'

Robyn's smiling as the car pulls away. Jon is smiling too; she can see him in the rear-view mirror. It's good, whatever it is that's happened between them tonight. Good, but tainted, because all she can see now is Sam's hand brushing against that woman's finger. A woman who is surely not his wife. And that way sorrow lies.

◆◆◆

Having said goodnight to Sam a little earlier than she'd hoped, Skye is sitting on her couch, staring at nothing. The knowledge he shared with her tonight in the taxi—that he isn't just married but a father too—lurks like a bruised mass somewhere behind her eyes. He has a baby girl.

He's off the table. Has to be.

And yet.

It touches her that he wants her so much, despite the pain of guilt it causes him. That's a lot of want right there. Almost enough to match hers.

Maybe if she doesn't think about you and your mother—if she works hard to actively forget about you both—she can turn you into an abstraction. A parallel reality that in no way intersects with hers.

She'd never ask him to leave you. A child abandoned by her father on her account is not something she could live with. Not after the childhood she had. All she wants is to have him look at her that way again.

There's a banging on the door.

Sam, she hopes as she pulls herself off the couch.

But the thumping comes again. Louder.

'Skye?'

It's Jethro.

Skye says nothing. Presses her ear to the door and waits.

'Skye? Open the door! Skye! Come on, I know you're in there.'

'Go away, Jethro!'

He's quiet for a while.

'I know,' he says. 'I'm being a dick again. I know I am. Sorry Skye.' Sounds like he's crying now. 'I'm sorry, I don't want to be a dickhead. Skye? Skye, please open up.'

'Jethro, you need to go home. Come and see me when you're sober, okay?'

'I don't want to go home.' He thumps on the door. 'Look what you've done to me, Skye.' He thumps on it again. Or was that a kick? 'Turned me into some pathetic arsehole.'

'Jethro! Go home before I call the police, or someone else does.'

'All right! I'll go the fuck home!' There's silence, then another thump on the door, and then silence again.

Skye's heart thuds. Takes a while to settle.

She wanders into her room, kicks off her shoes and climbs in between the sheets with her phone.

Trawling through Facebook, she contemplates stalking Sam and your mum on there. She goes so far as to type his name into the search field, but she knows that if she sees them together—

sees the evidence that her own existence in his life is peripheral—the whole thing will tilt off-axis.

A text comes through. From Sam.

Miss you already. Free Monday night?

Skye closes her eyes: the gratitude is vast.

She waits a while before responding. Gets up to brush her teeth first and fill a bedside glass of water. Thinks about what she might say. She should nip it in the bud, now—that baby girl—but it's as if someone has drawn a chalk circle around her and enacted some kind of spell; it's out of her hands.

She sends him a word, one little word that says nothing of the expansive feeling it gives her, knowing what it means.

Yes

That's how it goes sometimes, Isla. People do things they shouldn't do. They know they shouldn't do them even as they sketch out their plans.

19

After a long day's work at the paper, Robyn takes a detour and goes for a walk along the river, hoping to see Sam. She'd like to bring up the fact that she saw him on Friday evening. See how he reacts.

He's not there, and it unnerves her how disappointed she feels. She won't often admit it to herself, but Robyn loved Sam. A lot. With him, she wasn't just a motherless girl; she was a woman with a lover who made her feel fascinating. Alluring. Who showed her a lusty, vivacious part of herself she'd never known existed. He was funny and irreverent, not to mention well-read and spontaneous. She remembers listing these attributes to herself in the days after their first kiss, lying in her bed, buzzing with desire and astonishment.

The pregnancy scare wasn't his finest hour, no, but they'd only been together for three and a half months at that point, so it seemed fair enough; she chose not to dwell on it. He started running hot and cold after that, which was confusing, but even then, Robyn thought they were only at the beginning of something transcendent.

After I died though, he ran only cold. Robyn felt numb too. Unreachable. How could she touch his body when mine lay dead in the ground?

When it became clear that shock and grief had changed things between them forever—that a future together was mere fantasy— Robyn was sad, but not surprised. Sam was too remarkable to fit into an ordinary life anyway. She imagined him roaming the world forever, giving and taking exactly what he wanted—an untouchable, almost mythical being.

She cleared out of our haunted apartment and moved back home with Frank, and that's where she stayed, until she had her degree in her hand and a few pay cheques under her belt. Within a few years, she'd met Jon and moved across from print journalism to TV reporting. Life was humming along nicely, until Jon suggested moving in together. Robyn got twitchy. Began scanning the relationship for all the reasons why things might go pear-shaped. She packed it in too quickly, I reckon. They were great together, actually, most of the time. But you know what they say: once burned, twice ready to bolt.

Robyn and Sam didn't keep in touch, but she kept an eye on him online. She watched his career evolve from small publication wins to a series of book launches, after which came festival appearances, world tours, screen adaptations and multiple international translations. She was glad for him, though it stung a little, given that she'd imagined doing all those things with him one day: travelling and finding success; capturing it in ironic phrases somewhere exotic.

Driving homeward through his riverside suburb now, Robyn sees him, pulled over on the side of the road in the driver's seat of a navy SUV. He's talking on the phone. She pulls in behind a green Honda nearby and waits. When he's done on the phone, he glances over his shoulder and pulls out into the left lane. Robyn follows him as he winds along the tree-lined streets then turns off into the car park of a two-storey block of flats. She parks and watches him in her rear-view mirror. He sits for a while in the car, one hand still gripping the steering wheel, head lowered. Then he looks up, studies himself briefly in the rear-view mirror, and climbs out.

Robyn watches him head up the whitewashed stairwell and make his way along the open corridor, one hand nervously rubbing the back of his neck. She doesn't know exactly what he's up to, but after Friday night, she thinks she can hazard a guess.

Pulling out her phone, she turns on the camera function and climbs out of her car. She may be too late to stop him from making a ridiculous mistake, but if she can show him later what she's seeing right now, she may be able to stop him from doing it again.

He stops at number nine, glances around furtively, then knocks on the door. It opens and there's that dark hair again, that slender frame. The woman is wearing a blue dress and leaning up against the door. She's in no hurry to let him in but not intending to send him away either, if the tilt of her head is anything to go by. Sam says something, his hand returning to his neck. The woman smiles, reaches across the gap between them and takes hold of his belt buckle, pulling him inside.

Robyn gets the whole thing in a series of snaps and then the two of them are gone, nothing to see but a row of identical doors.

The car park is quiet. Robyn climbs back into the car, shakes her head and contemplates sticking around, just to see how long it is before Sam comes back out. Maybe he's only there to tell the woman he can't see her anymore.

But as the minutes tick by, she tells herself not to be so naïve—that's the role of the conned wife—and heads for home.

Along the way, she struggles to account for the sick feeling in the pit of her stomach. What is Sam to her anyway? What does she care what happens to his marriage? Really it has nothing in the world to do with her. She's hardly even his friend anymore, to be honest.

Even so, it's troubling. Hard to get her head around. First of all, seeing him with a wife and child destabilised the whole roaming-god narrative; that, in itself, was confronting. Logically then, this affair he seems to be having should settle the score a bit, situate him back within that seraphic, boundless realm Robyn always imagined for him. And yet it doesn't. Because actually, what Sam's doing is as base and fallible as it gets. It's nothing but mortal disrespect. And not just towards his wife and child, waiting at home, but towards love itself. Towards the most basic human quality of giving a shit about someone other than yourself.

✦✦✦

Skye's place is small and lovely, decorated with Klimt prints and little paper lanterns draped across window frames. She has an easel in the corner where a painting of an orchid rests, mid-composition.

Her bed is covered in sheets the colour of storm clouds. They smell of something Sam can't put his finger on. Something floral but not too heady. Some or other mild spice.

Her skin is warm and firm. All over.

Kissing her, in that bed, he is drugged. By her smell, her way of looking at him. Her arms around him. Her legs.

Her voice.

Nothing is known here.

For the first time in an age, his inner monologue goes quiet. That endless looping track falls away. Every part of him is awake to her softness. Her desire for him. It's a miracle. All of it. A strange, holy, awful miracle he'll have to live with forever. And while it's happening, he's fine with that. He'll take all the consequences that come, just as long as he doesn't have to stop.

But afterwards, lying there, gazing up at the ceiling, the guilt comes quickly.

Any man in my situation, he thinks ... but he stops himself there. He knows that plenty of men in his situation would not have taken Skye's number off that bottle in the first place, much less set up a series of liaisons culminating in this. And as sensational as it's been—small aftershocks are shimmering through his body even now—it's terrible. Terrible what he's done. The thought of Tori waiting at home, probably making dinner or feeding you, sends something else coursing through him: fear over what he's put on the line. Tori's secret may have cut him deep, but this has taken things to another level.

He looks at Skye there beside him, on the edge of sleep, and wonders at the strange blend of tenderness and self-loathing that rushes in, churning, eddying in his belly. It's all so rich and wrong he still can't speak. All he can do is lie here and marvel at how he can feel both elated and gutted at the same time.

Maybe he can get used to it. No one else has to know; no one has to be hurt. Plenty of other men carry on like this, don't they?

Skye rolls away, over onto her other shoulder. Sam traces a line from her hairline down the scoop of her neck and across to the top of her shoulder. Jesus. He's not proud, but also he's not sorry.

'Look out,' Skye murmurs, shifting her shoulder out from under his hand and rolling back to face him again. 'You might wear an actual groove into my flesh there.'

'Sorry.'

Eyes closed, she rests a hand on his cheek.

'It's okay,' she says, intuiting his torment. 'It's good that you feel guilty. If you felt nothing, *that* would make you a monster. This, between us, this makes us human.'

'Feeling bad about being a shit doesn't make me less of a shit.'

'Your other life … I'll never step on it, okay?'

Sam nods and opens his eyes again to look at her, the fine line of her nose, the turn of her mouth. Her eyes—now open too— are an astonishing green colour, framed by the longest, darkest lashes. They hurt him, those lashes. Because in them he sees your mother's fine, blonde ones, the ones she coats in mascara with a regularity that borders on ritual. He feels a surge of tenderness for Tori. He always tells her she doesn't need the makeup, and yet here he is, mooning over something she lacks.

He sits up and drops his head into his hands.

This can't be undone. Forever, as life spirals onwards, there will be this. And his marriage will bear the mark of it, even if he never tells Tori, and if she never finds out in some other way.

Because he will know.

The funereal march of a requiem sounds in his head: the solemn vocal harmonies, the ominous dragging of horsehair across strings. Something has died here tonight. Something beautiful; he has killed it. And he can never undo it, nor is he entitled to weep about it.

He shakes his head and stands up. Retrieves his boxers from the bottom of the bed. As he gets dressed, he looks back at Skye. One arm under her head, she smiles at him with a depth of compassion he feels unworthy of. So unworthy. And yet it might just be the only thing that can save him from this new place he's chosen to inhabit, this new role. It's like a home he didn't need or want but went out and bought anyway, and now he has to live there forever.

❖❖❖

The next morning, Skye's pillow smells of Sam. His absence hurts her, but in a good way. In a way that means something big is happening. Something cosmic. She finds it reassuring to know she's capable of whatever this is, after so long trying and failing to find it.

'Don't jinx it,' she tells herself, trying to silence the voice in her head saying: *It can't last*; *it shouldn't have happened*; *he has a family*.

'The man had a choice,' she says to the tapestry owl on her wall. 'You saw him; he wanted to be here.'

She wonders what he's thinking right now. Maybe while he's making coffee or reading the paper, he'll allow himself a moment to revisit last night.

Please, let it be without regret.

Guilt: okay.

Shame: if need be.

But not regret.

Making the bed, she pictures him getting up early to have a shower, or to make your mum a remorse-fuelled breakfast, and she finds herself plumping up the pillows more vigorously than usual. Tugging roughly on the sheets. She has to remind herself to stop thinking about them: you; his family. The ones who have a prior claim. And she can do that: create a space in her mind for only her and Sam to inhabit, a space into which reality may not intrude. You and your mum will henceforth belong in another dimension, a parallel existence that has no bearing on this one. She can't afford to dwell on her second-tier status, because as much as she'd like to think she could take or leave this thing with Sam, it already feels important. Necessary. Like oxygen.

20

Four days after witnessing your father crossing Skye's threshold, Robyn is in her cubicle at work, gazing at an image of him and Skye on her phone. She's uploaded the pictures onto her laptop at home as well, and she can't stop looking at them. Savouring the sting of betrayal, though she knows it's not hers. She's studying the look on Skye's face when Jon speaks behind her.

'Is that Sam Favier?'

'Jesus, Jon,' Robyn says. 'Don't do that to me.'

'Do what? Approach your desk and start talking to you?'

'No, sneak up behind me and start talking to me about what's on my phone.'

'Fair enough. Although I did approach from the front, you know. Is it my fault if you don't look up when you see me coming?'

'I didn't see you coming. That's the point.'

'Got it; sorry.'

'Good.'

'I texted you a few times this week.' He's pushing for upbeat, but the tone of his voice betrays him. 'Did I do something to offend you the other night?'

'No, you were fun. And kind. Can't have been easy, considering.'

'So, what then?'

Robyn says nothing, wondering where to start.

'Does it have something to do with your picture of a lauded author with a mysterious woman in blue?'

Robyn logs off and stands up.

'Do you want to grab a coffee?' she says. 'I'll try to explain.'

Downstairs, outside, the glare is intense. Robyn rummages in her bag for her sunglasses. Jon seems to have magicked his onto his face in his usual way of getting his shit together before Robyn's even found her bearings.

They walk along a concrete footpath until they reach a café nestled in the footings of a hexagonal building. The coffee aroma envelops them before they reach the café itself. It's so rich and alluring, it's hard to believe it's being brewed in the depths of this space with its cold gleaming planes and sharp angles. Hard to believe the place has any depths in the first place. But then one finds the café, epicentre of the spreading fragrance, and all is forgiven.

They order and sit opposite each other. Jon studies Robyn from below raised eyebrows—bemused, hopeful—and smiles. He pulls back the sleeves of his navy shirt, working his forearms free.

'Bit warm in here,' he says, glancing around as if hoping to find a window. Instead, he spots the water cooler and glasses on the bench a few metres behind him. He looks left and right before approaching it, as if he's doing something illegal, then he chooses two glasses carefully, holding them up to the light to check for lipstick residue.

'Not so fresh,' he says after drinking his down.

'Better than dry-mouth though, right?'

'Marginally.'

Robyn laughs. 'I'd forgotten you were such a water nazi.'

'I prefer connoisseur, but whatever.'

'I think maybe you're a little bit fussy.'

'Discerning?'

'Okay, discerning.'

'Thank you.' He smiles as if that is all he's ever wanted to hear. Looks down at his hands as they rock the empty glass back and forth.

'So,' he says, looking at her again. 'You were going to explain about that photograph. And last Friday night.'

'Which one first?'

'Friday's the one I've lost sleep over. I mean … you started off a little tense, then you actually smiled once or twice, and then out of nowhere you drew up the barricades again and slunk off home. What did I say? Or do? Please tell me; I'm so confused.'

'That's not a good review, is it?'

'Three stars at best. But I don't expect eternal sunshine from you, Robyn. Never been a fan of UV rays anyway, you know that. It's just, I need to know if it's me you're reacting to. If it's not me, I can roll with it, but if it is me, I need to know what I'm doing wrong.'

Robyn sits back to make space for the arrival of their coffees—froth-capped and enormous.

'It was you, Jon,' she says. 'But only the middle bit. The bit when I smiled once or twice.'

'Well, that's good to know.'

'The rest of it, well … I'm just a little edgier than I used to be. And not in an avant-garde kind of way, if that's what you're thinking … I know you and your little jokes.'

He nods. 'That is what I was thinking.'

'I knew it.'

'So that explains the first bit,' Jon says. 'And then what happened when we left the …' He lowers his voice to a whisper. '… the Pleasure Garden? I feel weird every time I say that.'

Robyn leans in and says in an exaggerated, sultry whisper, 'Take me back to the Pleasure Garden, Jon.'

'Exactly.' He shifts in his seat and glances around the café.

Robyn laughs. 'And you call me neurotic.'

'You call *yourself* neurotic, but stop trying to change the subject. What happened?'

'Okay, well, this kind of relates to the photo as well actually.'

'I'm listening.'

'When we were walking along James Street, past the Paradiso, I saw Sam Favier emerge with that woman from the photos.'

'Photos plural? I only saw the one.'

'Well, I took a few.'

'Why?'

'Evidence. To show him, you know? Make him realise what he's doing and maybe stop doing it.'

'Married, isn't he?'

'Yes. With a daughter.'

Jon shakes his head, eyebrows up.

'He's so sweet with her, you know?' Robyn says. 'His daughter.

So doting. I'd never have imagined him as father material, back when … when I knew him.'

'You guys go back?'

'Yeah, we were at uni together. We were an item for a little while, but it kind of fizzled out. We lost a good friend—I might have told you about Gracie?'

Jon nods.

'After she died, I guess grief overshadowed everything else, including my relationship with Sam. Not that it would've lasted. He wasn't head over heels, put it that way. There was a moment when I thought I might be pregnant.'

Jon studies Robyn's face as she stirs her coffee.

'I'm guessing he didn't go down on one knee?'

'He did not, no.' She rests the spoon on the table and clears her throat. 'Anyway, when I got back to Perth and saw him with his baby girl, I felt this weirdly intense rush of emotions. Seeing that he'd found someone he *did* want a baby with stung for a bit, but it was also nice, you know? To see something so simple and sweet. There's so much shit raining down everywhere, all the time, and seeing this small pocket of tenderness was … reassuring or something.'

'The world's so crazy, you'll cling to anything that even remotely resembles a life raft.'

'Exactly. Plus, you know, after Gracie died the way she did, I always had this feeling that we owed it to her to make our lives amazing. Otherwise, we'd be wasting what she lost. Seeing Sam as a doting father instead of a perpetual bachelor … it seemed right and good. And then when I saw him with a woman who could only be a mistress, I felt so … betrayed. And then angry.'

'I guess that all makes sense.'

'It really wasn't you.'

'I'm glad. I've been starting to question my sanity a little bit.'

'That's one of the three signs of wisdom.'

'Is it?'

'Should be.'

Jon laughs and leans back in his seat. 'I guess the next question is, when will we see this on the front page? Local personality fools around with younger woman ...'

'Um, never.'

'Why not? Good photo; great story.'

'What would be the point?'

'Aside from the fact that it's news many people will be interested in?'

'Tabloid fodder, Jon.'

'And what do you think our paper is, Robyn? I hope you haven't been labouring under the misapprehension ...'

'I know what our paper is, Jon. But I can't see who wins in this situation. He's a good man, just ... stupid or weak or going through something. And he has a child. I don't want to be responsible for her growing up one day and finding these pictures.'

'We publish stuff that scars people all the time, Robyn. It's called journalism.'

'I know. You don't have to tell me that, Jon. I know that. But you're forgetting the public interest test. There's public *curiosity* here, yes, but no real public interest. No one wins.'

'The paper wins. Improved sales mean we can minimise the next round of redundancy damage ...'

'Jon, it's not happening, okay? No way am I publishing these pictures. I haven't even decided if I'll show them to Sam yet, though that's why I took them in the first place.'

'Okay, well, they're your pictures. But I would urge you to reconsider.'

'You're free to do that, Jon, but I'd prefer to drop it, okay?'

'Consider it dropped.'

'Good.'

'For now,' he says, smiling and raising his eyebrows over his coffee cup.

Robyn reaches for his hand. He's been so careful around her till now. Kind of meek. It's good to see him standing up for something again. Even *this* something. 'Now is all we have, right?'

'It is. And I'm not complaining.'

✦✦✦

That evening, Robyn is chopping garlic and ginger in the kitchen while Frank pulls out the spices and gets the rice going. They're listening to Pink Floyd while they cook—still Frank's favourite soundtrack to most activities. It's been a hot day, but at last the wind's picked up and is bringing the ocean's coolness in through the kitchen window.

Feeling it on her skin, Robyn remembers me, standing at the window of my bedroom, waxing lyrical about summery night breezes. I remember it too—the jasmine scent on that breeze, and the look on her face as she teased me:

'A romantic *and* a poet,' she said. 'Are you really studying Marine Science?'

'Since when are science and poetry mutually exclusive?'

'Since forever.'

But science and poetry are all over each other, aren't they? Both wrapped up in observing and recording life, and love. Trying to understand existence.

Robyn pushes the chopped garlic and ginger into a pile on the side of the board and slices the ends off an onion, pulling the papery peel away from the hard, white flesh.

'Do you remember my friend Gracie?'

Frank, rinsing vegetables in the sink, replies over his shoulder.

'Yes, I remember Gracie. Lovely girl.'

'She was, wasn't she?'

The onion succumbs to the methodical dance of Robyn's knife until it's a milky mound on the board, finely chopped.

'You okay?' Frank asks, drying his hands and putting an arm around her.

'It's the onions, mostly.'

She moves away to wash her hands and splash the sting out of her eyes.

'You know it wasn't your fault,' Frank says.

'Maybe not, but if I'd been there, maybe I could've saved her.'

'Honey, you were here studying; you weren't to know.'

Robyn sits on a bar stool. Looks up at his kind face. He doesn't know she wasn't studying the whole time. Doesn't know that Sam came over and spent the night. Sam knew she had her final exam the next day, but he also knew she would have no trouble acing it. Indeed, even as Marla was discovering my body in the apartment the next morning, Robyn was tearing through her Communications 120 paper, nailing it like a queen.

'It was terribly hard on you,' Frank says, putting his arm

around her. 'Losing your best friend like that after losing your mother … that's a lot for a young woman to take. Try not to be so hard on yourself.'

Robyn leans into his shoulder for a moment.

'I know,' she says. 'I'll try.'

'Good,' Frank says, then he pours oil into a pan and places it on the stove to heat. He rests the washed veggies on a tea towel then pushes her chopped ingredients into the oil, adding the spices and stirring them as they begin to sizzle.

Watching him, Robyn wonders how he worked through his grief when Heather died; how he kept it together enough to help her through hers. Maybe she can get him to talk to Cohen, share his wisdom.

No—Cohen would feel uncomfortable about the whole thing.

But maybe he'll come around to her other idea, the memorial get-together. Especially if Sam's on board too.

Pulling out her phone, she scrolls through her contacts list. Then she taps Sam's name and stands up, wandering away from Frank and all the sizzling and chopping.

Sam doesn't answer.

But as she hangs up, another call comes through. From a number she doesn't recognise. She heads out into the courtyard. 'Hello?'

'Robyn. It's Sam. How's it going?'

'Sam, hi. That's weird. I have your number in my contacts list …'

'Yeah, I'm using Tori's phone. Mine's charging. What's up?'

'I think we need to do something to help Cohen. I saw him a couple of weeks back, and he's still pretty torn up about Gracie.'

There's a pause.

'I don't know what we can do for him, Robyn. I think he needs professional help.'

'Well, I thought we could get together at the cemetery, have a couple of drinks with Gracie, you know? Reminisce, celebrate the time we got to share with her. It might help him move on. Might help all of us.'

Robyn looks at Frank through the kitchen window, standing over the steaming pan and stirring the sizzling vegetables around.

'Sam?' she says, wondering if the signal's dropped out.

'Seems like it'll make things raw again.'

'I understand your reluctance, Sam. This isn't easy. But Cohen's our friend, and he's a mess. And I don't know about you, but I'm still haunted by what happened to Gracie. This might be good for all of us.'

'Okay,' Sam says at last. 'If you think it'll help.'

21

Robyn arrives at Karrakatta Cemetery early, planning to visit Heather's grave before meeting Cohen and Sam at nine. Maybe they'll head out for lunch somewhere afterwards, if they feel up to it. She can show Sam those photos. Give him a chance to pull his head in.

Her bag is heavier than usual, owing to the bourbon and coke she premixed, and the four cups. All tucked into Frank's mini cooler bag.

It's like a small town, this place, arranged according to denomination and cut through with roads and byways. Some areas of the rambling hectares are lawn-covered and spacious, with mature trees shading the graves. Deeper in, sun-baked stretches of earth are crowded with cracked slabs and steel railings, all rusted and bent. Dark, streaky stains run down the faces of finely carved stone angels and children, frozen in time and abandoned to this slow-crumbling place of shadows.

It's been a while, but Robyn knows the way: walk down the wide promenade, past the office, and veer left towards the rose gardens.

Sometimes, there are crows, hopping between the stones. Robyn saw one once, glossy black, perched on the edge of a vase built onto the side of a gravestone—a permanent place for flowers. There were no flowers that day, but it had rained and the vase was full of water. The crow bent over and drank from it then looked up, straight at Robyn, as if to say, *What? It's only death.*

The memorial gardens are lush with layered greenery. There are no gravestones here, only a winding multitude of plaques embedded in benches, rocks and garden beds. Deeper in, the traffic noise is a background hush, overlaid with wind in the trees and the intermittent trill and chatter of birds, but here, cars hum past on the four-lane road just the other side of the fence.

Heather's memorial is a bronze plate set into a rock. Robyn kneels in front of it. Wipes two dried leaves off the top and runs her fingers along the inscription: *Beloved wife and mother, taken too soon, forever missed.*

'Hi Mum,' she says softly. 'How's it going?'

The wind shuffles the trees behind her head, a gentle rustling.

She's brought a bottle of bronze polish and a small soft cloth with her. Her hands are shaking as she takes them out of her bag, and some of the liquid spills on the grass as she tips it onto the cloth. But as she rubs the bronze, making small circles with her fingers, her breathing slows and the tremble eases off.

'Sorry I haven't visited in so long,' she says. 'I've been away. Quite a few places. You'd have loved it. Well, not all of it. Not the wars and stuff, obviously. But the history, the architecture. And the people. You'd have loved the people.'

It feels strange at first, this one-sided conversation. She can't picture Heather's listening face anymore, though she remembers the way her mother cherished her thoughts and ideas. Drew them out of her.

She lies on the grass in the dappled shade, resting her cheek on her upper arm and her hand on Heather's plaque.

'I'm visiting Gracie today too,' she says after a time. 'With Sam and Cohen. Gracie was great. You'd have liked her a lot, I reckon. She was funny.'

The trees above are not enormous, not like the ones deeper in, but they're lovely still. Reassuring and steady against a bright backdrop of sky and drifting clouds. It's been too long since Robyn did this—lay back and gazed upward.

'I wish I hadn't gone back to Dad's that night, you know?'

Time drifts; Robyn's skin grows warm as the sun pulls the shade away.

'I have to go, Mum,' she says, sitting up. Brushing leaves from her arms where they cling. 'I don't like to leave you here, but I bet you've made some fine friends, knowing you.'

✦✦✦

She's the first to arrive at the Flynn family plot where my cremains are buried, beneath a square plaque lined up neatly beside those of my grandmother, my great-aunt and one of my uncles.

Robyn checks her watch, then she gives my plaque the same love she gave her mum's. She's still at it when Cohen arrives, hands in the pockets of his black shorts. Robyn recognises the T-shirt he's wearing. It's dark blue with a faded print of a shark on it. Nothing special, except that I gave it to him for our first and only Christmas together. I didn't think he liked it a whole lot. I assumed he'd chucked it out before the new year rolled in. But there it is.

'Robyn,' he says, glancing at the bronze square with my name on it.

'Cohen,' she says. 'Glad you made it.'

He smells of beer. Scratches his cheek and looks around at the rose clusters edged with plaques. Sinks his hand into his hair and rubs his scalp.

'I don't know if I can do this.'

'We can stop at any time, Cohen,' Robyn says. 'If it gets too hard.'

He nods. Holds out his hand for the cloth.

Tenderly, he rubs at the bronze, getting right into the inscription with the tip of his finger.

Neither of them notices Sam approaching.

'Sorry I'm late,' he says. 'Isla's cutting about six teeth at once at the moment.'

'No worries,' Robyn says. 'You're here now.'

'Yes, I'm here.'

Cohen works his way down to the bottom right corner. When he's finished, he drapes the cloth over the bottle and stands up. Wipes his hands on his shorts.

'So,' Robyn says. 'Here we all are, together again.'

They look down at my plaque, which completes the awkward circle.

'Shall we sit?' Robyn says. 'I brought some bourbon and Coke—remember? Gracie's favourite. I thought we could drink a toast and sort of hang out for a bit.'

I can tell she's close to tears, because of the awfulness of everything, and because she's desperate for this to go well. To help shift something inside her. Inside all of them. She unzips the cooler bag and pulls out the litre bottle.

'I guess I'm thinking of this as a little wake,' she says, lining up the cups and filling them with the dark fizzy liquid. 'The one we never had. We were so young and it was all so full on. I know I didn't know how to deal with it.'

Sam nods. Picks up his drink. Cohen takes his too. They're both about to drink when Robyn lifts her cup in a toast.

'To Gracie.'

Sam and Cohen echo the words, then all three of them sample the sweet, rich drink. With his free hand, Cohen picks up the fourth cup and pours the contents into the dry soil in front of my plaque. How I'd love to taste it.

Robyn's made a playlist of my favourite songs; she plays it, quietly so as not to disturb anyone else. Not that there are many people about. Cohen plucks at the grass, remembering how we planned to wander around the Roman Forum together one day; to explore the ruins of Machu Picchu; to settle eventually into marriage and kids.

'I don't know about this,' Sam says after a while, looking around. 'I think I prefer to remember Gracie the way she was, not cremated and dug into the soil next to Merle and Effie and Harold.'

'She is dead, you know,' Cohen says. 'It's not as if she's just off somewhere, living some brilliant life. Too busy to send a postcard ...'

'I do know that,' Sam says.

'... so what you prefer is not that important.'

'I miss her too, Cohen.'

Cohen scoffs. 'You're still at it.'

'Still at what?'

'Trying to claim her for yourself. Acting like you shared some special bond with her too. Like what I had with her was nothing special.'

'Cohen ...'

'I know something happened between you two down in Yallingup. I don't know what exactly—Gracie didn't want to talk about it—but I know it was something.'

Sam shakes his head. Lifts his hands in surrender.

'But you know what?' Cohen continues. 'I don't care. Whatever happened, she still chose me. And you hate that more than anything.'

'Why would I hate that?'

'Because you get what you want, and I mess shit up, and that's how it's always been. But Gracie was fucking brilliant, and whatever you did, she loved *me*, not you.'

In the silence that follows, Robyn clears her throat.

'Gracie,' she says, 'we're here today to let you know we haven't forgotten you. We hope you hear us, and know that we still love you.'

She catches Cohen's eye when he looks up. The devastation on his face is as fresh as if no time has passed at all.

'She did love you, Cohen,' Sam says. 'She loved you, but she also wanted me. And *you* hated *that*.'

Cohen doesn't talk himself around the way he usually does when it comes to Sam. Instead, he lets his resentment rush through him, thick and hot, and I'm glad. He lunges past Robyn and grabs Sam by the collar, knocking the drinks over and crushing his knee into Robyn's bag.

'You don't want to do this, mate,' Sam mutters through his constricted throat.

'It's like reading one of your books,' Cohen says. 'One cliché after another.'

Sam shoves Cohen with one hand, trying to free himself, but Cohen lunges again and presses him to the ground. He pauses, as if he wasn't expecting to gain the upper hand so easily, and in that moment, Sam grabs hold of his torso and uses his hips to push Cohen off. He's on top and pressing Cohen's wrists into the ground, Cohen's feet scuffing wildly at the lawn, when Robyn gets to her feet.

'Jesus, you two,' she says. 'Remember where you are, would you?'

They both stop and look at her, still locked in the wrestle but motionless. Sam drops his head and pulls back off Cohen.

'This is meant to be about Gracie right now,' Robyn says, packing up the drinks and throwing her bag over her shoulder. 'Not some pathetic bloody feud.'

22

An unseasonably cool breeze toys with the trees in the dark, down by the river. In your house, upstairs, your mum closes the bedroom door carefully behind her and waits. This is always a precarious moment: either you will whimper and soon be bawling or you will accept your gradual submergence into sleep. Tori yawns at the very thought of it—that blissful sinking.

Hand on the doorknob, she waits, primed to go in, but the silence stretches on. Her long hour of feeding and rocking and humming has been rewarded this time. She raises her hand like an athlete on a podium, nodding to an invisible audience, then tiptoes along the corridor in the direction of bed, past the window overlooking the river. It's a view that catches hold of her every time she goes past. Particularly at night when the layers of darkness are so mesmerising, shifting and drifting there, eternally benevolent.

So restful.

A dark layer of cloud slips across the sky.

Sam's study light is still on under the door. Tori considers going in and sliding her hands down inside the front of his shirt. She needs to do something about the state of things; he's been unreachable for weeks, ever since he saw that message. But then she remembers: he's not there. He went out. Again. Without offering an explanation. Again. As if she's no longer entitled to one.

And maybe she isn't.

Sighing, she turns back to the view and rests her head against the glass. If only she'd dropped Pete into a conversation with Sam early on in the relationship. Or more recently, she could've shown Sam one of his messages and let him help her craft a reply, one that might've dampened Pete's enthusiasm. Instead, she let things carry on, meandering pointlessly, gathering momentum and meaning along the way.

The cloud is almost gone behind the shaggy darkness of trees beside the water. There's something moving down there: dark figures, heading in a south-westerly direction across the esplanade. No eluding the moonlight for these two—nowhere to hide.

She recognises the gait of the figure in front. The shape of him.

It's jarring, the sight of Sam out there. Doesn't fit with the picture she's so far had in her head, of him sitting in a pub somewhere with his mates. Even more jarring is the woman trailing behind him, walking fast to keep up. She's almost nothing in that great expanse of green, just a wisp of a shadow, as though she shouldn't mean much at all.

◆◆◆

Sam and Skye walk across the esplanade. Blades of grass reach in through Skye's strappy shoes and scratch the skin of her feet. Ahead, the water is dark and waiting. Small waves lap up against the concrete bank. The small family of boats rests in the darkness, rocking gently and turning, turning on their anchor ropes. Skye can hear their unsettling lullaby from here—that arrhythmic tap-tapping of steel on steel. The distant gurgling, washing sound.

Sam walks fast. Almost as if he's angry.

But then he slows down and reaches back for Skye's hand. Smiles a little.

Maybe she shouldn't have asked him to show her his boat. She can't think of anything more blissful than floating with him, out on the water, where no one can see or hear them, but it took a lot for him to agree. He looked away when she asked over dinner. Looked down at his hands then back over his shoulder, both ways, as if something invisible were chasing him down.

'Maybe,' he said. 'Maybe. Some time.'

'Some time, like right now,' she said, leaning towards him across the table, dropping her voice. 'Is there a place to lie down on your boat?'

'There's a cabin.'

'Don't you want to take me there then? Take off this dress? See how little I'm wearing underneath?'

'I do,' he said. 'I really do, but ...'

'What?'

'It's moored out the front of my house. Tori's at home ...'

'Will she see us taking it out?'

'No, probably not in the dark ... but ...'

'What then?'

'*I'll* see us. Home will see us ...'

'What, the house has eyes?'

'No. You know what I mean.'

'Are you referring to your conscience?'

'Maybe. Yes.'

He looked at her, as if he might vocalise the question in his eyes, but then he looked away again. Rolled his fork over and over on the white tablecloth.

'I haven't taken Tori out on the boat since Isla was born.'

'So it's your special place then? Yours and Tori's? Is that it?'

'Kind of, yes. Taking you out there might be one betrayal too many.'

'I get it,' Skye said, leaning back into her chair. Holding his gaze. 'I do. But you know what? If your feelings for me are not strong enough to get past this guilt or whatever it is, then maybe they're not strong enough at all. Maybe it's time we walked away.'

There was power in the statement. And God knows she needs a bit. Mostly, your dad holds all the cards, and the idea of him roping off a sacred place for his wife—one that Skye is not allowed to breach—is unendurable. Tori is the one who gets to wake up with him every day as it is. She gets the leisurely mornings and the holiday plans, while Skye—it's already clear—will have to be satisfied with whatever's left. An hour or two on his boat is the least he can do, right? She's not asking that much.

Sam looked at her then. Stopped thunking the fork on the table. Pulled his hands in and rested them in his lap.

'I don't want to walk away,' he said. 'I should, but I don't think I can.'

'I don't want you to either, Sam,' Skye said, reaching across the table, offering him both hands. 'All I want is you, in the moonlight, out there on the water.'

So now here they are, approaching the jetty, just across the esplanade from Sam's house where Skye assumes Tori is sleeping. Or maybe not sleeping; lying awake, feeding or rocking her baby. Skye wants to ask which house it is, but she doesn't want to risk making Sam change his mind. In the end, she doesn't have to. He looks up at your house at the end of the row, buried right up in the bush of Birdwood Park. It's a commanding piece of architecture, up there in the hillside, tall panels of glass reflecting the night sky and the water down below. There's such sorrow in his eyes as he looks up at his home, as if he's been exiled, that Skye wonders why he's carrying on with this at all. One foot in front of the other he walks, like a man approaching the gallows.

She should put him out of his misery. She should say, let's not bother about the boat. Let's not bother about any of this anymore. Go back to your life. But she doesn't say it. This boat trip has become significant now. She is making him choose.

They reach the gate—a strange sight, halfway along the narrow jetty, with nothing by way of a fence around it. They could, in theory, hold on to the frame and step around it, but Sam pulls a key out of his wallet and unlocks the padlock. The gate swings open, making a devilish groan.

'Tori keeps saying we should bring Isla out here. Before she's crawling and it's too difficult.'

Skye nods. She can't work out how best to respond so she focuses instead on the gently churning water below.

Stargazing is moored up against the creaking jetty. Sam climbs on first then holds out his hand for Skye. She waits until his grip is firm, then steps down onto the small fibreglass deck.

As they pull away from the jetty, Skye shivers. It's colder out on the water than it was on the shore. Bracing, with the cold air whipping her hair around her face.

'Bet it's warmer down below,' she says, nodding towards the cabin, dark and beckoning.

'Would be, yeah,' Sam says, concentrating harder than he needs to on getting *Stargazing* out into the open water. It would be great, Skye thinks, if he wasn't doing all this like a man at gunpoint, right hand on the helm, eyes on the water.

They leave the sheoaks behind, needle-leaves jostling in the breeze. The abrasive hum of the engine relieves them of the need to put words to the tension. Skye expects Sam at any moment to steer them back to the jetty, where he'll banish her from his boat, and his life. But instead, he takes the boat west around Dalkeith and cuts the engine halfway to Keanes Point. He eases the anchor rode into the water and they watch it slide over the side of the boat. Skye wonders if Sam feels it too—the sense that something important is going with it, down into the inky water.

Watching him, Skye wonders at the nature of her feelings for him. Love would manifest itself more kindly than this, surely. After all, it's within her power to end his misery. Now, on the boat, and in general, on land. The words hover behind her lips—*let's go home, Sam.* But she doesn't allow them to form. She has other ways of attending to his misery. Ways she prefers.

Once the anchor has found its place, Sam runs the boat back a touch then cuts the engine. He looks at her at last. Gives her that much. His sorrow is too lovely, Skye thinks. Lovely in the tenderness it evokes in her.

Sam smiles and holds out his hand. Skye stands carefully, searching out stability with her feet, and takes it. She laughs as the boat dips a little on Sam's side so that she falls against him. He touches her face where the smile creases her cheek; he smiles back; kisses her there. She kisses him too, though not on his cheek, then moves away, towards the hatch. She casts a look back at him over her shoulder then steps down into the cabin, out of the cold.

There's not much down there, just a low ceiling and a built-in bed with a faded doona.

This could go either way: either she's pushed him too far—into the realm of what he can't forgive in himself—or he'll join her there.

She waits, listening to the waves against the hull and the deep groaning noises *Stargazing*'s body makes at the whim of the tide.

She sees his shoe first, on the top step. Then his other one. And then he's there, with her. He seems calm now. As if he's found his way to a resolution of some kind. She can't tell whether he's decided to accept his fallibility and go with it, or to make this the last time and find some way to atone for it. Either way, he's here and she's glad.

Later, they lie on the gently rolling bed inside *Stargazing*'s belly. It's restful. They can see the dark night of stars through the open skylight. Skye drifts on the rise and fall of Sam's chest. It's out of sync with the motion of the waves and the thud of his heartbeat, but somehow, it's harmonious. Enough to bring her to sleep, or bring sleep to her.

✦✦✦

Meanwhile, your poor mum can't leave the window. She should go back to bed. She's tired; she's cold. But Sam is not here. Sam is out there. On their boat. With someone else. She *saw* them: Sam reaching out behind him for that woman's hand as they crossed the esplanade—that most tender of careless gestures. Tori thought it was reserved for her alone, but there it was, unthinking, generic. And that shadowy other woman took it the way Tori always does—accepting his terms, his pace. Because why wouldn't you? They're good terms. Usually.

Maybe it wasn't him, Tori thinks. Maybe he *is* in a pub somewhere.

But she knows.

How could he do it? On the boat, of all places? He might as well have brought that woman up here, right into their marriage bed. Tori closes her eyes on the agony of it. It's like a serrated, rusty blade, hacking at the sacred place in her belly, the place where you grew. Where love now is dying.

It's not, of course, Isla. Not really dying. Love goes on and on and on, you see, whether you want it to or not.

23

Having crept late into bed, Sam wakes to the sound of you fussing in your bassinet. He's groggy, but Tori is dead to the world. Watching her sleep, Sam realises his pain over her betrayal with Pete has lessened, mitigated no doubt by the guilt he feels over his own. In which case, he thinks, you *could* argue that his infidelity has been constructive. Just what the marriage needed.

Shaking his head, he rolls out of bed, wondering if he's always been this gifted at rationalising his bad choices.

He decides to take you down to the river, let Tori sleep in. Lifting you out of the bassinet, he holds you close for a moment— your baby cheek against his stubbled one—before he heads out to change your nappy and make you a bottle.

Checking his phone, he notices a text has come through, from Robyn.

We need to talk, Sam, ASAP

She'll want to process what happened at the cemetery last weekend, most likely. Fair enough, he can do that.

I'm heading to the river with Isla now, meet you there?

On the way down, the breeze makes you gasp and blink. There's no chill in it, but it's stronger than usual. You gnaw on your fist and whimper a while, then you go quiet. Feeling your trusting weight on his hip, Sam feels his guilt intensify: by cheating on your mum, he's thrown your cards into the wind as well, letting fate decide where they fall.

He slips his pinkie finger into the curl of your grip. You hold on tight and he wants to stop time, halt everything. And then he wants to wind it back, just a few days. Or maybe weeks. Or is it months? It's hard to tell anymore. How can everything have unravelled so fast, and so comprehensively? It feels as if all he has now is this moment: the solidity of you; the sweetness of your head on his shoulder. Your hair against his cheek is the softest thing in the world. How could he have been so reckless?

With an intensity that throws him, he remembers how much he loves your mum. He loves the way her hair falls down her back. He loves the steadiness of her gaze, and the way she knows things. The way she moves to music, with her arms in the air and that smile on her face. Will she ever smile at him again, once she knows about Skye? Will her love for him shut down entirely? Will she take herself and you back to London, to be with her family and Pete, if that's where the bastard is? *When can I see you again?* Why not? Why would she stay here?

He takes you to the water. Dips your toes in it. Smiles as you splash water on his legs. The light is clear and sharp on the water. It reaches the eye in dazzling bursts as the waves rise and fall.

'Bah-bah-bah,' you say, kicking out, straining towards the water with your arms.

'Okay, I'm on it,' Sam says, letting you sit on the sand. You love it, particularly like this, with the water lapping at your feet.

◆◆◆

Walking from the car, Robyn is still mulling over what happened at the cemetery last weekend. Sam and Cohen brawling on the grass … She's felt uneasy about it all week. Distracted at work and unable to figure it out. She always knew there was tension between them, but it used to come and go, and it was ill-defined back then. Last weekend though, the friction was palpable. And anything but vague. All that stuff about me wanting Sam, and something happening down in Yallingup—it's been looping through Robyn's mind all week, round and round, regardless of her stern notes-to-self that it doesn't matter now. Sam is no longer the centre of her world.

Today, she feels stronger. She still plans to show Sam those photos, but while her initial impulse was to help him see the error of his ways before it was too late, there's something else driving her now. Now, she wants to show him what he's done. How low he's sunk.

'Robyn,' he says, looking up into the morning sun.

'Hi, Sam.'

They're quiet for a moment, watching you.

'I have something to show you,' Robyn says, sitting down too.

'Yeah?'

'You're not going to like it.'

Fear curls in Sam's belly. What might Robyn know of his ugly mess of a life?

'Okay,' he says as she pulls her phone from her pocket. He checks on you—still sitting there, working the sand—then looks back at the screen Robyn is holding out to him.

'Oh God,' he says, seeing himself on Skye's threshold.

'I saw you together in Northbridge,' Robyn says. 'And then I spotted you in your car the other day and I followed you.'

'You followed me?'

'I wanted to know,' she says, watching you kick at the tiny waves. 'Not only what you were up to with that woman, but who you are, exactly. When I left, you were this elusive, creative enigma I loved and respected. And I came home to find you'd become a lovely, gentle father. A person you said you'd never be.'

'Is that what this is about? I know I was awful to you, Robyn. I'm sorry about that ...'

'But even that wasn't the real you, was it, Sam? The selfless family man. Because next thing there you are, carrying on with some other woman. I mean, what are you doing? We owe it to Gracie to be *more*, Sam, you know? To be better.'

'I know it looks bad,' Sam says. 'But in my defence, there are extenuating circumstances.'

'Of course there are.'

'Tori and I hit a rough patch.'

'The point of marriage is that you work through those.'

'You been married then, have you?'

'No,' Robyn says, though she and Jon came close. Sort of. Not long before she left Perth, he asked her, ring and all, but she said no. The relationship felt so frayed by then, it would've been farcical to try to fix it with vows. 'But the concept is not alien to me.'

'Look, you're right, okay? I know what I've done is inexcusable. I don't need photos to show me that.'

'Well, good.'

'What's your plan with them anyway? The pictures?'

'This *is* my plan: to show you what you're doing. So you can fix it.'

'I can't fix it. There's no going back.'

'You can try though, can't you?'

Sam scoops you up and begins wiping the sand off your hands with the bottom of his shirt.

'I don't know, Robyn. Where do I start? Do I tell Tori?'

'Can you forgive yourself if you don't? Is her pain worth more than your absolution? What's best for Isla?'

'Jesus, I need answers, Robyn, not more questions.'

'Stop what you're doing and go from there. Don't tell Tori if it's not over yet. But also, don't let it not be over.'

Sam strokes the wispy hair out of your eyes.

'Would you mind deleting the pictures, Robyn? Could you do it now? It's not that I don't trust you. It's just that, you know, you might forget and they might fall into the wrong hands.'

'I understand,' Robyn says, opening them up and beginning to delete them one by one. He doesn't need to know they're on her laptop as well. She'll get rid of them as soon as she gets home anyway, now that they've served their purpose.

When Sam gets back, Tori's up. She's made coffee and scrambled eggs. He puts you on your playmat and goes to hug her but she moves away. Doesn't meet his eye.

'I've eaten,' she says, picking you up and disappearing upstairs to settle you for a nap.

The eggs are good, but if it wasn't for the coffee, Sam would be unable to get them down. Something's happened. Tori's either had enough of his sulking and she's decided it's her turn, or else she knows something.

He's doing the dishes when she comes back down.

'Tell me about her,' she says, digging into a pile of washing and beginning to fold things. Sam turns to face her. Dries his hands on a tea towel.

Misunderstanding his hesitation for denial, Tori scoffs.

'Don't pretend you don't know what I'm talking about, Sam. Give me some credit, okay? I saw you. From the window.'

Sam shakes his head, closing his eyes as if it might erase the memory. Maybe even the night itself.

'Tori,' he says, taking a step closer, 'I'm so sorry … I didn't want to take her out on the boat. She … well, she insisted.'

It's pathetic; he knows before he says it.

'Oh, she insisted did she? Fair enough then. What else did she insist on, if I may be so bold as to enquire?'

'God, Tori … it's hard to explain.'

'Shall I go upstairs and find your old Human Biology textbook? Would that be helpful?'

'Tori, please don't be angry. It's been a crazy few weeks …'

'Has it?' Tori says, realising she's folding a pair of Sam's trousers and dropping them back into the basket. She pushes her hair back from her face and crosses her arms across her chest. 'You want to tell me about it?'

'Well, there was finding out about Pete, obviously, which was full on.'

'And then …?'

'And bumping into Cohen again … that was … that's stirred up a lot of difficult memories.'

'Oh, what's this? A past I've heard nothing about? How traitorous.'

'Tori, you're angry, I understand …'

'Who is she?'

'Someone I met in a bar.'

'When? When did you meet her?'

'About a week after I saw Pete's message.'

Tori looks at him, shakes her head. 'Didn't take very much, did it? For you to break your vows. I mean, we only just made them for Christ's sake … what, nine months ago?'

'It's not like I planned it, Tori. I wouldn't have been in the stupid pub in the first place if it hadn't been for your ongoing flirtation with your ex-lover of … what was it, nine years? Don't forget about that now.'

'The key word there is *ex*, Sam.'

'No, I think you'll find it's *ongoing*, Tori. And then refusing to let me see what you've been saying to each other … What did you expect me to think?'

'I don't know, Sam. But I expected you to give us a bit more than a week to work it out before you went and jumped into bed with someone else.'

'Who says I jumped into bed with her?'

'Well, didn't you?'

Sam rubs his left eye which has started twitching. 'Not straight away.'

'Well, someone give the man a medal.'

The silence stretches between them until Tori speaks again.

'You know what, Sam? Forget about it. I don't want to know who she is. She can have you. You and that stupid boat.'

'Come on, Tori, I'll end it with her right now. I'll go up and call her ... I was planning to do it today anyway.'

Tori looks at him. 'For some reason, Sam, I don't believe you.'

'Tori, please, you have to believe me. It was a stupid mistake. I was angry and upset. I felt like our whole marriage was just a rebound farce. Everything I thought we were ... disintegrated. But I've realised that it doesn't matter. What I *thought* we were doesn't matter. It's what we *are* that matters, right?'

'And what is that, Sam? What's it called when a husband runs off with another woman the moment his ego is dented?'

'It wasn't about my ego.'

'Really? I think it was. I think that's exactly what it was about.'

'I'm not proud of it, Tori. You and Isla are everything to me.'

'Not quite everything, clearly.'

'Jesus, I'm sorry. I don't know what else to say. I'll end it with her right now. You can listen in if you want to. It was a mistake. A stupid mistake.'

'Do what you like, Sam, as long as you pack a bag while you're at it.'

'You want me to move out?'

'For a while, yes. I think that's probably best for both of us, don't you?'

'But … you and Isla …'

'We'll be fine.'

'Where will I go?'

'I think you can work that out for yourself, don't you?'

She returns to the laundry pile and picks up a towel. Sam reaches out to touch her on the arm, hoping she'll soften and let him console her, but she regards him coldly, first his hand and then his face, and it's clear that she'd sooner set his clothes on fire than fall sobbing into his arms.

◆◆◆

Upstairs, Sam shuts himself away in his office. Still struggling to process what's happened, he leans against the door for a minute or two before finding his way to his chair. With trembling hands and a throbbing head, he pulls out his phone and deletes the message thread between himself and Skye. Then he taps her number.

He's not called her before, only texted; the sound of her voice hurts him, like driving a knuckle into a bruise.

'Sam?' she says. He can hear the smile in her voice. She's surprised he's called, pleased.

'Skye,' he says. 'How goes it?'

She's quiet before she responds, probably thrown by his tone.

'It goes well, thanks,' she says cautiously. 'And how goes it with you?'

'Not so well with me,' he says, picking up a pen and beginning to draw spirals on his notepad.

'What's up? Or do I need to ask?'

'Maybe not. Maybe you know.'

'You can't see me anymore?'

Outside the window, a parrot chatters loudly.

'Yes,' Sam says. 'That's it exactly.'

After a silence, Skye says, 'I see. Well, that's not altogether surprising I suppose, is it? Given your circumstances.'

'I'm sorry, Skye. I wish ...'

'You'd never met me?'

'No, of course not.'

'You weren't married and a dad?'

'No. Not that either.'

'What then? That infidelity was acceptable?'

'Well, I guess that would solve a lot of problems.'

'This one in particular.'

'Exactly. This one in particular.'

'I don't like to think of us as a problem though, Sam.'

'Me neither, but you can see how it complicates things.'

'I can, although like I said, I have no expectations ...'

'It's not just a matter of expectations though, Skye. I can't live with the guilt. And Tori knows. She saw us the other night.'

'Oh shit, Sam, I'm sorry.'

'She's asked me to move out for a while. Give us some breathing space.'

'Far out.'

'She's an amazing woman, Skye. She deserves better than all this. Isla does too.'

'I don't need to hear how amazing your wife is, Sam, thanks anyway.'

'Of course. I'm sorry.'

'Where will you go?'

'*Stargazing*: free lodgings, close to home.'

'You could stay with me if you like.'

'I'm trying to save my marriage, Skye, not destroy it completely.'

Skye goes quiet again. 'Well,' she says at last, 'if that's how it has to be ...'

'It is, Skye. I'm sorry.'

'Okay. Well ... that's it then I guess. Go well, Sam.'

'You too,' he says. It's the right thing to do, but as he hangs up, he feels more wretched than relieved. Wretched, and culpable. As if he's muted a symphony before the final movement.

24

Cohen's at home, and he's not in a good way. The accumulation of stressors over the past few months has him sweating, pacing, not sleeping.

After another restless night, he's in bed, feigning sleep until Jewel goes to the gym. Once he's heard her car leave, he reaches under the bed for his second phone, taped to the underside of the bed frame. He turns it on. Ninety-three emails and sixty-five texts since this time yesterday. He doesn't reply anymore; doesn't even read them. They're all the same—panicked, outraged, threatening—and he has no good news, so what's the point?

The hole he's dug for himself is deep and wide, with sides so high he can't see over them. The question is, what now? He can't see himself fronting up to the cops and going down for the crime, spending night after night in a cell, surrounded by who knows what kinds of creeps and filth, and for who knows how long ... it would be the end of him. He'd rather be the master of that end and make it quick. Avoid having to look any of his victims in the eye. Avoid the long, humiliating trajectory of a trial. He can't imagine telling Jewel everything either. She's more likely to dob him in than cover for him. *You're not my problem anymore*, she'll say after hearing him out. She'll be cold. Contemptuous. Practically hissing.

No; he's on his own. It's a relief, in a way.

Outside, with maggies chortling overhead, he positions the phone on a stump and smashes it with a hammer. He cuts the SIM card into pieces then puts the whole lot into the oven on high for a while, just to make sure. He's reasonably confident the bank account he used can't be traced to him now; he used fake credentials to set it up and has since closed it down, having moved the money into a handful of fake accounts linked to small non-existent businesses, all of which disbursed the income through cash payments for services not actually rendered. Once he's destroyed his laptop, fingers crossed he'll be home and hosed.

Aside from Sam, who'll be smarting after that humiliating set-to in the cemetery. Cohen shakes his head; he shouldn't have lost his shit like that. Can't afford to alienate the one person who knows what he's done.

Still, Sam should be manageable. If he's anything like he used to be, Cohen just needs to get a good grovel on. An apology and a good feed somewhere classy should do it. Then, once things die down and he's sure Sam won't dob him in, he'll change his phone number and convince Jewel that they need a good, long holiday. Somewhere amazing, like Prague or Venice. She'll go for that—beautiful buildings and an endless string of social-media moments. And if the heat follows them, he'll find a way to lose himself somehow.

Failing that—if the cops come knocking before he can get it together—he has that other plan. That package behind the toolbox. He'll feign willingness to go with them but it will be right there in his jacket pocket, ready for him to pour into the coffee or water they're sure to offer him: his solution. His way out.

The sun moves across the sky, asking no one's permission, as usual. Cohen contemplates his plan to take Sam out for a placatory dinner, but the idea of sitting opposite him, pretending they're still the mates they once were … he doesn't think he can do it. A phone call will have to do.

'Yeah, look, all good, mate,' Sam says after Cohen's stilted apology. 'I know this has all been hard on you.'

Understandably, there's a degree of wariness behind his words.

'How are things with Tori?' Cohen asks.

'Not so good. I'm in the doghouse. Well, the boat actually.'

'Hang on, I'm confused. Isn't Tori the one who stuffed up?'

'Well, yes, initially. But … let's just say it's complicated.'

The Rosemount is packed, mostly with women: fishnet tights, denim shorts, tight black numbers and leather boots. Big hair, short hair, white hair; lots of skin; dark-ringed eyes. It's hot in here, though the ceiling is high. Everybody's moving to the rapid-fire beat generated by two women on stage, Jude and Asha. They're Skye's friends from music at uni, performing as the Electric Bits. Skye feels both stirred up and slightly embarrassed by Jude's crass lyrics, which is exactly what the Bits are all about: shock value *über alles*.

Skye nearly didn't come tonight. Had to drag herself off the floor where she'd lain weeping as the sun went down and the moon rose to check on her. But drag herself up she did, because this is a big night for her friends. You don't get to launch an album every day. She wasn't going to let them down because a man had broken her heart; that went against everything they all believed in. So she rested an icepack over her eyes until the swollen redness eased off enough for her to layer eyeliner and mascara over them, and headed out the door.

Now, she squeezes into a gap between bodies at the bar. It's a cut-throat affair, trying to get a drink tonight. A girl might have to reach across and take the barman by the collar just to get an order in.

While waiting, she contemplates the Sam-shaped hole in her life. What shape is it, exactly? He was everything she wanted in a man, if you discount his capacity for infidelity, though he assured her he'd never have strayed for anyone other than her. Meaning she's irresistible; what woman doesn't want to hear that?

Maybe that's why he said it. Maybe it was an easy lie and he's not the amazing man he presented himself to be, just another opportunistic philanderer having a bit of fun. But if that's the case, why would he have called it off, given that the opportunity remains right there on the table? She made no secret of her willingness to continue as before. Under whatever circumstances he wants. Surely a man without integrity would keep her on the line for as long as possible.

He got found out—yes—which has thrown a spanner in the works, but it doesn't have to mean the end. If you can lie once, you can lie twice, right?

So maybe he got bored.

But he didn't seem bored. Not when he was kissing her. Not when he was pressing her down by the hands and gazing at her, the moonlight through the window catching the side of his face. The look in his eyes … it wasn't something you can manufacture out of nothing. She moved him, she knows she did. She knows because she's not an idiot; she's a watcher too, like him. She can spot a conman from twenty paces.

Which leaves only two options.

Either he still wants her but is honour-bound to pull himself away, for his wife and child, or he was using her as material for his writing. Shaking things up for himself. Escaping some sinking, suburban malaise. But now something's spooked him and all that predictability isn't looking so bad anymore. In which case: dickhead.

Kiyo materialises beside her. Leans up against the bar. She lifts her eyebrows at the look on Skye's face.

'You okay?' she says into the lull between songs.

'Not exactly.'

Kiyo lifts her hand for the barman's attention. He shuts the till, wipes his hands and comes straight over, as if she's wearing some kind of halo. Skye mulls over the injustice while Kiyo orders gin and tonics and hands over her card, but her indignation is half-hearted at best. Taking possession of the drinks, Kiyo steers Skye out into the courtyard—a large space framed by a timber awning covered in grapevines. Low benches, adorned with Moroccan-style cushions, line the walls.

Kiyo leads the way to the farthest corner.

'You look like you got slapped with a wet fish tonight,' she says. 'Is it Sam?'

'Yes.'

'Did he break it off with you?'

Skye nods, swigs from her drink to force her throat open and give herself a chance to blink the tears away.

'Guilty conscience?'

'Yes.'

'Not cos he thinks you're ugly then?'

Skye laughs. 'No. Well. Maybe. Who knows?'

'Sucks that you have to feel this way.'

Skye nods again.

'But he's doing what's right, yeah?'

It's true enough. It was wrong, what they were doing. All kinds of wrong. And Skye's dodgy compartmentalisation was only ever going to get her so far. But still. Everything felt so calm, so predestined when they were together. No awkward moments. No ambiguities. Just easy synchronicity. As if the stars up there in space were finally taking on some kind of comprehensible formation. For the first time in a relationship with a man, Skye felt understood. Recognised.

'I guess I deserve this,' she says. 'Betraying the sisterhood and everything.'

'He's the one who made vows, not you. You don't deserve this any more than the fuckwit deserves you, which is to say: not at all. In both cases. I don't know if that made any kind of sense.'

'I don't know,' Skye says. 'But I think I might need to get shit-faced.'

'I've got you covered, babe,' Kiyo says. 'Sit tight.'

She returns with beer and tequila on a tray.

'Did somebody say shit-faced?'

Skye laughs. 'That might have been me.'

The tequila is sharp and bracing, and as it begins to fuzz away the edges of her anguish, Skye thinks maybe she won't be sad forever.

But later, back home, ears still buzzing from the gig, she sits in the dark with her guitar, trying to come up with something new, hoping she can make all this count for something. All her songs so far have been about some kind of heartbreak or disillusionment, but this is the first time she's ever truly felt it. And now—now that she's actually trailing her way through that valley—it's worse than any of those imaginings. She can't even begin to turn it into a song. It's too big and dark. Murky and impossible to articulate. Worst of all, it's confusing, because if she was so content to be Sam's bit on the side, why should it hurt so much to find that she's nothing to him at all?

If you ask me, Skye was kidding herself from the get-go with all that stuff about never wanting more from Sam. She was simply doing what needed to be done—calmly setting up the kind of internal dichotomy that's been part of her survival for so long. Because the kind of childhood Skye had, it leaves scars. Scars, and empty spaces in the heart. And do you know what loves those kinds of spaces? Loves nothing better than to fill them up, like groundwater, seeping up when you dig too deep? Self-doubt, that's what. And shame. Not to mention powerful feelings of inadequacy. No matter how tough Skye became, and how creative she managed to remain, there was always the sense that nothing she could ever do would be of any consequence to anyone, anywhere. And then Sam came into her life, a walking antidote. Cool honey on a hot wound. And though she'd had relationships with men before, in all of them *she'd* had to be the salve, the one doing all the soothing and all the healing. I mean, Sam was preoccupied at times, yes. Of course. He had a lot to process all of a sudden. But there was a different air to his preoccupation. It was self-contained; he wasn't looking to her to fix it. For the first time in her life, Skye's role was not to uplift or to reassure. All she had to do was *be*.

She never told Sam what that meant to her. Instinctively, she knew what he'd feel compelled to do if he knew how deep her attachment was becoming. So she kept it quiet. Made him think she could take him or leave him. Because she knew that anything else would force his hand, and she'd lose.

And now she's lost anyway.

She slides the guitar off her lap and leans it up against the sofa. Picks up her pen and notebook and tries to draw something instead of writing it. A castle on a hill in a storm. But it's lame, inept, falling way short of what she's asking of it—namely, to pull the toxic storm out of her body and mind and contain it on the page.

Needing some other strategy, she finds Björk's *Vespertine* and puts it on loud. Lies on the floor of her lounge room, watching the play of shadows and light on the far wall as the streetlight shines through the restless tree outside. In places, the music is an acoustic equivalent of being inside a crystal: chimes in the upper register imitate light, bouncing, refracting inside a giant translucent mass. The choral harmonies contrast with the electronic tipple tripping along in the background while melodies overlap and skip across each other, made from instruments Skye can't identify. They could be from another universe. Another time. She closes her eyes to see it all better, allowing the soundscape to form behind her eyes: blues and grey washes, light glimmering on a far-off horizon. She feels herself breathing more deeply, drifting down into the carpet. Everything is fine. Everything just is.

But then the album is over, and once again, nothing is fine. She picks up her phone and writes a message to Sam, reminding him of the night they lay together in his cabin, admiring the ghostly clouds through the open skylight. His voice, when he spoke, was so close to her head, she could almost feel its vibrations against her skin. Literally could feel them when he shifted over and whispered in her ear. The warmth of his breath, the hum of his lips, sent ripples of pleasure down her back.

She sends the text. Sees it stack up below the rest of her sad little offerings on the screen. All of them have been delivered. None has been deemed worthy of a response. Surely Sam, as a writer, knows how much that stings. To go without feedback. And if he thinks it's hard for him, he has no idea how hard it is on this end, dealing with the silence. Now that he's not available to her anymore, it's as if he's changed his frequency. Gone to a new dimension. Willed himself out of existence. His absence is huge. And if she could summon the energy to scream into that void, no one would hear her. Least of all him.

25

Cohen wakes up late and alone. Jewel is away on a girls' weekend in the Swan Valley; he hasn't seen her since she left yesterday morning.

Must be around eleven by the time he's downstairs, making coffee and toast with butter. He watches an Attenborough doco while eating. Sort of thing that usually gets him out of his own head. Today though, he doesn't notice when it ends and the next show begins; finds himself watching some sort of heist film.

Flicking it off, he sits staring at the dark screen.

He needs to snap out of his stupor. Make things happen.

After a cold shower, he sits on the edge of his bed and picks up his phone. He searches online for bed-and-breakfasts down south, scrolling through the options. He's unsure what he's looking for; his plan is too nebulous. But there are plenty of places available for a single guest with no expectations, so he decides to defer that decision till he gets down there and focus for now on booking a flight out of the country. Which he does, locking in a ticket to Rome for Tuesday night. In case his luck extends that far.

Next, he packs some clothes and toiletries into a suitcase. Just the basics. Whatever won't be noticed by Jewel when she gets home.

Finally, he goes down into the under-stairs storage room and retrieves the package. You can get anything online these days, including this small white container with its twist-top lid.

In the kitchen, he reads the label then scans the small page of instructions. It's riddled with typos, but he gets the drift. He pulls open the cutlery drawer, takes out a teaspoon, and reaches into his pocket for a ziplock bag.

Beyond the window, while he works, the late afternoon light skims across the river's surface, catching the edges of the shifting trees. Cohen avoids looking at it. Appreciating small moments of loveliness opens him up to other feelings. Paralysing ones he has no time for right now.

He dips the spoon into the container and scoops out some of the powder, sliding the tiny white crystals carefully into the ziplock bag. One teaspoon is supposed to be enough, but he adds a second one and then a third, just to be sure. He drags his fingers across the tracks to seal it shut and holds the bag up to the window. The crystals inside it gleam, almost yellow in the vanishing light.

Watching him with this stuff, I'm fearful. If he elects to take it—if he's ever cornered—he'll become dizzy, nauseated, tight in the chest. He may convulse, throw up, double over in pain. The poison will make his blood unable to funnel oxygen around his body, turning it brown while his lips and fingers go blue. His breathing will slow, he'll sink into a coma, and eventually, his cardiovascular system will collapse. I'd never choose death for Cohen, but if he insists on choosing it for himself, I wish he'd do it some other way. But I'm powerless to warn him as he wipes down the benchtop, tucks the bag into his jacket pocket, and drapes the jacket over his suitcase in the entrance hall.

He's looking around the room, realising how little he'll miss it, when his intercom buzzes. Robyn is there in the greyscale screen.

'Hey, Cohen,' she says. 'Thought I might drop round for a cuppa.'

Cohen can't think of a good reason to say no.

In the kitchen, once he's let her in, he turns on the kettle and grabs some cups from the cupboard. 'You just caught me,' he says, spooning coffee grounds into the plunger and pouring hot water over it. 'I was about to head off. Getting out of the city for a while.'

'Nice,' Robyn says, sitting on a barstool at the kitchen island. 'Quality time for you and Jewel?'

Cohen concentrates on warming some milk in the microwave. 'She'll come down later,' he lies.

'Well, I'm glad to hear you're taking some time away,' Robyn says. 'Sounds like a good idea.'

Cohen hands her one of the mugs and sits on a stool beside her.

'How are you doing, anyway?' Robyn says. 'I meant to check in before now, see how you're holding up.'

'I'm good. You know. Just sorry I lost it with Sam at the cemetery. You made all that effort ...'

'Hardly an effort,' Robyn says. 'But I hope you two managed to resolve things after I left?'

Cohen shrugs. 'He left soon after you did. I stuck around

though. Felt a bit weird talking to a plaque, but I was calmer when I left. Things seemed clearer.'

'That's good,' Robyn says. Cohen feels her studying his face for evidence of this new clarity.

'I wanted to ask you something,' she says. 'You and Sam were going on about something that happened down south ... Was it that time we all went there for swot vac?'

Cohen nods, staring at the cup in his hands. Rustic blue with daisies on it.

'What was it that happened?'

'I don't know for sure,' Cohen says slowly, 'but I think something went down between Sam and Gracie. There was this vibe about them—remember?—when they got back from surfing. Gracie brushed it off and I didn't push it.' He looks at Robyn; she's watching him intently. 'After she died, I asked Sam about it. He said I was being paranoid. But I can tell when he is lying.'

'What do you think it was?'

'I think he tried it on with her, that's what. And last weekend was the first time he's ever come close to admitting it.'

Robyn bites the inside of her lip, no doubt picturing Sam with me, in high-fidelity; the kind of self-torture she's always been good at.

'So ...' she says with a small shake of her head. 'Are you saying you and Sam were warring over Gracie that whole time?'

'We weren't warring over her; she had a choice, and she chose me. But Sam was always trying to get between us. He'd act like he was kidding, but he wasn't.'

'All those months I was going out with him ...?'

'He was into you, Robyn. Don't think he wasn't. Wanting

Gracie was about winning, that's all.'

Robyn sits there, staring at the small pool of tea at the bottom of her cup.

'You really didn't know?' Cohen asks.

'Nope.'

'Sorry to burst your bubble.'

'Water under the bridge, I guess,' Robyn says, picking at the skin beside her thumbnail. 'And not overly surprising. Did I tell you? I saw him in the city with a woman. Not his wife.'

'What, recently?'

'About two weeks ago.'

'You're sure?'

'Yes. And then again, a few days later, arriving at her apartment. I took pictures and confronted him about it.'

Cohen lifts his eyebrows. 'What did he say?'

'He was ashamed, I think. Said he'd end it.'

'Does Tori know?'

'I don't know. I said he should fess up.'

Cohen stares at his hands around his cup. 'Tosser. I mean, to be fair, he reckons Tori's been having an affair with her ex, but that was just a texting thing.' He shakes his head. 'That'll be why he's sleeping on the boat.'

'He has a boat?'

'Yes, and he's been banished to it.'

Cohen pictures Sam on the water, suffering over the love of two women, while Cohen's packed his whole life into a suitcase, ready to ghost a wife who'll hardly notice he's gone.

'He'll be pretty rattled,' Robyn says.

'Serves him right. He has a wife who loves him, and a kid, and he goes around acting like he's still working out what he wants for himself.'

'It's funny, isn't it?' Robyn says, picking up a rogue yellow crystal on the benchtop and rolling it around between her thumb and forefinger. 'You think you know someone, and then you realise you just have no idea.'

'Or maybe,' says Cohen, 'you turn out to be right.'

1996 Saturday, 13th July

Sam is fourteen, riding his bike to Cohen's place on the outskirts of town. He cycles past the small cluster of shops—post office, pub, general store—then a row of rustic houses, their chimneys sending woodsmoke thinning out over lush greenery full of birdsong. The air is cold and damp after rain, but Sam is warm in his puffer jacket and beanie. Hot by the time he gets to Cohen's place.

Cohen hops on his own bike and they head out into the forest, where the trees are taller, the hollows deeper. Some days, they walk along the derelict train line, overgrown with moss and leaf matter. They go fishing or raid the marron traps in a neighbour's dam. They skim stones across the river, when there's a river to speak of.

Today they're building forts down near the abandoned railway bridge for Capture the Flag. Sam's mum made them a pair of calico flags for this purpose, but usually they forget to bring them and use whatever is at hand. Today, Sam's flag is his beanie, while Cohen's is one of his blue fingerless gloves.

The game is played with gings and projectiles: small gumnuts only, gathered up before the game begins. Headshots are banned—instant disqualification—but if you get hit anywhere else, you have to drop to the ground, out of action for ten seconds. The first to capture the other's flag wins.

The trees are still dripping wet, but the wind has shaken lots of small branches down. The boys gather up the damp pieces and spend a good half hour building their structures, fifty metres apart in the forest.

Sam gives the hoot that signals his readiness. A minute or so later, Cohen hoots back. The game is on.

Usually, Cohen takes a fairly direct route to Sam's fort, hiding behind trees and keeping low. It never goes well, but he doesn't trust his aim enough to adopt Sam's strategy, which is to hunt Cohen relentlessly, keeping him down often and long enough to reach his fort and claim victory. But today, Cohen has a new plan. There will be no beeline for Sam's base. Instead, knowing that Sam will be expecting the usual easy target, he drops down low and crawls outward, pausing now and then to listen for Sam's footfall. He moves slowly and steadily. He hears a shuffle and the snap of a branch followed by a muttered curse, but it's some way off. He keeps going.

When he's sure he's close to Sam's base, he listens again, locating Sam somewhere near the mid-zone. Looking up, he spots him behind a tree, facing the wrong way. Carefully, Cohen lines up his shot. For once, his aim is true and Sam flinches, feeling the ping on his thigh. He turns to see Cohen make a dash for his base. Cohen is almost there, then he *is* there, with five good seconds to spare. He grabs Sam's beanie and shoves it on his head triumphantly.

Sam should still be on the ground, waiting out the last few seconds of his downtime, but instead he's right there, tackling Cohen to the ground, pinning him down by the wrists. Sticks and rocks jab into Cohen's back and arms.

When Sam releases Cohen's hands, he yanks the beanie off his head.

'Don't want your headlice thanks, mate,' he says, then he gets up and watches while Cohen gets to his feet.

'Finally got you, though,' Cohen says, smiling as he brushes leaves and twigs from his jacket.

'Guess again,' Sam says, pointing to his temple. 'Headshot.'

'Bull-crap. I got you on the leg.'

Sam turns and starts walking back to their bikes near the path.

'Yeah,' he says. 'Whatever.'

'Don't be a dickhead,' Cohen says, indignation welling up. 'You know I won.'

'Keep telling yourself that,' Sam says, mounting his bike. He nods back toward the forest. 'Leaving your glove out here for next time?'

'Shit,' Cohen mutters, turning back.

It takes him a while to find his fort and retrieve the glove, and when he returns to the bike spot, Sam's gone. Cohen shakes his head as he sits back on his saddle, muttering *bloody sook*, but there's something wrong; his bike feels bogged. Looking down, he notices his front tyre's flat, and his pump isn't where it lives on the down tube. There's nothing for it but to push the bike all the way along the forest track and home along the road.

When he gets home, Sam's bike is on the porch and he's inside, drinking hot chocolate with Cohen's mum.

'There you are,' Libby says when Cohen comes in. 'We were worried about you.'

'You don't look worried.'

'Sam says you took off and left him in the forest.'

'That's not what happened.'

'Why don't you have some hot chocolate? We can talk it all over once you've calmed down.'

Cohen looks at Sam at the table, leaning back in his chair with his hands behind his head.

'Your bike looks a bit cactus,' Sam says, looking past Cohen out the door, smiling at him. 'Need a hand fixing it?'

Then he gives Cohen a wink, as if they're in it together. It's Sam's gift, that wink. It draws you in; you can't stay angry.

Cohen would've told anyone who'd asked him while he was pushing that bike home that Sam had gone too far this time, but once his belly's full of hot chocolate and he's watching Sam pump his tyre back up, he finds he's over it. No one got hurt, and Sam's putting things right. You have to have a sense of humour about things, that's all. And remember it's Sam who wins the games.

2001 Thursday, 22nd November

I finish my final exam and step out into a blue-sky afternoon, pulling a sunhat from my bag. The walk home is uncomfortably warm after the air-conditioned hall, but there's a willie wagtail chattering on a wire overhead, and I have nothing serious to think about for a good two months. Life's good.

When I get home, Robyn's on her way to meet her dad.

'Hey, Gracie,' she says, bag on one shoulder, lever-arch file in her arms. The rest of us are done, whereas she has one more exam to sit, so she's getting away from temptation and studying at home tonight. 'How'd it go?'

'Pretty good, I think. So good to be finished.'

'Lucky duck.'

'You're next, and then we'll have that party.'

'You lot will be all partied out after tonight.'

'No chance. I'll save some mojo for you, and for when Cohen gets back.'

Cohen's gone south for his uncle's funeral. Car accident on one of those narrow, winding roads down there, with the giant trees right alongside the tarmac. Sublime, but deadly. The funeral's today. Even as we speak. I feel bad going out celebrating, but Cohen says I've worked hard and I deserve a night out. So, Marla and I have big plans. We'll kick things off with margaritas at home, followed by jugs at the tavern. After that, we'll follow the action down to Steves Bar or the city, or wherever it leads us.

'See you, Robyn,' I say, giving her a quick hug. 'Good luck.'

'Thanks. Have fun tonight.'

'I will, though I've got a headache coming on.'

'I have paracetamol in the bathroom cabinet if you need it,' Robyn says. Then she blows me a kiss and bobs off down the stairs.

I have a drink of water and a long soak in the bath, then I lie down on my bed for a while, hoping the headache will go away. It's still there when Marla gets back from the bottle store, so I hit that paracetamol and we start getting ready.

Gwen Stefani blaring, we work through a few outfits before settling on my favourite silver dress and Marla's go-to skinny jeans with a strapless top. All made-up and fragrant in Marla's jasmine-scented perfume, we get busy filling a glass jug with tequila, lime juice and orange liqueur. Marla reaches into her bag by the door and pulls out a box of plastic cocktail glasses from the party shop on the highway.

'Nice touch,' I say.

'Nothing if not classy, darling.'

I grind salt onto a plate and roll the plastic rims in it.

'Good mix,' I say after my first taste.

'Love it,' Marla says.

We sit on the balcony while the heat of the day lifts away, knowing we have a whole summer to laze on the beach. I'll probably take on some extra shifts at the Windsor, but other than that, the only things I'll need to plan around are music festivals, outdoor movies, and Sunday sessions down at the Cott.

Once it's dark, we stash the leftover margarita in the fridge and skip down to the Tav, which is heaving, full of students jostling for beer and shouting to each other over the band. Two jugs in, things are starting to blur at the edges. We yell names and hug people and dance, and we get a jug of soft drink to improve our chances of making it to a second venue. Which we do, miraculously enough, staggering along the river road to Steves.

We're there for what feels like hours but also mere seconds, drinking, dancing, shouting over music. So many bodies, so close together; such heat. At some point, I lose Marla—she finds her boyfriend and disappears into the night. I'm there for a bit longer, propped up against the bar, until it sinks in that the party is over; I'm alone. I head outside and start walking, hoping the fresh air will sober me up. The laughter and music fall away. I'm zoning in on the twin rhythms of my footfall and my breathing when someone calls my name behind me.

'Thought that was you ducking out,' Sam says, catching up with me.

'Jesus,' I say. 'Where'd you come from?'

'I spotted you just as you were leaving. Thought you might need someone to walk you home.'

'I'm fine.'

'Sure you are; you can barely put one foot in front of the other.'

We walk in silence for a while, the night air cool around us. Halfway home, I stop and close my eyes. I feel like I'm going to be sick, but after a few deep breaths, it passes.

'Finished exams then?' Sam asks once we've resumed walking.

'Yeah. You?'

'Two days ago,' he says.

'You been out drinking alone? Sad-sack.'

'No. I was with Matty. You know Matty?'

I squint at him; he's pretty straight, all things considered. 'You're sober as.'

'We weren't really drinking. Matty's not into alcohol.'

'Course he isn't.'

'He prefers to play the chemical field.'

'He's an idiot.'

'He knows his stuff though. Ask him anything about any drug, and he can tell you.'

'I'm sure he can.'

'For real, though. Some of the stuff he messes around with, it can take you pretty close to the line. But I trust him; he knows what he's doing.'

'I wouldn't trust him.'

'You're *you*—of course you wouldn't.'

He laughs at the look on my face. Dodges the punch I try to land on his shoulder.

By the time we reach my door, I'm feeling steadier on my feet and lucid enough to want the evening to go on.

'Do you want to come in?' I say, unlocking the door. 'We have margarita in the fridge.'

'Sounds like a plan.'

'Just as a friend though, okay? Yallingup was …'

'Yallingup was amazing.'

'It was a mistake.'

'A fun mistake.'

'Stop it, Sam. I'm with Cohen, okay?'

'Okay, Gracie, I hear you. We'll drink margaritas and just be friends … if that's really what you want.'

2019 Sunday, 17th February

Cohen watches Robyn absent-mindedly roll that sodium nitrite crystal around in her fingers then brush it off on her leg.

'Do you ever wonder what he's doing now?' he asks, resting his elbows on the counter.

'Who?'

'The guy who was responsible for what happened. To Gracie. He must've seen it on the news. Must've known he'd killed her.'

'If there's any justice, he's dead himself. Or at least consumed with guilt in a hovel somewhere.'

'Maybe. Or maybe he's evolved into a more complex predator.'

'It's possible,' Robyn nods, 'for sure.'

'For a while there, I thought it was Matty.'

'Me too, but so many people saw him at his house that night. From quite early on, like before Gracie and Marla even got to Steves. They had that afterparty, didn't they? Heaps of people were there.'

'Yeah. I had to let that theory go in the end.'

'I think it was just some random guy, Cohen. Just, wrong place, wrong time.'

Cohen nods.

'Although ...' Robyn continues.

'Although what?'

'Did you ever think it might've been Sam? If he had a thing for Gracie ...'

'He spent the night at yours though, right? The times didn't fit.'

'Yeah, I know. It can't have been him.'

'I mean,' Cohen says, running his hand across his jaw, back and forth. 'I'd be lying if I said I'd never considered it, but ... if he was with you, then ...'

'Yeah, he definitely was.'

Cohen remembers the torment of it all, that vortex of questions and speculation. He's surprised when Robyn reaches across and squeezes his arm. Compassion is a rarity for him these days. As is physical contact of any kind.

'Anyway, I should let you go,' she says. 'You were about to hit the road.'

'Yeah, I should head off. Thanks for coming by.'

'Get some proper rest, okay? You've had a rough time.'

'You can talk.'

Outside, Robyn climbs into her car and returns Cohen's wave. He smiles at her before closing the door, but even he can tell it's unconvincing.

26

Let's take a detour now—a small one—and drop in on Skye. She's okay. I mean, she's sad, but she's endured worse things. She'll survive.

Tonight, she lies on the sofa, watching *Seinfeld* reruns while finishing off a leftover bottle of wine. She's hoping to nod off and save herself the trouble of having to lie in bed, thinking. But it doesn't happen. When the fourth episode begins—that chunky bassline thwacking into her skull—she turns it off and stands up. Sleep is not even knocking on the door.

There's only one thing for it: a night stroll. Get that dark sky to fill her mind instead of Sam. She slips her phone and keys into her bag, slings it over her shoulder and heads out. The air is fresh and the sky is dark, though the trees are darker. She finds comfort in their silhouettes beneath that toothbrush-spray of stars.

She heads down Broadway towards the river then takes the footpath beside the dark expanse of water. The fact that she's on her way to *Stargazing* and Sam doesn't occur to her—or so she'd tell you—until she's three or four blocks away.

Jethro is also there. It's only natural that he's following Skye, given that he was outside her apartment when she left. He was loitering in the shadow of a red gum, having talked himself out of banging on her door again. He maintains a good distance behind her now: far enough away that she won't hear his footfall, but close enough that he doesn't lose her in the darkness.

He knows she'd be unimpressed if she saw him. What he's doing is indefensible; it amounts to stalking. But it's not of the threatening variety; he'd never hurt her. That's not what it's about. It's about knowing she's okay, that's all. Knowing she's still there, in the world, going about her business.

He's planned what he'll say if she spots him hanging around one day. He'll be surprised to see her, of course, then he'll ask her how she is and explain that he's following up on a job application. Gardening or something. But would she like to grab a coffee? Just to catch up. Yes, he knows he stopped turning up for rehearsals, but he's still drumming. Found a new band … This is almost true: he's made a few enquiries, so it will be true soon. Hopefully. Because without drumming, he has nothing. *Is* nothing. And though it comforts him to see her like this, from a distance, it hurts too much to be in the same room as her, much less the same band.

She's taking them towards the river now, not bothering to stick to the shadows the way Jethro is doing. He wants to call out to her, advise her to be less conspicuous; she looks so solitary up ahead. So exposed. But of course, he holds his tongue. She'd freak out if she knew he was there. She'd flip him the bird and tell him to get out of her life, once and for all. She has Sam now, after all.

Fucking Sam.

Jethro has spent many sweet hours dreaming up ways to eliminate the guy. He could wait just outside his property, for example, until the gate rolled open to let a car in or out. Then he could nip through and bide his time. Thump Sam on the head with something heavy. Knife him, maybe. Or he could opt for something less messy. Tamper with the brakes of his car. Tie him up and shove him inside one of those giant freezers. They're not exactly everywhere, those freezers, but Jethro has hospitality connections; he could find one. For days now, he's lain in bed, listening to his neighbour's incessant sweeping of her driveway, indulging in these possibilities. Assuring himself that he could make them happen if he had to. Called upon to rescue Skye from heartache, he'd be capable of anything.

Skye approaches the yacht club from the west, wondering if Sam will let her talk to him. What she'll say if he does. There are hardly any people about, aside from a woman walking her poodle and a man zipping past on his bike. Skye senses movement in the shadows near the skatepark, in her peripheral vision, but there's nothing there when she turns to look.

The river is so peaceful in the dark, lapping quietly on the bank and up against the timber stumps of the short jetty. Three or four small boats are moored there, bobbing gently with the movement of the water.

Skye steps onto the jetty and makes her way along it carefully until she sees Sam, sitting on the deck, drinking a beer. He rolls the bottle around in both hands then works at peeling off the label, idly, his mind on something else.

The gate is open. When she reaches the boat, Sam puts the empty bottle down and stands up, reaching out to steady himself. He knocks it over as he goes. As if in slow motion, Skye sees it fall and roll, then disappear down into the hatch.

She's prepared for irritation in his voice, but when he speaks, he sounds more confused than angry.

'Skye? What are you doing here?'

'I need to talk to you, Sam.'

'I really need to not see you anymore.'

'Can I come aboard? It's hard to do this from up here.'

'No, Skye ...'

'Please, Sam. I'm not going to ask anything of you, okay? That's what I wanted to say to you. Things can be easy between us, I'm not going to ...'

'I have a daughter, a wife ...'

'I know, all right? I bloody know you do.'

They stand a long moment in silence then Sam glances up at the house.

'Okay,' he says, reaching a hand towards Skye to help her on. It's warm and firm. That familiar charge courses through her body at his touch.

There's a thud, near the back of the boat.

'What was that?' Skye says.

'What was what?'

'That noise. Didn't you hear it?'

'I wouldn't worry about it. *Stargazing* makes a lot of settling noises. She's not a new boat, put it that way.'

'I didn't hear anything last time.'

'We were a little preoccupied though, weren't we?' Sam says, smiling at her. Skye smiles back; it's been so long. But then Sam glances at his house again and unties the rope that connects them to the jetty. 'We'd better take her out a bit. If Tori sees you here, she'll never forgive me.'

◆◆◆

Much later, Skye comes to. She doesn't know where she is, but she can smell the briny water. Feel the throb of pain at the back of her head.

When she opens her eyes, there's the moon overhead and pins and needles in her hand.

She manages to pull herself onto her knees. That's when she notices Sam's shoe, and the rest of him.

Crawling over, she touches his face, feels for a pulse. There's nothing. Just the slap and gurgle of the water against the boat. The incessant rocking.

The lights are still there on the shore, but they have no answers. There's only panic for guidance, and the panic says *swim*.

◆◆◆

Head still throbbing, Skye staggers out of the shallows. She's breathless and cold, aside from the heat of her tears. She starts walking home, her canvas shoes rubbing through her wet socks. Pain seems right though, given the circumstances. Because whatever's happened to Sam might be her fault. Though it can't be, surely. She'd remember if she'd done something to hurt him. Wouldn't she?

One foot in front of the other, she walks, until she reaches her apartment. She walks up the stairs and makes her way along the open corridor, past the familiar terracotta pot plants outside her neighbour's door and the dated ceramic figurine bolted to the wall.

Outside her door, she digs around in her bag for her keys, same as always, except now the bag is sodden, and Sam is dead.

Inside her apartment, there's a heavy, turning sensation in her belly as she peels off her wet things, puts them in the washing machine and mops up the water she's dragged in. After a hot shower, she wanders around, touching things at once familiar and strange—a stick-vac attached to the kitchen wall; her laptop closed on her desk; the remote control on the heavy oak coffee table; the woollen throw on the sofa. As the sun pushes the dawn light out of the sky, she makes tea, staring at nothing while the kettle boils. Lifting and lowering the teabag to some in-built rhythm. She takes the mug to the sofa, where she sits, watching curls of steam catch the light as they lift off the surface. She should call someone. Tell someone. But who? And what difference would it make? He's gone, and all that's left is this ache, spreading the way the universe spreads. Into space that wasn't even there before.

27

Tori wakes up slowly. The morning light is thin. With any luck, it'll be a mild day today, though Tori doesn't like her chances.

She rolls onto her back, wondering if she'll ever get used to these Perth summers, not to mention this exhaustion, day after day. Last night was a horror-show, though this time it wasn't your fault, Isla. It was your blessed father's. And Tori's too—her inability to let things go. She stayed up way too late, stewing, unable to switch off. She made a decision in the end though, so that's something.

Sitting up, she reaches into your bassinet, giving you a thumb to wrap your tiny fingers around.

'Morning, sweet pea,' she says, leaning across to watch the emotions flit across your face.

Downstairs, she gives you some milk and makes a quick phone

call. Then she blends warm apple puree into a small bowl of rice cereal for your breakfast. Sipping coffee, she wonders if Sam's awake yet, lying in *Stargazing*'s airless cabin.

Feeding you with a small, rubbery spoon, she pictures herself, older, sitting across the table from a teenaged version of you, the pair of you eating in silence. All grown up, you'll be distracted, thinking about something else: décor for your other bedroom maybe, the one in your father's house; or a conversation you've had with the people who live there. Your other family.

It wouldn't be the end of the world for you; plenty of people grow up like that and thrive. Possibly their lives are richer for it.

But the thought of Sam having children with someone else fills your mother with despair. Makes her throat ache with tears not yet shed. She should've taken his calls yesterday. Should at least have heard what he wanted to say.

'Come on,' she says, lifting your solid little body out of your highchair. 'Let's go see Daddy.'

When she reaches the reserve, Tori picks up the pace: she needs to see him *now*, to talk to him, to ask him to come home before he decides he's happy not to.

Before she reaches the jetty, she spots *Stargazing*, not at her mooring but anchored some way out. Weird. Her feet sink into the sand as she approaches the water.

She calls out: 'Sam!' Twice, three times. She waits, willing him to emerge from the cabin. He'll smile, give her a wave, and bring the boat back in. He'll be so happy to see you both. So relieved.

But there's no sign of movement, other than *Stargazing* turning slowly on her anchor.

'Sam!'

With a trembling hand, Tori takes out her phone. She goes into her recent calls list and taps Sam's name. It's reassuring to see it on the screen, as if it guarantees something, but from across the water, slightly muffled, comes the sound of his ringtone: a distant, strumming sound, on and on.

'Hi love,' Tori says when it goes to voicemail, trying to steady her voice. 'Give me a call when you can.'

◆◆◆

Robyn is out walking along the river path, making the most of the cool morning air before work. She's approaching the grove of trees when she hears a woman shouting, fear catching at the hope in her voice. There she is, up ahead, with a baby on her hip.

A hand shielding her eyes, Robyn follows the woman's sightline and sees the boat on the water. She heads towards her. The woman seems oblivious, but then she speaks.

'My husband,' she says. 'I think he's out there.'

She calls out again: 'Sam!'

'He won't hear you from here,' Robyn says, her heart racing as she fits the pieces together—the boat, the baby, the name. 'You'll need to get closer.'

'I phoned him,' Tori says. 'He didn't pick up.'

'I'll hold your baby if you want to go in?'

Tori looks at her as if she's speaking in tongues.

'I'll look after her, I promise. Can you swim?'

Doubt flickers across Tori's face.

'He might be injured out there,' Robyn says, pulling off her trainers and socks, dropping her hat and sunnies on the sand. The sand is coarse between her toes. 'I'll go.'

The water is colder and choppier than it looks. Robyn has to work hard against the drag of her waterlogged clothes. Her heart thumps in her throat, and not just because she's never been a strong swimmer. Who knows what she'll find? And what's the plan if Sam's there with Skye? She'd like to turn back—let him sort his own shit out—but something isn't right, that much is clear. And she knows first aid; whatever's gone wrong, she might be able to help.

If she could only swim faster.

She pulls her arms through the water, kicks as steadily as she can and tells herself not to think about what else might be in the water with her. She's almost there. She can see the vessel, the name *Stargazing*, rocking on the waves.

Reaching it, she manages to grab the gunwale when it rocks down low enough. She holds on, trying to figure out how she's going to drag herself up and into it. After a minute or two hanging on like that, she floats her legs up and hooks her right ankle over the edge. Drawing on her last bit of strength, she rolls herself up out of the water, landing hard on her shoulder.

In the strange hush that follows, she turns her head and sees Sam, stretched out on the deck of the boat. A fly crawls across his cheek. It's as if all the silence comes from him.

Maybe he's asleep, Robyn thinks. Maybe he drank so much last night he crashed out and hasn't woken up yet, despite the sun on his face. She allows herself this possibility, though even as she registers the relief of it, she recognises it as a diversion. A deferral. Something to ease her transition from one reality into another. Because such a transition is necessary; she's seen enough death to know what this is, and it's not the languor of sleep.

Pulling herself up onto her knees, Robyn looks back at the shore. Tori is watching, craning her whole body. Robyn looks away and moves towards Sam. His bluish skin is cool to the touch. She feels for a pulse, shifting her fingers over his wrist, still hoping for that flicker beneath the skin, though she knows already it isn't there. It doesn't matter that the people who love him most are on the shore, waiting; it changes nothing.

Tori gestures at Robyn with her free arm: a question.

Robyn shifts her weight—how to communicate what she's found? Pointing down at Sam, she shakes her head. She's not sure at first if Tori will be able to see what she's doing, but something about the time she's taken, and her body language ... it's enough.

Tori covers her mouth. Robyn looks away. Concentrates on pulling up the anchor, dripping and heavy. She studies the controls, starts up the engine.

Steering that boat back to shore is surely the most mournful thing she's ever done. There's nothing for it but to avoid looking at Sam and wonder, as she draws closer, if she should keep Tori from seeing him like this too. But the boat embeds itself in the sand before she can figure out what's best and by then Tori has waded knee-deep into the water, still in her cotton pyjamas. The belt of her robe has come untied.

'Please,' Tori is saying, over and over.

Robyn turns off the engine and stands up awkwardly. She climbs out and joins Tori in the shallows.

'I don't think you should see him,' she says. 'I don't think you should look ...'

But Tori is passing you over now and climbing into the boat.

She slips and falls in her haste then she drags herself to Sam across the deck until she's holding him in her arms, still murmuring *please, Sam, please*. Quiet for a moment, she studies his face, feeling for a pulse under his jaw, and then she drops her head onto his chest and moans, a primal wail, welling up from the depths of her being. She doesn't stop for a long time, even when you join in, distressed at the sound of your mother's pain.

'Hush little one,' Robyn says, holding you against her shoulder and rocking gently. 'Hush-a-bub.' She's never held a baby before, but it feels okay. You take in gulps of air—shuddering breaths— and rest your head on her shoulder. Tori's weeping abates too after a while, giving way to an eerie quiet, filled only by the lapping of small waves on the shore and up against the boat. Robyn lowers her cheek to your soft baby hair and wills the universe to let her carry all the grief that lies ahead for you: the long nights you'll spend wishing you knew your dad. It's brutal—the cruelty of your loss, the way it will shape you. But all she can do is bounce you gently and echo the whispered hush of the waves on the shore, saying *it's okay*, though it isn't.

Once you've settled, Robyn reaches down awkwardly for her phone amongst her things on the beach. Looking back at Tori, curled over Sam, she calls one of her police contacts.

'Detective Marella,' she says, speaking quietly. 'I'm afraid I've found a body.'

Sofia Marella listens while Robyn explains.

'Stay where you are, okay?' she says. 'I'll be there asap.'

◆◆◆

As the sun climbs and the morning's shade recedes, the four of you occupy the small stretch of riverbank together, like a mismatched cast in some awful play. The boat is wedged in the sand, its stern rising and falling with the movement of the waves so that it pivots ever so slightly on its embedded bow.

Tori won't leave Sam. She lies there, clutching his body as if that might bring him back, or at least allow her to slip away and join him, wherever he is.

At last, Detective Marella arrives with some officers and a crew from Forensics. One of the officers helps Tori out of the boat. He's firm about it, borderline forceful; they need to get in there to figure out what's happened. Tori can't make out much of what they're saying, just *the body* this and *the body* that. Someone wraps a blanket around her; she's shivering.

'Sam,' she murmurs through her clenched teeth.

'Beg your pardon?' the officer says.

'His name is Sam! Stop calling him *the body*. Please stop calling him that.'

She's cold, though she can feel the heat of the sun burning her skin. God knows what time it is. A sudden fear moves through her.

'Where's Isla? My baby?'

'She's okay; she's fine. Your friend has her.'

He points over at Robyn. Tori heads over through the sand. Wordlessly, she holds out her arms for you; you murmur as you're handed over then settle back to sleep against the skin of Tori's chest.

Tears stream down Tori's face—she can't stop them—and all anyone can do is stand around looking at her. She can't stand the way they look at her. All that compassion and sympathy mean that she hasn't imagined the whole thing.

Detective Marella suggests they go back up to the house. Tori thinks she'll be glad to get out of the sun and lie down—her legs are trembling—but her relief seems unforgivable. Sam is dead; everything else should stop too, including mortal challenges like thirst and sunburn.

'Can Sam come too?' she says, her voice thin and childlike. She wants to take him somewhere cool and still. Somewhere he won't be without her. The idea of leaving him behind, rocking in that boat, widens the chasm that's opened up inside of her. She wants to collapse, scream, something—anything—to get this anguish *off*, out, away. But she can't do any of those things; you are clinging to her even in your sleep, one little hand gripping her nightshirt.

'I'm sorry, Mrs Favier,' the detective says. 'Not yet. But we'll get him off the boat as soon as we can, I promise.'

For me, this is the worst bit. I don't feel much on Sam's account, but I know you and your mum did nothing to deserve this. Still, what's done is done and there's no turning back. As any decent grief experience will teach you, time moves one way only.

'Okay,' Tori says, or tries to say. She can't be sure she's made a sound.

Detective Marella and an officer walk behind Tori on the footpath. They reach the top of the steps and there's the house, looming over them like the extravagance it is. *Nobody needs a house this big.* That's what Sam said when they were looking at it to buy, and again once they'd moved in. Tori always said it's not a question of need though, is it? We can afford it. And when we want to sell it, it's the kind of house people expect in this area. But he was right, she thinks now, looking at the stretch of pool gleaming cyan at the foot of those two vast storeys whose walls of glass overlook the river. They were so important to Tori, those walls of glass. But now, all they're good for is reflecting the quiet slide of clouds, ushered across the sky by a brooding south-westerly.

'I need to sit down,' she says, suddenly dizzy and fearful that she might drop you; you're awake now and whimpering.

How can there be no more Sam? Only these scudding reflections, like something out of a nightmare. And that's what this is, Tori thinks. It must be. Surely, she will wake up soon and draw close to the warmth of her husband in bed beside her. Breathe in his scent. Thank God, she'll think—it was a dream. Just a dream.

'Come,' Detective Marella says, holding out her arm.

Tori passes you over then because she can feel its approach—a great wave of darkness, coming to take her away. She welcomes the relief of it because this is not a dream and she knows it. It's all real and it will be like this forever. Sam is never coming home.

When Tori drifts back to consciousness, she's in her house and her mouth is dry. She's on the couch. Her neck aches. The detective is there, and the officer too, walking up and down the room with you in his arms. You're giving off little yelping noises, reaching for your mum.

'Here,' Tori says, sitting up and reaching back.

The officer's relief is obvious as he passes you over.

'I'm sorry, my darling,' Tori murmurs, wrestling open her nursing bra with one hand while trying to contain your enthusiasm with the other. You cry at the injustice of having had to wait so long. You drink, then come off to cry a little more before searching for the nipple again.

The detective, Sofia, brings Tori some tissues and a glass of water then sits on the chair opposite her.

'I'd like to leave you in peace,' she says. 'But I do need to ask you a few questions. Do you think you can manage that?'

'If you promise me you'll work out what happened,' Tori says.

'I'll do everything I can, Mrs Favier. Tori?'

Tori nods again. 'What do you want to know?'

'When did you last see your husband alive?'

'Sunday morning,' Tori says haltingly. 'We had an argument, I asked him to leave. He packed a bag and went to sleep on the boat.'

'Have you talked to him since then? Did he say anything about taking the boat out for a spin last night?'

'No,' Tori says. 'I don't know why he did that.'

'Was he on his own?'

Tori thinks of that woman the other night, trailing behind Sam, taking his hand.

'Of course he was,' she says, louder than she means to. 'You found him on a boat in the middle of the river. Alone. You think someone killed him then disappeared into thin air?'

Sofia looks at her steadily. 'Perhaps they swam to shore. Or used a second vessel.'

Tori bows her head. 'I'm sorry. This is … a lot.'

'Was there anything unusual going on for your husband, Mrs Favier? Was he depressed, perhaps? Or can you think of anyone who might've wanted to hurt him?'

'He wasn't depressed, no,' Tori says. 'Exhausted maybe, but … you know, we have a baby, so … nothing out of the ordinary.'

He was having an affair. The words form in her head, but they don't come out of her mouth. She should say them. It might be important. Sam said he was planning to end the relationship that same day; an abrupt rejection—people have killed for less. But it can't be relevant. Surely not. If Sam really wasn't alone, if he took that shadowy woman out on the water again, knowing how it had hurt Tori the first time … She can't bear to think that of him.

'Mrs Favier, I have to ask: what were you doing last night?'

'I was at home all night, with my daughter.'

'Is there anyone who can verify that?'

It takes Tori a moment to process this question. The suspicion it implies.

'I called my mum in the UK at some point,' she says. 'Can't tell you what time it was, exactly. Maybe around eight? I can call again and ask her.'

'That won't be necessary; we can check the phone records. Thank you, Mrs Favier. You've been very helpful.'

Once the detective has left, her questions linger in Tori's mind. *Was* Sam alone when he died? And where was she, Tori, in his hour of need? Not there for him, that's for sure.

She drifts around the living room, then the kitchen, feeling unmoored. Anchorless. It's unsettling to think she's a suspect, but it's no surprise. They always look at the spouse. Who else has loved the victim enough to swear a lifelong allegiance? Or felt love bleed into fury when that faith was betrayed?

28

After a fitful sleep, Skye wakes up some time around midday. Still blinking on the couch, she's otherwise motionless when there's a knock on the door. She checks her watch, as if it matters what time it is.

Another knock. She'll ignore it; whoever it is will eventually give up and go away, God willing. But there's a third knock, louder this time. Skye rolls herself off the couch and heads to the door.

'Hello?'

'Hi.' It's a woman's voice, quick and unapologetic. 'My name's Robyn Tinsley. I was hoping to have a word with you.'

Skye opens the door, just a fraction, although Robyn doesn't look particularly threatening.

Skye clears her throat. She can still taste the river water. 'This isn't a great time,' she says through the gap. 'What is it you want to discuss?'

'Do you mind if I come in?' Robyn says. 'It's about Sam.'

The ground falls away at the sound of his name—a cold, disorienting rush.

'May I come in?'

Skye loosens her white-knuckle grip on the door and steps back to let the woman in.

Robyn walks across the room and stops not far from Skye's sodden handbag and its spilled-out contents on a towel on the floor. 'Been swimming?'

'It's a long story,' Skye says, heading back towards the kitchen. 'Can I offer you some tea?'

'No thanks,' Robyn says. 'But you go ahead.'

Skye leans against the kitchen bench for a moment, then she fills two glasses with tap water and returns to the living room, where Robyn is pulling a laptop from her bag.

'Do I know you?' Skye says. 'You look familiar.'

'I used to be on telly sometimes. Foreign correspondent for the ABC.'

'You're a journalist?'

'Yes, but that's not why I'm here.'

'Why are you here?'

'Like I said, we need to talk about Sam,' Robyn says, accepting the water, putting it on the table.

Skye looks at her warily. 'Is this an interview?'

'No, I won't be writing about your relationship with Sam. Not for your sake but for Sam's. And for his wife and daughter.'

Skye bristles at the way Robyn lets these last words settle on her, watching her for a reaction.

'This is making me quite uncomfortable, to be honest,' Skye says. 'I mean, how do you know who I am? Where I live?'

'I think that will become clear once I've shown you these,' Robyn says, opening the laptop and a folder on the desktop, revealing a handful of thumbnails. She opens the first one and stands back with a sweep of her arm. The first image is a little blurred, but the rest are sharp and clear. Skye recognises herself, the tattooed bird on the inside of her wrist, which Sam is holding to his mouth. She's taken aback by the coquettish look on her face, and the sight of Sam, still alive.

'I found him dead on his boat this morning,' Robyn says, glancing again at Skye's things on the towel. 'And I think you might know something about that.'

Skye closes her eyes for a moment.

'I was out there with him last night,' she says slowly. 'But I don't know how he died.'

Robyn frowns. 'Can you elaborate?'

Skye hesitates, then she tells Robyn how it went, all of it—how the water rippled as the boat cut through it. How the moon was steady, watchful as the water stretched and pulled its reflection apart.

A short way out, Sam cut the engine. Skye watched him pull the small anchor towards himself and throw it over the side with a heavy splash. The rope uncoiled rapidly, slipping coarse and snake-like into the water, until the anchor hit the riverbed and the rope went still.

'Sam,' Skye said into the quiet. 'I know it's not cool, me turning up like this, but I didn't know how else to get you to talk to me, you know? You've been ignoring my calls, and my emails, and my texts ...'

He nodded, looking morose.

'I have to ignore you, Skye.'

'No, you don't.'

'You think I don't think about you? All the time? But when I'm with you, guess who I think about?'

'Tori?'

'And Isla. She's my daughter, Skye. She needs me. She's part of me, and what she doesn't need is for me to mess things up with her mum because I can't keep my hands off some ...'

'Some what?'

'Someone else.'

'I like it that you can't keep your hands off me, Sam,' Skye said, standing up and moving towards him.

'Skye, I need you to stop this. Please. Tori's my wife. I made vows ... I need to make amends before it's too late, and if I keep spending time with you, I won't be able to tell her it's behind me.'

'She never has to know, Sam. I'll never tell her. Never. I'll never ask anything of you except that we don't have to stop seeing each other.'

Sam dragged a hand down his face then looked at it, squinting, as if he expected something to have come away on it.

'I don't feel good, Skye.'

'I know Sam, but doesn't it feel worse being apart? It does for me.'

'No, I mean ... I feel sick ... dizzy ...'

Robyn watches Skye, who seems entranced by her own words, staring past Robyn at nothing.

'That's when I noticed how pale he looked. It was hard to tell, even with the moon so bright, but he'd gone kind of grey. He was rocking forward, holding his stomach, saying he was going to throw up. I said to take a deep breath, to slow it down, but he couldn't do that. Almost couldn't breathe at all. Or speak, trying to tell me something was wrong. I said we needed to get back to shore and I'd call an ambulance on the way, if he could pull up the anchor, start the engine. But he said I'd have to do it, so I told him we should swap places, but slowly … And he tried, but the boat shifted beneath him so he staggered sideways a bit, then he righted himself and I thought he might be okay, but then his head … his head slumped forward.'

She stops talking. Looks at her hands.

'And then?'

'He swayed there for a moment, as if his strings had gone slack, and then his legs gave out. I tried to catch him, but he was so heavy. I guess we went down together. I hit my head. Must've been hard. I remember this pain, and then nothing.'

She reaches for the tender place at the back of her skull. Presses on it gently, as if she too needs convincing.

'Show me,' Robyn says.

Skye takes Robyn's offered hand and places it over the sore spot. 'Just … ow!' She flinches at the pressure Robyn applies. 'Not so hard! Bloody hurts.'

'Sorry,' Robyn says, looking less sure of herself.

'I woke up with a thumping headache and Sam was … lying there … without a … without a pulse.'

Outside, some kids yell out, their bicycle wheels whirring past along the uneven concrete pavement below.

'Did you have any symptoms like his?' Robyn says. 'The

nausea and gasping for air? Maybe you should see a doctor.'

Skye shakes her head. 'No, no nausea. And the pain's easing off.'

'Do you think Sam might've taken something?'

'I don't think so. He was upset about his family and stuff, but it wasn't like … he hadn't given up.'

Robyn frowns as she packs her laptop away.

'Have you shown those to the police?' Skye asks.

'Not yet. I think you should go in. Tell them what you've told me. They need all the evidence to figure out what happened.'

'What if they think I did it?'

'They might, but if you don't tell them, I will, and they'll come knocking anyway. And they'll be a lot less inclined to believe your story that way.'

Robyn pulls a card out of her wallet and puts it on the table.

'That's the detective in charge of the case,' she says. 'I'll give you half an hour to call her. After that I'll be showing her the photos. Text me when you've done it.'

Leaving Skye's place, Robyn feels deflated, though it was naïve to have hoped for some great revelation or confession in there. Still, at least she knows now—assuming Skye's telling the truth—that Sam was alive when he got in the boat.

She parks Frank's green Honda in partial shade outside the low-slung red-brick police station and waits to hear from Skye. With nothing to distract her, she is assailed by memories: Sam on a blanket in the sunshine, pulling pollen from her hair; only half listening to her while reading some enormous text for one of his units; the look on his face just before he kissed her. All of it still exists for her, but it's dwarfed now by the horror of finding his body. Of her powerlessness to revive him. Numbly, she watches a fly come in through the open window. It buzzes noisily along the dashboard, thwacking itself repeatedly against the windscreen.

Finally, a text from Skye comes through: *Called the detective. Do what you need to do.*

That's good, Robyn thinks. She will—she'll do exactly what she needs to do. As soon as she knows what that is.

She pictures Adira's face if she lets this opportunity get away from her. That steely gaze over her glasses. From a professional point of view, Robyn really should take this story and own it. But if she does that, is she exploiting Sam's death? Just one more instance of profiting from someone else's misfortune? The very thing she came home to avoid.

Of course, Adira need never know about Robyn's proximity to the story. Robyn could wait for it to break in some other way— disentangle herself from all these ethical brambles. But that would mean letting someone else trample all over it. No one else will have you and Tori in their thoughts as they write it. Robyn is the only one who will do that.

Which, in a way, makes it the opposite of exploitation.

So that's what she'll do. She'll cover the story as if preparing it for a time capsule with your name on it. As much as she can, she'll hold the line between public interest and curiosity.

She pulls out her laptop and gets the words down. Row after row, they stack up on the screen, each more gutting than the last. Journalistic detachment feels cold at the best of times, and Sam's death is barely a blip on the global-trauma radar, but Robyn's history is caught in the teeth of it, like skin in a zip; the cool tone she needs is even more eviscerating than usual.

Still, she does it. She gets it all down and reads it through for accuracy and flow, then she fires it off to Adira before she can change her mind.

'Good stuff!' Adira replies a few minutes later. 'It's up. No one else is on it yet. Keep digging. And get it on Twitter now.'

Breathing deeply, deliberately, in and out, Robyn composes a tweet. She adds a link to the article already on the paper's website and hits publish. Within minutes, *Popular author found dead* has been retweeted many times over, replete with tear-streaked and shocked-face emojis.

Robyn leans back in her seat. She'll have to talk to Tori as soon as she can. The thought of encountering the poor woman's grief up close again is overwhelming, but Robyn chases it off with the formulation of a strategy. She'll knock on the door with flowers, commiserate, and then explain that she happens to be a journalist. But a journalist who cares. Who has Tori's best interests at heart.

Her phone rings.

Seeing Jon's name on the screen, Robyn remembers she's not the only one who knows about Skye. Her heart thuds faster. She lets it ring out, but he calls again straight away. On the third ring, she picks up.

'Hi Jon,' she says.

'Robyn, hi.' There's a pause. 'Sorry, I've ... I didn't expect you to pick up ...'

'I tried not to, but I know you too well.'

'Nothing if not persistent?'

'I was going to say relentless, but we'll go with persistent.'

'A generous concession. I'll take it.'

There's another pause. Robyn pictures him heading down the stairwell, making for fresh air and coffee. She's surprised how relieved she is to have him there, on the other end of the line.

'So,' he says, 'I imagine you can guess why I'm calling?'

'You want those photographs on the front page?'

'I was going to ask how you were holding up, actually. Given that Sam Favier was your friend and all.'

Robyn glances out the window at the police station sign and the cars cruising past. Her heart still feels as if it's relocated to her throat.

'Are you okay?' Jon says.

'I've been better.'

'Come meet me at the beach,' Jon says. 'You need some company.'

29

Robyn pulls up in the beach car park off the main Cottesloe drag. Must be the most expensive real estate in all of Perth, this car park, given its location and the view: a great sweep of sea and sky. It's a little choppy out there today, small white horses jagging across the water's indigo skin. Before getting out, Robyn flicks on the radio; it's news time and she wants to know what's made the bulletin.

'In breaking news, Perth author Sam Favier was found dead this morning.'

It's one thing for the story to be skipping across the internet like a stone across water, leaving a trail of concentric ripples in its wake, but hearing it broadcast in the perfunctory way of radio news makes it more permanent somehow.

Robyn turns it off. The world, no matter which part of it you choose, is full of death and loss and grief. How does anyone bear it?

She sits in the car, letting her eyes rest. Seems they don't want to be open right now. Something to do with the woeful sleep deficit she's accumulated over the past few days. Strange—disloyal, really—how proper rest eludes you just when you need it most.

The sea air should help, she thinks, slipping her laptop under the passenger seat before opening the door and stepping out onto the bitumen. She waits for Jon, leaning up against the stone wall.

When his car pulls up next to hers, she's surprised, again, at the extent of her relief. He's here, just as he said he'd be.

'Hi,' he says. 'You okay? You look … vanquished.'

'That about sums it up.'

They head south along the footpath, behind the tea house and through the dense shade of the towering Norfolk pines.

'If you say something about these trees being iconic but alien to the region, I'll pummel you,' Robyn says.

Jon smiles. 'Would I say a thing like that?'

'Every time we've ever been here.'

'I solemnly swear to never ever mention the iconic-yet-alien status of the pine trees ever again.'

'Good. Thank you. Although I should thump you anyway for sneakily mentioning it just then.'

'Fair enough. You have one free hit. Shoulder only though.'

Robyn gives him a half-hearted knuckle to the upper arm. They walk in silence along the footpath, past the stretch of coast marked off as a dog beach. A man in a straw hat hurls a ball into the surf for a labrador; a family walks in the shallows, trailed by a bounding cavoodle.

'Guess what I did this morning?' Robyn says, forcing a smile, hoping it'll keep her together.

'Aside from breaking a massive story?'

'Yes, besides that.'

'I think you'll have to tell me.'

'I swam out to Sam's boat and found him there,' she says. 'I brought the boat in for his wife.'

Jon stops walking. 'That's terrible, Robyn.'

'Yeah, it really was.' She lets him take her in for a hug until the tears seem imminent and she pulls away. Keeps walking. Blinking into the wind.

Further south, they reach the end of Marine Parade and turn to step off the footpath, walking toward the ocean over a rise of dry, spiky grass, past yellow beach daisies and clumps of saltbush. The hardy scrub carpet gives way to sand and they stop on a small summit overlooking the water. Rottnest Island is a long flat shadow on the horizon.

'I was a bit surprised, actually,' Jon says, 'to see your by-line on the story.' He gazes out at the ships lining up in the distance for access to the port. 'I thought you were going to keep clear of writing about him.'

'I thought about leaving it, but I decided it would be safest with me.'

An aeroplane drags through the blue above. There are no clouds, just a cool breeze and a half day-moon hanging above the cranes to the south.

'I know, I know,' Robyn continues, seeing the way Jon's looking at her. 'I probably should've mentioned in the story that I knew him.'

'Knew him,' he says, 'and also swam out to his boat to bring his body to shore while his family looked on. You're part of the story, Robyn. You can't ...'

'I know, okay? I've not been a hundred per cent ethical.'

'You need to tell Adira. And you need to disclose your involvement in the next piece you put out there.'

'I know you're a stickler, Jon, but do you have to get so … het up about it?'

'It's not only about the rules, Robyn. You could get into trouble. I'd be worried about your job.'

'Well, I'm not worried about that, okay? Let's just … let's head back.'

'Seriously though,' Jon says, once they're back on the footpath. 'What are you going to do about this?'

'I'm going to keep hold of the story and do what I can to make sure Sam's name isn't dragged through the mud. He doesn't deserve to be remembered that way, and his family … they're going through enough, don't you think?'

'You can't protect them from this, Robyn, but you can protect yourself. Let someone else do it.'

'Who says I can't protect them? Skye's not going to say anything, and neither am I.'

'Don't be naïve, Robyn. There'll be an investigation, a post-mortem … You can't control this narrative.'

Robyn studies Jon's face a moment. 'I told you about Skye in confidence. You wouldn't go and tell anyone else, would you?'

He's silent.

'Did you talk to Adira about me?'

'I may have …'

'What did you tell her?'

'Only that you may not be the best person to be on this story. And she might like to consider giving it to someone else.'

'Someone more committed to giving the readers what they want, is that it? Even if it's none of their bloody business?'

'I'm worried about you, Robyn. That's all. I can't see how it's good for you to be covering this story. You care too much about the people involved. Jesus, you are one of those people. I'm sorry if you feel I've betrayed your confidence in going to Adira, but I was worried about you, and I knew you wouldn't listen to me. So, sorry-not-sorry, because it's worth it if it means you'll stop and think about this a little bit. Step back. Protect yourself.'

'Sorry-not-sorry?'

'Yes.'

'Fine.'

They walk in silence for a while. A motorcycle's low growl cuts through the wind's sound-blanket just as Robyn's phone buzzes in her back pocket.

'Robyn,' Adira says when she answers. 'What's this I hear about Sam Favier having a mistress?'

Robyn looks at Jon.

'I'm, uh ...' she says. 'I've not ... I'll look into it. Who's your source on this one? Just so I can ...'

'Be sure you do. Must go.'

Jon is still beside Robyn, watching a couple up ahead, pushing a pram.

'Tell me, Jon,' Robyn says, slipping her phone back into her pocket. 'How exactly did that conversation with Adira go? I can imagine it now, the pair of you looking all smug and concerned: *I should tell you, Adira, Robyn's holding out on you ...*'

Jon frowns, shakes his head.

'Why did you tell her, Jon? I told you about Skye in confidence.

The decision to take it to Adira was mine to make, not yours!'

She starts walking, back towards the car.

'Robyn, hang on a minute ...'

'No, Jon!' She turns to face him, indignation flaring up into something more potent. 'I asked you to wait. I asked you to trust me. But you couldn't do that could you?' She turns to go. 'Just because we know something, doesn't mean everybody else needs to.'

'Robyn!' Jon calls again, but she ignores him and walks faster.

30

Jon is right, of course, Isla. No one can control life's narrative, and many have ruined themselves trying. Human beings are unpredictable. They're often unreasonable. And everybody wants what they can't have.

It's early afternoon and Skye still hasn't eaten. To start with, she had no appetite, but more recently, the issue has been a lack of opportunity. No sooner had she texted Robyn, letting her know she'd rung the detective, then two police officers arrived to take her statement.

'That was quick,' she said, letting them in.

'We were on our way back to the station after another job,' the female officer said, glancing around the apartment. 'Just around the corner.' She remained standing near the door, watching as her partner pulled out a dining chair and set his paperwork down on the table.

'Would you like a tea or coffee?' Skye offered, her throat suddenly dry. 'Water?'

'We're fine,' the male officer said, pulling a pencil from his chest pocket.

Skye sat opposite him and relayed everything as succinctly and chronologically as she could. He stopped her now and then to clarify things, and she answered him plainly, burning under the steady gaze of the policewoman at the door. Towards the end, she began to wonder if she should've been quite so free with the details. Should perhaps have found a lawyer.

The thought nags at her again, now, as she scrolls through the take-away options on her phone. Did she say too much? But she shrugs it off; too late now. And anyway, she has nothing to hide.

She's narrowed down her lunch options to Italian or Asian when Robyn arrives at her door again.

'I thought you were done with me,' Skye says, sliding her phone back into her pocket.

Robyn shakes her head. 'Not quite,' she says, following Skye into the living room. 'I wanted to ask you something. And give you a warning.'

'Sounds ominous.'

'Have you told anyone else about you and Sam?'

'A couple of my friends know. Why?'

'Might they have told anyone?'

'I doubt it. I mean, they didn't approve but … it's not the sort of thing they'd do.'

'Did you ring anyone in the press about it, after I left? Or since then?'

'Why would I do that?'

'I don't know. Money, attention …'

'No.'

Robyn slips her glasses up onto her head and rubs her eyes with the heels of her hands. 'Fuck's sake, Jon,' she mutters, reaching for the phone now buzzing in her bag.

'Thanks for ringing me back, Sofia,' she says, raising her eyebrows in apology at Skye. 'I know you're busy … I had a question about Sam Favier. I'm guessing you won't get anything back from Toxicology for a while yet, but I was wondering if you're ready to release a statement about probable cause? The public will be wanting to know if there's been foul play.'

She waits a moment, paces the room, takes in the view of the sky from the window.

'Yes, I'm still here,' she says. 'Really?' She raises her eyebrows. 'And what are you thinking in terms of how it got there?' She nods and murmurs, 'Of course, Sofia, thanks a million.'

Robyn meets Skye's gaze with her own.

'They think he was poisoned,' she says.

'Jesus.'

Robyn watches Skye closely, but her surprise seems genuine.

Both women jump at the sudden knock on the door.

'Police?' Robyn says.

'Been and gone.'

It's Jethro. He's shaved off his beard. His hair is still wild, almost matted, but he brings a waft of shampoo into the room with him, along with a faint smell of laundry detergent. He looks sheepish, but also determined. Resolved and therefore relieved.

'Skye,' he says. 'I'm sorry to …' His words dry up when he sees Robyn. 'Who's this?'

'This is Robyn. Robyn, this is Jethro.'

Robyn holds out her hand; Jethro shakes it.

'What am I interrupting?' he says.

'Don't worry about it,' Skye says. 'What did you want?'

Jethro shifts in his shoes and glances at Robyn. Clearly, he'd prefer to do this without an audience, but the look on Skye's face makes it clear that he doesn't have a choice.

'I wanted to apologise,' he says, 'for everything, and let you know I'm leaving. Moving to Melbourne. Some friends of mine are there and their drummer's shot through so ... they want me to play with them.'

'That's awesome, Jethro.'

'A new chapter or whatever. And I'm happy for you too, Skye. I know you're seeing someone new, so ... Whatever you want to do. All good.'

Skye glances outside. Struggles to say it. 'Sam's dead.'

Jethro looks bewildered. 'For real? How? I mean, when? He looked alive enough last night ...'

Skye frowns.

'You saw us? Were you following me?'

He avoids her gaze. 'I was making sure you were okay ...'

'God,' Skye says, glancing from Jethro to Robyn and back again. 'I suppose you were taking pictures as well? For your stalker-wall?'

'No, I wasn't. I swear, Skye, I was just ... being stupid I guess. But you know that about me already.'

'That I do.'

Jethro nods, stung by the edge in Skye's voice, though aware that he probably deserves it. 'So, what happened to him?'

'Looks like somebody poisoned him,' Skye says.

'Seriously?'

'Probably,' Robyn says, sending Skye a warning glance; for all they know, this Jethro guy could be the one who did it. Stalking Skye suggests a clear motive. Leaving town now is similarly suspicious.

Jethro looks at Robyn. For a moment he's on the verge of asking who she is again and what she's doing there, but he decides against it; it's not as if it changes anything.

'Could it have been … like … self-inflicted?'

'No way,' Skye says. 'He was really confused about what was happening to him on that boat. If he'd done it on purpose … it doesn't fit.'

'Maybe it was that other guy.'

There's a beat in which Robyn and Skye glance at each other then back at Jethro.

'What other guy?' Skye says.

'There was a guy there. Once you were on the jetty, he came out of the trees. Near the skatepark, I think. Came right towards me.'

'I thought I saw something in there,' Skye says, 'but I wasn't sure.'

'Did he see you?' Robyn asks.

Skye shrugs. 'I couldn't say.'

'Don't think so,' Jethro says. 'I ducked behind a tree.'

'Bit dodgy, was he?'

'No, it was more of a reflex. He wasn't, like, dangerous looking. Just walking away pretty quick.'

'Did you get a good look at him?' Robyn asks. 'Enough to describe him to the police? It could be important.'

'Not me,' Skye says, shaking her head.

'Light hair, and wearing a jacket,' Jethro says. 'Denim, I think. Dark.'

Heart pounding, Robyn remembers Cohen's jacket on the night of the fireworks. It was draped over his suitcase in the hall yesterday evening, too. Black denim, wasn't it?

Could he have been there last night, visiting Sam before Skye did?

No, he was heading away for the weekend. Leaving right away.

'Surely not,' Robyn mutters, tapping her phone. She holds the phone up to her ear then pulls it away again, looking at Skye. 'Anything else I should tell Sofia?'

'Did they find a beer bottle? When they searched the boat? Sam was drinking a beer when I got there … If he was poisoned, maybe that's how.'

'Sofia didn't mention anything about a bottle,' Robyn says. 'Hello, Sofia? Shit. Voicemail … Sofia, it's Robyn Tinsley again. Sorry to hassle you, but I have some information. Call me when you get a chance.'

She heads towards the door. 'I have to run,' she says. 'Skye, will you keep trying Sofia at Claremont station? Detective Marella? You still have her number? If you get hold of her before I do … fill her in, would you?'

'Okay.'

'And Jethro? Can I suggest you front up at the station before you head east? They're going to need your statement. They might ask you to stick around for a little while, but it's your best option. Last thing you want is to be picked up the moment you land in Melbourne.'

Robyn pulls up outside Cohen's gate. She looks over at the intercom but doesn't get out to press the button. It's unlikely he'll pick up, but what if he does? It'll mean he didn't leave the city after all, and the implications of that … She doesn't want to think about it.

Sitting in the car, feeling the heat press in now that the aircon's off, she remembers Cohen in his kitchen yesterday afternoon.

He seemed so lacking in energy, and more distracted than usual … if that was even possible. So distant when she said goodbye. After that, she was glad to find Frank at home, thawing something in the microwave. He watched her drop into a chair at the kitchen table.

'You look zonked,' he said.

'Yeah. I am, I guess. I just saw Cohen. I'm worried about him.'

'This soup will be a while yet, but I'll make you some tea and you can tell me about it. Or we can watch something, get your mind off it.'

'Thanks Dad, but I think I'll head straight to bed.'

'It's only seven,' Frank said, pretending to be shocked. 'Early, even for you. You can usually make it till nine.'

'Only on special occasions,' Robyn said, giving him the smile he was after. 'Either way, I'm off to bed.'

Upstairs, she was pulling on her nightshirt when a thought that had been drifting and gathering formlessly all evening finally took on a shape: a possibility she'd not considered before. Because Frank was right. Usually, at nine pm or thereabouts, unless something exciting was happening, she was out like a light.

Sitting on her bed, she pulled out her phone. She typed a message, deleted it, rewrote it, let it sit for a minute or two, then pressed send. She yawned and sat watching the screen, waiting. In reply, those three little animated dots appeared and hung around for a minute. Then they disappeared. And they didn't return.

In the morning, she found she'd fallen asleep on top of her covers, phone in her hand. And still no word.

Now, parked on Cohen's driveway, Robyn checks the message thread again, in case she's missed something, but there's nothing. Just her own stupid message, which she should've known better than to send.

She tries to call Cohen, but it rings out.

Slipping her phone into her bag, she decides to bite the bullet. She climbs out of the car and tries the intercom, in case he's there, waiting for someone to come. She tries again, but there's nothing. Nothing but the heat and the distant sound of traffic on the highway.

Back in the car, she heads to the river, pulling up in the car park near the skatepark.

Shielding her eyes against the late-afternoon glare, she approaches *Stargazing*. The small boat is anchored in the shallows and watched over by an officer, who waits, shifting on his feet and waving flies away. He shakes his head when Robyn gets too close. Skye must've reached Sofia though, because Robyn can see the detective through the small cabin windows, moving around, looking for something.

The wait feels interminable in the heat, but finally, Sofia emerges from the hatch, holding up an evidence bag with a beer bottle inside it—brown with an oval label. So ordinary you could weep.

31

The afternoon is still hot, but finally there's a breeze, trailing the finest drapery of clouds across the sky. Funny isn't it? Even as terrible things unfold, weather keeps happening. People keep walking around, thinking themselves important. Birds keep flying. And babies keep needing things—milk, cuddles, baths.

On this hot, indifferent day, since that detective and her officer finally left the two of you alone, Tori has been marking time, fulfilling those needs of yours before putting you down for a nap in your downstairs bassinet.

Watching your blinking slow as you drift off to sleep, she finds it difficult to step away and leave you alone, because what if you're not breathing when she comes back? She's lost Sam; what's to say she won't lose you too?

Lying down on the couch, she feels it rushing in—that dark, crushing feeling that nothing will ever be okay again. Who knew she had it in her, this capacity for grief? This limitless darkness, pulling away in all directions, hungry to drag her in. She thought nothing could be worse than the agony of Sam's betrayal, but now there's this … How can she hold it all? Who will she be if she survives it?

An hour later, she's still there, stretched out on the couch. Not sleeping. Not even resting exactly. Just reminding herself to pull air into her lungs, right down into her belly, then let it out again. Hoping it's enough.

A gentle breeze off the water stirs the muslin sheet draped over the bassinet. Watching it, she feels as if she might sink into something resembling sleep, but then her phone buzzes on the coffee table. For a mad, heart-thumping moment, she hopes it's Sam, but it's not. Of course. It's the police liaison person.

Kai Watson, he says. Kind voice.

He explains that Tori's been ruled out as a suspect. For the time being, at least. A witness has reported being with Sam on the boat when he died.

'A young woman,' he says carefully. 'She came forward and identified herself of her own volition. Confirmed that you weren't there.'

'I see,' Tori says, wondering if he expects her to sound surprised.

'Also, I thought you'd like to be kept in the loop on this; it's looking like your husband was poisoned.'

'Poisoned?'

'It's too early to say for sure, but I'm afraid it looks that way.'

Tori says goodbye and thank you, but in truth, she's not grateful for this new information. She doesn't know what to do with it. It circles above her like a mosquito in the dark: Sam … murdered. And that woman, with him on the boat. Again.

It's difficult to get a handle on it, to figure out the logic. If he'd ended the relationship on Sunday morning, as he said he was going to do, it's possible the woman had wanted him dead. Hell hath no fury, et cetera. But if she'd killed Sam, why did she voluntarily come forward, and put Tori out of the frame? And if it wasn't her, then who the hell was it?

It doesn't make sense. It gives Tori nothing. All it means is that Sam spent his last moments alive with some other woman, instead of where he should've been. Here. At home. With his daughter. And who is to blame for that? Well, the person who asked him to leave, of course.

Tori sits up and puts her head in her hands. It's all too much. She stands and wanders towards the kitchen. Turns on the kettle, though she has no interest in tea. Listening to it heat up, comforted by the ordinariness of the sound, she walks over to the sliding door and rests her forehead on the cool glass. She takes in the familiar view of the pool, the river, the distant city, and thinks about the phone call she made to that newspaper editor. First thing this morning, before giving Isla her breakfast. She'd spent an almost-sleepless night, pacing through the hours at the mercy of a mind stuck on a looping track, round and round: Who is she? What's her name? Eventually, the idea had come to her: ring up the papers. Let them dig around on her behalf and deliver the answer to her door. That way, she might get some sleep.

Seemed genius at the time. And it had worked—she'd nodded off, knowing she had a plan.

Now though, it seems ludicrous.

Like inviting the wolves in through the front door; a foolish act of self-sabotage. It's bad enough having to endure in private the humiliation of Sam's infidelity—to marvel numbly at the awful alchemy of anger and grief simmering away, hot and cold, inside her—but now, thanks to her own actions, she'll have to endure it in public too, reflected in all the eyes and newspapers she comes across, and for God knows how long. It's unbearable, she thinks, turning her head and looking over at you, serene in your bassinet. Unbearable, all of it. But here she is and there's no changing it.

◆◆◆

Near the front of Tori's house, Robyn parks on the verge, in one of the few spots not yet taken up by news vans and cars. The reporters and their crew are mostly sitting in their vehicles, but a few of them are milling around, drinking coffee out of takeaway cups. It's a strange scene, this huddle of journos on an otherwise empty street of manicured verges and carefully trimmed trees.

Robyn gets out of her car and heads towards the gate.

'Good luck with that,' Harry says as she approaches the intercom. He's a reporter from one of the commercial networks. 'She's stopped answering.'

The intercom is flat and grey with a small camera eye at the ready. Robyn pushes the rectangular silver button. There's a low hum, then silence. She pushes it again; nothing.

'You're right,' she says to Harry, returning to her car. 'The drawbridge is up.'

Maybe she should drive around to the other side and approach the house via the river path. But that would be even more of an intrusion; she'd have to trespass on Tori's lawn before knocking on the door.

She wishes she had Tori's number, then remembers she does. Sam called her from it when his own phone was low on charge. It's a cold strategy, but it's worth a try. She scrolls through her received calls and finds the most likely candidate—one that came through on the evening of Friday the eighth.

The phone rings a few times before Tori picks up.

'I'm so sorry to disturb you, Tori. It's Robyn Tinsley. Do you remember me? I swam out to your boat this morning.'

There's a long silence, then Tori says yes, she remembers.

'I'm wondering if we can have a word.'

'This is not the best time ...'

'I know. I know, it's an awful time, but I'd like to help.'

'How?'

'It's probably best if we discuss it in person. If you're up to it? I'm outside the front.'

There's a pause, then Tori says, 'Those reporters still there?'

'Yes.'

'Think you can slip through the gate without letting any of them in?'

'I'll manage.'

◆◆◆

Up at the house, Tori answers the door, hanging back to avoid the cameras beyond the gate. You're on her hip, gnawing on a teething rusk.

'Thanks for seeing me,' Robyn says, holding out the flowers that seemed so necessary on the way over, but which now seem more a bribe than an offer of condolence.

'Well, how could I not?' Tori says, taking the flowers without really seeing them. 'After what you did for us ...'

'Anyone else would've done the same.'

'They're saying he was poisoned,' Tori says, leading Robyn through into the kitchen and putting the flowers down on the bench.

'Yes, I heard that too.'

'You heard that? Where?'

'There's something you don't know about me,' Robyn says. 'Which is why I'm here. Because I think you should know. Two things actually.'

'Okay.'

'First of all, I'm an old friend of Sam's, from uni days.'

'Oh,' Tori says, looking confused. 'Right.'

'And the second thing is, I work for a newspaper. I'm a reporter.'

'I see,' Tori says, adjusting your weight on her hip.

'I heard about the poison theory from the detective, on the phone. I've been ... I'm covering the story for my paper.'

Tori shakes her head. She's so weary, so stricken, almost nothing can surprise her, and yet, here is this woman, this trojan-horse journalist, claiming to have known Sam. Tori glances at the flowers. 'Is that why you're here?'

'Well, in a way, yes. But also, I've been thinking about you two here on your own, wondering if you have anyone else around to give you a hand.'

'No,' Tori says. 'My family's all back in the UK.' She wants to be outraged. To throw Robyn out and slam the door. But Robyn's concern seems authentic, and if she has some hidden agenda, she's hiding it well.

'Have you spoken to them?' Robyn says.

'Who?'

'Your family.'

Tori blinks. 'Yes,' she says. 'Yes, of course. My mum wants me to come home.'

'Will you go?'

Tori looks around the living space, the open-plan kitchen. Sam's hat is still hanging on a hook near the door. His shoes—three pairs—are still on the shoe rack.

'I don't know what I'll do.'

Robyn puts a hand on her arm. 'You'll be okay,' she says. 'Eventually. I know it sounds impossible, but … you will. Why don't you sit down? I'll make you some tea. Can I do that?'

Tori nods, heads towards the couch. Robyn watches her lower herself onto the sofa facing the window. There, she rests her cheek on your head as you nuzzle into her shoulder.

Robyn finds the kettle. Turns it on and finds the teabags and cups.

Waiting for the tea to draw, she lets her gaze settle on the pool beyond the window. Sunk into the deck that runs the length of the house, it's overlooked by a few vacant sun loungers. The water gleams, a sky-blue eye, wide open.

When it's ready, she brings the tea to Tori in the living room where they sit for a while as you suck on what's left of your rusk.

'So,' Tori says at last. 'Which paper do you work for?'

'The *Times*.'

Tori nods slowly. 'Editor's name Adira?'

'Yes,' Robyn says, surprised. 'Do you know her?'

'Not really,' Tori says, then she shakes her head more definitively. 'Never met her.'

'She's very good at what she does.'

Tori nods again. Robyn adjusts her legs to sit more comfortably.

'I'm guessing you want to interview me then?' Tori asks.

'Well, not necessarily. I was thinking I could help you prepare a statement. Expressing your shock and grief and asking for privacy. Might get rid of that mob outside your gate.'

'I'm not going out there.'

'You don't have to. We can release it electronically. They should leave you alone after that. For a bit.'

Tori looks at her warily.

'I can understand why you might not trust me,' Robyn says. 'But I promise you, my interest in covering this is to protect you and Isla. And Sam's memory.'

Tori gazes at a spot on the floor.

'I don't need this story, Tori. I don't want it, believe me; I wish it didn't exist. I truly just want to help.'

Tori nods then looks away again, out past Robyn's shoulder, at the sky beyond the window.

'How did you and Sam meet?' Robyn asks.

'Is this for the statement?'

'No ... I mean, it can be, if you like.'

'He was on a book tour,' Tori says, almost smiling. 'He came to see my show with some of his friends and waited out back to meet me. Swept me off my feet with his Aussie charm.'

She looks at her wedding picture on the coffee table. The ivory dress that showcased her baby bump so beautifully. The thigh-high slit. Her cowgirl boots. And Sam, gazing at her, one hand on her belly, proud as anything.

Once the statement is drafted and Tori's happy with it, Robyn packs everything into her bag.

'I can stay if you like?' she says. 'Help out with some chores or rock the baby or something while you sleep?'

'Thanks, but she's going to sleep now anyway. I'll nap with her.'

'Is there anyone I can call for you?'

'Actually, there is one thing,' Tori says, rubbing her forehead with her free hand. 'It's awkward ... but can I ask you to pass on a message for me? To your editor? In case I don't get around to calling her myself.'

'Adira?'

'Yes, Adira. Please tell her it was all a misunderstanding.'

Robyn tilts her head.

'I rang her this morning,' Tori says. 'Told her that Sam had been seeing someone else. I saw him with a woman, from the window, and it was doing my head in not knowing who she was. I had nothing to go on but a silhouette. I thought maybe a journalist might be able to find out for me ... but I don't actually want it in the news.'

Robyn pictures Jon's face while she yelled at him on the beach. She was so sure, then, of his betrayal. So self-righteous.

'I'll tell Adira,' she says, trying to hide her dismay, 'but it might be good if you call her too, if you get a moment. She may not believe me.'

'Okay.'

Robyn pulls her bag over her shoulder, wondering where Jon is now, and what to say to him. Why is she always so quick to think the worst of him?

Before turning to leave, Robyn looks at your sleeping face—the sweet bump of your nose, the twin curves of your resting eyelids—then she looks back at Tori. No words can communicate the things she'd like to say. Hope and forgiveness: these are things we have to find on our own.

32

The newsroom is alive with the sounds of typing and telephone interviews rippling across the rows of cubicles. Adira waves Robyn into her office. As usual, she's sitting behind a stack of newspapers on her desk and she's dressed in black, her jacket draped over the back of her chair.

'What news?' she says. Her favourite greeting, delivered with a wry smile.

'Massive development,' Robyn says, closing the door behind her and approaching the desk. 'And a message from Tori Favier.'

'Sam's wife? Just got off the phone with her, actually. She wanted to apologise for the other-woman bum steer. Seems fishy to me, so I say keep digging ... but sit tight for now. What's this massive development?'

'I spoke to Detective Marella. They found the beer bottle I told you about and they have a suspect in mind. They'll have people out looking for him any time now.'

'Good stuff. I want it online yesterday.'

'On it. But there's one more thing.'

'Yes?'

'I knew Sam, Adira. I knew him, and I was the one who found him in his boat.'

Adira looks at Robyn, eyebrows raised. 'That so?'

'Yes. I'm sorry, I should've …'

'Some kind of disclaimer was in order, don't you think?'

'Yes. Absolutely.'

Adira studies her for a moment then shrugs. 'Spilt milk,' she says. 'Get a disclaimer on there now. And I want a feature all about it, some immersive narrative journalism, bringing it to life and expanding on the investigation as it goes. For next weekend's magazine. Got it?'

In her cubicle, Robyn updates her online piece and adds the disclaimer. She spends a few minutes wrangling over a tweet before sending it out into the world, like Moses in a basket. Two minutes later, Adira gives her a thumbs-up through the glass. It's gratifying, but she could sleep now for a week. And sooner or later she's going to have to find Jon and apologise.

For now though, deciding she'd best get started on the feature Adira wants, she opens a blank document.

Staring at the page, she wills her fingers to move, but her mind keeps drifting away, mentally drafting an apology text to Jon instead of getting down to business. She checks her phone again; still nothing. She heads across the nylon-carpeted floor towards his office, but he's not at his desk. Didn't come back after lunch, apparently.

Back at her desk, she tries ringing him, twice, but he doesn't pick up. There's nothing for it but to get serious about this article. When Jon's ready, he'll call.

Closing her eyes, she takes herself back to this morning by the river. The trees behind her. The sun on the water. People, dogs ... and Tori, shouting, with you on her hip. The cold river water. The waiting boat.

She gets it all down in high definition, everything she can remember, followed by a list of questions readers might ask, to guide her when she resumes work on it. It's rough—only a draft—but it'll do for today.

After saving it in two places, she emails it to herself so she can work on it from home for the rest of the week, then she shuts down the computer and checks her phone again. Nothing but some dreary emails and press releases, all of which can wait till next week. She's getting better at that, at least—calling it a day, and meaning it.

Back at home, the house is quiet. Frank's left a note—he's out visiting a friend. Robyn drops her bag on the table and heads over to the fridge, turning on a light as she goes. Frank has done a shop, meaning she could whip something up for her dinner, but the thought of it brings exhaustion rolling in. Much easier to collapse on the couch and order in a Thai curry.

That done, she picks up the remote and flicks through a few

channels before settling on something about gardening. Benign. No surprises. Nice and calm.

Even so, the knock on the door makes her jump. That was quick, she thinks, checking her watch. But it's not her dinner. It's Jon, bottle of wine in his hand, hair standing up slightly higher than usual.

'I was just around the corner,' he says. 'I brought wine.'

'Excellent,' Robyn says, taking it from him and examining the label, though they're all the same to her. This one is beige with a smudged-looking pencil sketch of a leopard on it. 'Hmm, leopard wine. My favourite.'

Jon follows her into the kitchen area where she takes two glasses from the back of a cabinet and sets them up on the benchtop.

'Haven't been here for a while,' he says, looking past Robyn at the night-time view of the trees in the courtyard. 'Where's Frank?'

'Playing poker with some friends,' Robyn says, handing him a corkscrew.

She watches as he fills the glasses with the dark liquid; it glows ruby-red where the light gets through.

'Come,' she says, heading back to the couch. 'Sit. I'm watching something about aphids ...'

Jon follows, pausing to study Robyn's photograph of the Pinnacles on the wall. 'Is this from our Cervantes trip?' he says, leaning closer.

'Must be,' Robyn says. 'I've only been up there the once.'

'Good photograph.'

'Thanks. Dad must've thought so too. Pride of place.'

'That was a fun trip,' Jon says, moving towards the sofa and lowering his glass to the table to remove his jacket.

'Hungry? I've just ordered dinner.'

'Hope you did your usual over-order?'

'You know me.'

'Lucky I'm here to help.'

◆◆◆

Dishing up is messy. They sit opposite each other at the table, eating. Jon fidgets with the soy sauce.

'Robyn, I need to apologise. I know I overstepped the mark. I kept pushing you to do what I thought was right rather than trusting your judgement.'

'I guess that pissed me off,' Robyn says, 'but I was wrong too, accusing you of telling Adira about Skye. I should've known you wouldn't do a thing like that.'

'I wouldn't.'

'I know. That's why I called you today. I wanted to apologise.'

'I forgive you.'

'Technically I haven't apologised yet …'

'Forgiveness on stand-by.'

'I'm sorry, Jon. I should've had more faith in you.'

'Can I forgive you now?'

'You may.'

'Thanks.'

'No worries.'

They eat for a while in silence, enjoying the food, and the easy contentment between them. It's familiar, and yet it feels different. Back in the day—she can see it now—Robyn was suspicious of anything like happiness. All her life, it had been fleeting, inseparable from heartbreak. So, when she was with Jon, fear shadowed everything that was good between them. It was a sad little dance, and she was the one leading it.

Tonight though, at the table, Jon drinks his wine and smiles at Robyn, and it's good. She's still convinced joy is ephemeral, and she's not seen the last of fear, but now, at least, she can see the pattern. She can spot the fear and name it. And if she's learned anything from Sam and me, it's that happiness is precious *because* it's fragile. Instead of sabotaging it to avoid the risk of pain, she must seize it. Do what she can to keep it alive.

'Hey, Jon?' she says, reaching for his free hand. 'Have you thought about the two of us? You know, having another go?'

Jon looks at their hands together on the table.

'I suppose I have thought it over,' he says. 'Once or twice. Just in passing.'

'Me too.'

'And? What do you reckon?'

'I will if you will.'

Remember what I said about those moments when envy gets the better of me, Isla? Well, this is one of them. You understand though, don't you? Love is … well, it's everything.

33

There are many things the authorities need to do, Isla, when someone dies the way your father did. Procedures that need to be followed to establish the facts. There'll be a trial, a verdict, a media frenzy … But don't fret; your mum will shield you from all of it. Until you're old enough. Then, you'll have questions, and she'll answer them. As faithfully as she can, I'm sure. Time will pass and the pieces will fit together, into a picture you can fold away and keep. But here are some pieces you'll never find anywhere else.

It's early morning in Yallingup.

In a white room with narrow windows and a jarrah desk, Cohen lies in bed, listening to the birds. Their calls fall across one another in an intricate weave, like the most delicate lace.

He checked in late yesterday, having spent Sunday night and most of Monday in his car. Sleeping and not sleeping. Driving

266

around dazed and hungry. He'd left the city as planned on Sunday night and driven south for what felt like a thousand hours but was probably more like five. At some point, eyes grainy, lids heavy, he'd taken a small side road and then another one before rolling into a space between the trees just big enough for his car. He'd managed a little sleep, stretched out awkwardly in the passenger seat, but it had been patchy and left him with a deep ache in his lower back. Yesterday, anticipating more of the same, he found an ad for this secluded bed-and-breakfast on an information board near the edge of town. He called the handwritten number, gave a false name and let himself in with the lockbox code the host provided, hoping that a hot shower and a solid night's sleep might revive him enough to make it to that sunken path, beneath those twisting branches. Where the dappled light seemed so ethereal; where I told him I loved him.

So, here he is, stretched out between these starched, white sheets.

The birds are getting loud out there. Not so delicate anymore.

Cohen sits up and pulls his legs off the bed. He scratches his stubble where it itches, wipes his eyes with the heels of his hands, then reaches for his jacket slung over the back of the desk chair.

He pulls out his wallet. From its leather depths, he slips out a piece of paper, its folded edges worn thin. The drawing has faded and it's lightly smudged all over, but it's still there, left by my pencil so many years ago. It's a sketch of the Roman Forum, accompanied by the words: *Can't wait to see the world with you.* I remember copying it off a postcard from my brother—those ancient columns towering aimlessly over the garden of ruins at their feet.

Cohen runs his finger over the sketch then folds it up again and slips it into his wallet. He wonders if he'll get there, or if the cops will be waiting for him at the airport. They'll be stern. Resolute. In no way interested in his excuses.

He reaches back and touches his turtle tattoo, closing his eyes to remember the one I had on my shoulder. He can picture it any time he wants to, more vividly than the exact shade of my eyes. Then he looks over at the unrumpled side of the bed.

'Nearly there now, Gracie,' he says.

Standing up, he goes to the window and watches the sun move over the treetops. He pulls out his phone and considers replying to Robyn's text. But reading it again, he finds he's still hovering somewhere between relief and anger. Though he doesn't blame her, as such. How can you blame someone whose only crime was believing someone else's bullshit?

There it is, on his screen. Black font in a long grey rectangle. Same as it was when it came through on Sunday evening. He was still at home at the time, sitting in an armchair, trying to find the will to get up and hit the road. Robyn had left nearly an hour earlier, and since then, he'd been stuck, his mind circling around all the old questions. The ping of her message snapped him out of it.

> *Hey Cohen,*
> *I know you're driving, but*
> *I just realised something*
> *and had to tell you.*
> *Since coming home to Perth,*
> *I've had to rethink everything*

I thought I knew about Sam.
Including the night Gracie died.

Reading this, Cohen's heart lurched. His breathing became shallow.

As you know, I was
studying at home that night.
I went to bed at around 9
and fell asleep, waking up
at some point to the sound
of Sam, calling me from outside.
He was under my window.

Cohen had to read this bit twice. All those years, he'd pictured Robyn working at her desk late into the night. Wide awake and interrupted by Sam knocking on her front door.

Interrupted being the key word here. Not *woken up.*

All this time, he'd pictured her checking her watch then going downstairs to let Sam in. She'd have smiled at him—indulgent as ever—before leading him upstairs and letting him climb drunkenly into her bed. After which, she'd have returned to her books while Sam worked up a snore behind her.

But that's not how it went.

I let him in and went back
to sleep. In the morning,
he was still there. I asked him

what time he'd come in.
He said about 10.
Maybe 10.15.
I had no reason to doubt
him Cohen. Never questioned it.
Now though, knowing about
his feelings for Gracie,
I'm not so sure.
I'm so sorry Cohen.
Until we spoke today
I'd forgotten how much
hinged on what time he
arrived. The fact is I don't
know what time it was.
I have no idea.

Now Cohen throws the phone on the bed as if it's scalded him. He won't reply; what is there to say?

After a long, cool shower, he packs his things again and heads outside, locking the door behind him. He looks around for signs of a police stakeout. There's nothing but trees and gravel. Cockatoos and early-morning sky. He deposits the key back in the lockbox. So far, so good.

He decides to leave his car behind in case someone's out looking for him. Soon, Jewel will tell the police he's missing, if she hasn't already, and the unravelling will begin.

Walking along the gravel road, hoping he'll spot a shortcut, Cohen remembers how he felt, standing up from that armchair on

Sunday evening. Robyn's text message and everything it meant seemed to pulse in his back pocket as he grabbed his suitcase and pulled on his jacket. He felt vindicated. Potent with certainty. Swept along on a floodwater rage, dark and rising.

There was room for doubt, of course. It was, after all, still possible that Sam had arrived at Robyn's house some hours before the window of suspicion, as he'd always said.

It was possible.

But was it likely?

No, Cohen thought as he took a final look up at Jewel's house and placed his suitcase in the boot. No, it wasn't.

He steered the Audi down the driveway, into the gathering dark, and drove along the quiet streets, remembering my mum at my funeral—unable to stand without the support of my brother. If it hadn't been for Sam, she would've been spared so much pain; they all would've. And Cohen would've had a completely different life. A life with me, a family.

Pulling into a drive-through bottle store, Cohen bought a sixpack of craft beer. Then he made his way to the yacht club. Sam had been a good mate, at times. Maybe he deserved one final chance to come clean. To hold up his remorse. Wave it like a flag.

Cohen's footfall on the timber jetty seemed loud as he approached *Stargazing*. The moon was large and pale to the east. Somewhere, there were sirens, ringing out across the evening. A mournful, reaching sound.

Sam sat on the deck, jabbing single-use chopsticks at something in a takeaway noodle box.

'Oh, how the mighty have fallen,' Cohen said, casting his eye around. 'Soft landing though.'

Sam nodded. 'Guess I can't complain.'

'Well, you can,' Cohen said, lowering the beers to the jetty so he could climb aboard. 'But who's listening?'

'Good point,' Sam said, smiling a little warily, no doubt recalling Cohen's wrath in the cemetery.

'I'm heading out of town for a couple of nights,' Cohen said. 'Thought I'd stop by and shout you a beer before I leave.'

'Romantic getaway with the wife?'

'Yeah.'

'Nice.'

Cohen sat opposite Sam, the sixpack at his feet. 'I've been thinking about the other day at Karrakatta,' he said. 'Wondering why I got so pissed off so quick. I think it's not knowing what happened to her, you know? It's done my head in.'

'Yeah, me too, mate,' Sam said. 'Me too.'

They sat for a moment, the boat rocking beneath them.

'You were out with Matty that night, right?' Cohen said.

'Right.'

'Drinking at the Tav?'

'Steves,' Sam said, resting his elbows on his knees. 'Then I went round to Robyn's.'

'Yes, that's what you told us at the time.'

Sam frowned. 'What, you don't believe me now? Robyn vouched for me, remember?'

'You're right,' Cohen said. 'And why would you lie to me?'

'Exactly.'

Sam rolled down his sleeves. Rubbed the bristles on his jaw and played with his wedding ring. Turned it round and round on his finger. Cohen watched him, remembering that this was what

Sam did when he was lying: fidgeted like a roach.

'Wish the CCTV was as good back then as it is nowadays,' Sam said, crossing his arms across his chest. 'We could've seen the prick Gracie left with that night.'

'Yeah,' Cohen said. 'I wish too. Then we'd know for sure.'

'It's the not knowing, like you said.'

'Hundred per cent.'

Sam rubbed the back of his neck. 'So how about that beer then?'

'Coming right up.'

Cohen pulled two bottles from the cardboard case and headed towards the hatch.

'You got an opener down here?'

'Down and to the left. In the drawer.'

The cabin was a small, airless space with a stale-sheets smell.

Glancing up at the perspex skylight, Cohen retrieved the little bag from his jacket pocket. He considered it for a moment and almost slipped it back again, but then he remembered Robyn's grief-tight voice on the phone, all those years ago: 'Something's happened to Gracie, Cohen. Something awful.'

Jaw clenched, he rummaged in the drawer. Closed his hand around the bottle opener.

'Thanks,' Sam said when Cohen handed him the bottle. 'Cheers, mate.'

'Cheers.'

'Nice of you to come by.'

'I had to see it for myself: the brilliant Sam Favier, tail between his legs.'

'Thanks a lot,' Sam said, taking a sip and grimacing. He checked the label. 'Tastes different.'

Cohen watched him for a moment before looking away.

'I'm guessing nothing tastes good right now,' he said.

'That's true,' Sam said, glancing at the sagging noodle box on the seat.

'Stress affects the tastebuds; did you know that?'

'No shit?'

'That's what they say.'

Sam looked over at Cohen, and for a moment it seemed he might apologise for everything he'd put his old friend through. Acknowledge it at least. But he didn't. He took a long drink, then he lifted his gaze and studied the clouds, those shadowy layers in the night sky. As if there was nothing more to say.

Cohen drained his beer and stood to go. 'Don't get up,' he said.

'Take care, mate,' Sam said, reaching up for a handshake.

Returning it, Cohen wondered if maybe he'd missed something essential—some redemptive act of Sam's that he'd forgotten. But nothing came to mind.

2001 Thursday, 22nd November

Inside the silent apartment, I turn on a light while Sam shuts the door behind us. He examines my 'Whales of the World' poster while I'm in the kitchen. I like that he's giving it such close attention— the olde-worlde style of the drawings; the Latin names: *Monodon monoceros, Balaena mysticetus*.

All the glasses are dirty in the sink, so I find two teacups in the cupboard and roll the chipped rims in the salt still on the plate. I manage to fill them without too much drunken spillage then we take them out to the balcony. Sam sits on the couch on the far end. I flop down next to him, careful to leave a good foot between us. I'm not immune to his allure; this we know.

We tap our teacups together and drink, listening to cars driving past below. The margarita is cold and fresh and salty. Strong. I know I'll regret it in the morning, but hey—that's what mornings-after are for.

There's a loud TV somewhere above us, and a man and woman arguing down in the street below.

'Fancy another one?' Sam says. 'That jug's not quite empty; be a shame to waste it.'

'Go on then,' I say. 'You pour them; I need the bathroom.'

When I emerge, he's back on the couch, fresh drinks on the table.

'Cheers,' we say, tapping cups again.

We keep talking, but the words begin to feel remote. Incidental. I feel expansive. Celestial. Life is fantastic and the night is perfect. Sam is here and nothing's going to happen between us, but it could. Sometimes, possibilities are every bit as good as actualities.

'Margaritas are magic,' I say, staring at the way the light plays across the salt crystals around the rim.

What I can't see is that it's not only margarita in that glass. It's not just the salt that tastes salty.

'Good, hey?' Sam says, looking at me with that smile of his.

I hate to admit it, but I want to kiss him again. I can suppress it well enough when I'm sober; I can remind myself that I love Cohen, and Robyn is my best friend, and Sam would not be good for me. But I'm far from sober right now, and, as it happens —thanks to Sam and a little vial of GHB Matty gave him earlier— there's a toxic aphrodisiac coursing through my veins, mingling with the alcohol in my blood.

The air is like silk against my skin. My silver dress is just a slip of fabric between my body and the world … and with Sam looking at me like that … I could lean across and kiss him, right now. I could touch his face, feel his body against mine the way it felt beside his car, after that surf. I could … except I can't. Everything seems to be slowing right down. I feel compressed, my arms heavy against the back of the sofa. I inhale, then I feel the air move out of me, all the way out, and I'm waiting for the next in-breath. Waiting. The pause feels so long. My head, so heavy.

'Gracie? You okay, Gracie?'

Sam's voice comes from a long way off. I open my mouth. Motion seems impossible, except inside my head, which is spinning, fast then slow, fast then slow.

Sam's saying something. 'Shall we go inside? You should get to bed.'

I can't even shake my head.

'Maybe not then, huh?' Sam pulls a beach towel off the balcony rail and drapes it over me. I hear the clink of our china cups, far away, as he washes them in the sink.

I'm not scared. I've felt this way before, more or less, when I've had too much to drink too quickly, or smoked a spliff when already hammered. No, not even scared, though I should be terrified. I should be clinging to consciousness, begging Sam to call an ambulance. Sam should be terrified too. And maybe he would be, if he knew what was happening—if he knew mixing GHB with alcohol could be fatal. Instead, he heads for the door, thinking he'll have to win me over some other time, some other way.

'Goodnight, Gracie,' he says, and he closes the door.

Walking along the road—bitumen now—Cohen listens to the pulsing drone of cicadas in the bushes around him. He marvels at their cooperation as a species. Their intensity, relative to their size.

The fragrances of coffee and buttery pastry waft towards him from the café near the campsite up ahead. He heads over. It's like stepping into a dream. The barista glows in the morning light; she smiles at him with angelic benevolence while continuing her chat with the manager, who laughs and shakes his head over his clipboard. Cohen almost doesn't want to leave, except that he has somewhere to be.

Coffee cup in hand, and what's left of the poison still in his pocket, just in case, he heads along the road towards the dead-end, where the path begins. If he had his bike, he thinks, he could really cover some ground. For a moment he's a boy again, flying along a forest track, wind in his hair, Sam just ahead. But he shakes off the memory. No matter what else happens, he needs to get to our place. After that, he'll accept whatever comes. Just as long as he's made it there.

And do you want to know what I'm hoping? Down where my deepest longings lie? I'm hoping something magical will happen when he gets there. On this cool morning, in our special place, the combination of his liminal exhaustion, my concentrated presence, and our history soaked up by the trees, will make it possible for me to finally reach him. He'll see me standing there in the gossamer light. He'll *see* me, and that will be enough.

ACKNOWLEDGEMENTS

The Ghost of Gracie Flynn owes so much to the land and river on which it is set. I'd like to acknowledge the traditional custodians of this magical place: the Whadjuk people of the Noongar nation. In their hands, the Derbarl Yerrigan has been central to many, far more important stories than this one.

Thank you to Fremantle Press, the City of Fremantle, and the WA Department of Local Government, Sport and Cultural Industries (DLGSC) for their support of emerging writers through the biennial Hungerford Award, for which this novel was shortlisted in 2020. I'm so grateful to the 2020 judges—Sisonke Msimang, Brenda Walker, Richard Rossiter and Georgia Richter—for seeing something worthwhile in my manuscript. Further thanks to the DLGSC, whose Creative Development grant gave me time and space to develop *The Ghost of Gracie Flynn* for publication, and to Claire Miller, Jane Fraser and the whole Fremantle Press team for their warmth, hard work and support.

I am indebted to Georgia Richter for her care, precision and sense of humour during the editing of *The Ghost of Gracie Flynn*. This novel is immeasurably better for her input and guidance.

I would not have written this novel were it not for the writers who've mesmerised and inspired me over the years. Nor would it exist without my parents, Barbara and Andrew Burnett, who read to me, sang to me, and planted an avocado tree that grew enormous, ideal for climbs and daydreams. I'm so grateful for their unwavering love and support, and for the many hours both spent reading multiple drafts of *The Ghost of Gracie Flynn*, brainstorming titles with me and, in Mum's case, following me around with a camera taking headshots.

Thanks also to my sister Ruth McKeown who has read at least three versions of this novel, and several other works in progress, thereby passing the sibling-endurance test with grace and style. And to my brother Mike Burnett, who invited me to join his band in 2001, which I did, and which loosely inspired some moments in this novel. All the musos depicted in my novel, though, are entirely fictional.

Many thanks to the band's bass guitarist, Aranda Morrison, who married me, blissfully ignorant that his future would involve reading multiple drafts of this and many other stories. Beta reading wasn't in the vows, but he does it anyway, and his feedback is invaluable. He's supported me in so many ways to pursue this crazy dream, and I'm so grateful.

To my sons, Rohan and Luke—thank you for being your wonderful selves and keeping me on my toes. I hope we'll have many more adventures together, both imagined and real. And I'm sorry, but yes, I will always cry at the end of *James and the*

Giant Peach. I love you two endlessly, more than all the hairs on all the bears.

So many friends have expressed support and interest in this work. Thank you to all who read early drafts, cheered me on or said kind things—Fleur Ledger, Tiki Dickson, Stephen Burnett, Janet Tagg, Shannon Knight, Teresa Flynn, Tracy Robinson, Helen Ramsey, Kelly Quayle, Louise Tinsley, Katy Kell, Emily Sun, Laurie Steed, Susan Morrison, Kali Ledger, Jacquelyn Angus, Anne-Sophie Deleflie and Leanne Brass, among others.

Thanks to my postgraduate creative writing supervisors, Deborah Robertson and Christine Owen, who inspired me and taught me many things, including the importance of tenacity, exacting feedback and long walks on the beach.

Finally, thanks to forensic pathologist Dr SA Collis and marine scientist Emily Gifford for their expertise; to my late aunt Mary Burnett, a traveller, a reader, and a journalist, and to whom I'd so love to send a copy; and to my early bookish friends, Kelly Quayle, Janis Holmes and Tamsin Harrington, who opened my eyes to whimsical epics and dystopian fiction, and to tragedies, hilarities and lyrics I might otherwise have missed.

ALSO AVAILABLE

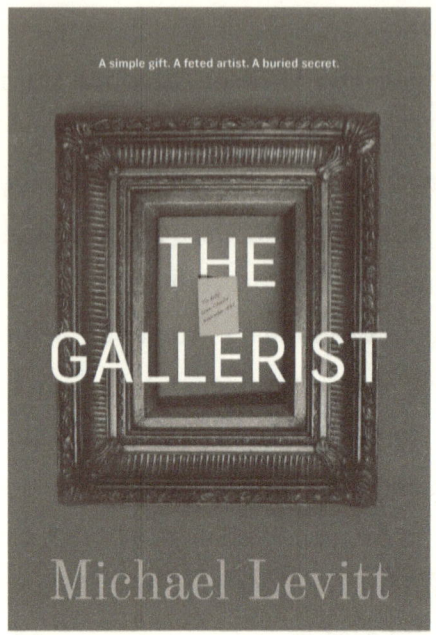

Mark Lewis, a former surgeon, has found solace in running a small art gallery. When Jan, a local woman, brings him a painting for valuing, it looks uncannily like a painting by the enigmatic artist James Devlin. Yet Jan claims it was done by a seventeen-year-old boy called Charlie. As Mark searches for the painting's true provenance, he is joined by the attractive and clever Linda de Vries. The pair will learn that James Devlin is a man whose past is as blank as an empty canvas, and he is determined to keep it that way.

'… a clever novel with an ingenious plot set in the Australian art world.' *Good Reading Magazine*

FREMANTLEPRESS.COM.AU

Fifteen-year-old Darren Davies is found facedown in the Weymouth River with a gunshot wound to his chest. The killer is never found. Ten years later, his mother Sandra receives a visit from local police. Sandra's best friend, Barbara, has been found dead on a remote Pilbara road. And Barbara's DNA matches the DNA found under Darren's fingernails. When the investigation into her son's murder is reopened, Sandra begins to question what she knew about Barbara. As she digs, she discovers that there are many secrets in her small town, and that her murdered son had secrets too.

'… the kind of crime novel which hooks you in from the first chapter and doesn't let up until the very end.' *Better Reading*

Literature professor Jack Griffen has recently suffered a nervous breakdown. His wife has divorced him and she and their adult daughter have moved to the USA. Into the void steps exchange student Hieronymus Beck. The pair spend hours talking about the anatomy of crime fiction, and Beck's favourite book of all time, *In Cold Blood*.

But everything changes when Jack finds Hiero's list. Five sheets of paper. Five ways to commit a murder. His student has told him he's writing a crime novel, but what else is he doing? Caught up in his protégé's dangerous game, how far will the mild-mannered professor go to save a life? As far as murder?

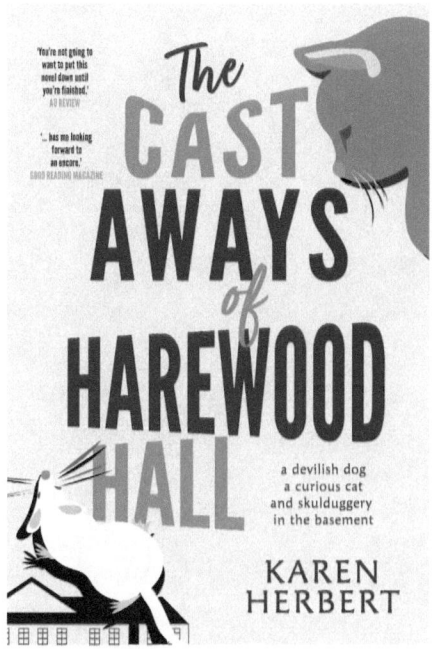

Josh is a sweet, well-meaning university student with a big heart. After he impulsively steals two research mice from a campus laboratory, he hides them in the basement of the retirement village where he works. The mice are happy and so is Josh, until he discovers that the lab mice could cause a deadly disease.

Enter a cat called Harley, a dog called Bobby, the arrival of some mysterious packing boxes, and a strange spike in the village's water bill. As the clock ticks, and disaster looms, can the Harewood Hall residents save the day?

Joanna Morrison has a background in journalism and a PhD in Creative Writing. Her short fiction has appeared in Australian literary journals and anthologies. In 2020, *The Ghost of Gracie Flynn* was shortlisted for the City of Fremantle Hungerford Award. Joanna lives in Perth with her husband, two sons and miniature schnauzer, Scout.